Praise for *Hunting Annabelle*

"With a protagonist you'll almost hate to love, and more twists than a foot-long corkscrew, *Hunting Annabelle* is a compulsive, deliciously addictive psychological thriller that pulls you in from the first page, and doesn't let go until you've reached the shocking end. A must read!"
—Hannah Mary McKinnon, author of *The Neighbors*

"Is *Hunting Annabelle* an unconventional romance, a creepy psychodrama, or a detective story about a good kid stuck in a bad situation? I devoured this thrilling debut in one sitting to find out, and it took me on a wild, twisty ride until the very last page."
—Amy Gentry, author of *Good as Gone*

"Wendy Heard's *Hunting Annabelle* is the best kind of psychological thriller—dark and twisted with a generous side of creepy. I had no idea where this story was going, only that I was rooting for Sean, the tortured hero whose search for Annabelle means releasing his own inner demons. Gritty, intense, and 100% surprising, *Hunting Annabelle* is one hell of a wild ride."
—Kimberly Belle, bestselling author of *Three Days Missing* and *The Marriage Lie*

"Wendy Heard's *Hunting Annabelle* is a twisted roller coaster of a ride with an utterly unique, fascinating narrator. You won't want to miss this genre-bending thriller."
—Heather Gudenkauf, *New York Times* bestselling author of *The Weight of Silence* and *Not a Sound*

"Gritty, intense, and full of multi-dimensional characters that will keep you guessing until the end, *Hunting Annabelle* is a must-read psychological thriller. Readers of Gillian Flynn and Caroline Kepnes will adore Wendy Heard!"
—Meghan O'Flynn, author of the Ash Park series

D0107743

HUNTING
ANNABELLE

WENDY
HEARD

mira

Recycling programs
for this product may
not exist in your area.

ISBN-13: 978-0-7783-6934-9

Hunting Annabelle

For questions and comments about the quality of this book, please contact us at CustomerService@Harlequin.com.

BookClubbish.com

Printed in U.S.A.

HUNTING

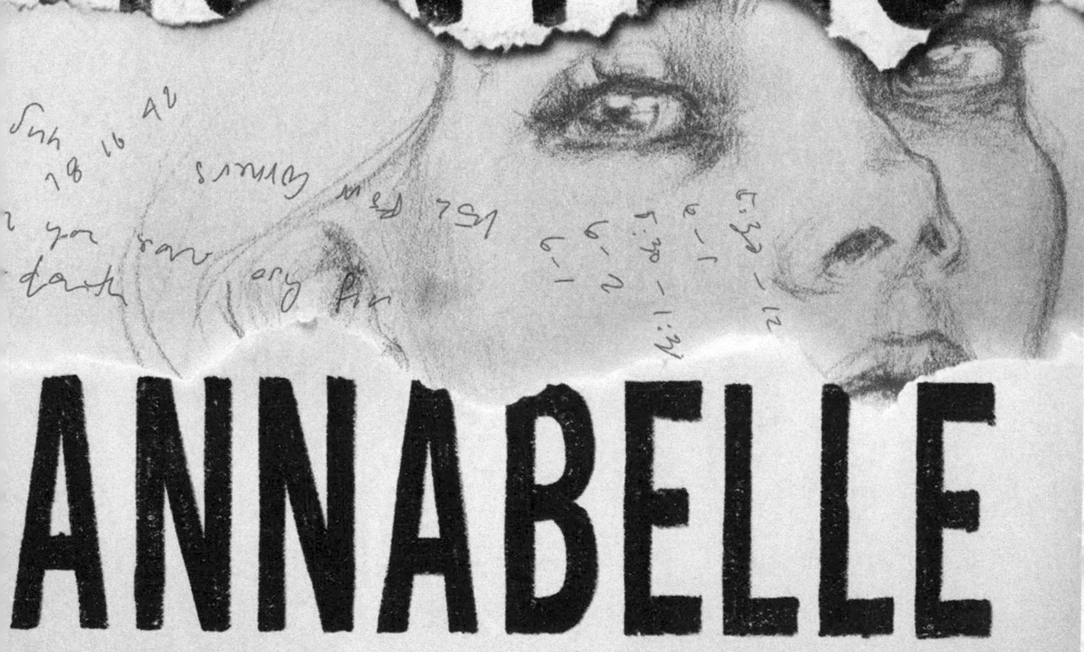

ANNABELLE

The moon never beams
Without bringing me dreams
Of the beautiful Annabel Lee.
—Edgar Allan Poe

CHAPTER ONE

1986

I lock my bike up near the gate underneath the giant Four Corners sign. Sweat trickles down the small of my back, slowly soaking through my shirt. At the gate, a bored-looking teenager casts an apathetic glance at my worn membership card and hands it back to me. I wonder if they recognize me. It seems like they don't, but you'd think at some point someone would wonder why I'm always here. So far it seems like I'm just another guy, another tourist, an uninteresting, invisible speck in the pulsating crowd.

I pass the entrance to Marine Land, Future Land, Jungle Land (everything here is a cheap Disneyland rip-off), and make my way to Halloween Land, where I always start my rounds. I sit on a bench in front of the crooked black haunted house with the wax museum inside, trying to blend into the crowd, or coming as close to blending in as an Asian can in South Texas. I get out my sketchbook and flip through the pages. Hundreds of drawings stare back at me: mothers with fanny packs, kids throwing tantrums, a young teenager with

a curly mullet taking aim at a plastic duck at one of the shooting booths, the fake rifle settled into his shoulder like he'd
done it a thousand times. I get in different moods, some more
colorful than others. Last year I went through a pointillism
phase that lasted two sketchbooks; next it was cross-hatching.
The subjects of the drawings are always the same, though:
people. Sometimes I draw their auras and sometimes I don't.

I cast my gaze around for likely subjects and it lands on a
middle-aged couple strolling with fingers loosely interlaced,
gazing around with the wide-eyed awe of Catholics visiting
the Vatican. They'll do.

I slip my headphones on, briefly annoyed as they catch on
my earring. I press Play with a satisfying *click* and pocket the
Walkman. The tape starts to roll with a hiss and a scrape of
static, and then the Smiths kick in, Morrissey crooning shrilly
above the bustle of the crowd around me.

I draw the couple with robot-quick strokes. Matching high-
waisted khaki shorts reveal doughy white legs squished into
white athletic socks. I bet they work office jobs; this is probably a wedding anniversary. The man's aura seeps red into the
air around him; his wife's blue is almost completely overpow-
ered by it. The shapes of their auras are interesting, almost
serpentine. I use colored pencils to illustrate them, although
it comes out wrong. Without motion, the auras always look
like flames.

A flurry of movement catches my eye. A family hops aside
to make way for a kid who runs past and trips, taking a majes-
tic, sprawling plunge onto the asphalt. He lands near my feet,
both knees scraped and bloody under cutoff jean shorts. He
curls his legs up to his chest and contorts his face into a grimace.
I can't help but smile. He looks to be around eight years old;
he's all elbows, like a scarecrow with a bush of sandy hair. I slip

the headphones off my head and snap the Stop button on the Walkman. I'm opening my mouth to ask if he's all right when a broad-shouldered man with a bushy mustache sidles up and toes him with a sneaker. "C'mon, Craig. Up."

Craig crunches his eyes into a dried-apple squint and shakes his head. Tears squeeze out from under his eyelids. He pulls his knees tighter into his chest.

"Hey." The toe nudges Craig again in the ribs, less gently this time. "Son. Up. It's just a coupla skinned knees." In response, the kid lets out a high-pitched sob.

The dad huffs a frustrated breath and looks around at the nearby mothers eyeing the situation. "Little sissy, his whole life, his sister's ten times tougher," he declares, earning a few maternal smiles before the women cast their attention elsewhere.

I don't like this dad. I lean forward and tap the kid on his arm. "You want me to get you some ice? Might help."

The kid opens his eyes, surprised, and looks me up and down. The sight of me is so unexpected that he actually stops crying. What am I, a werewolf or something?

"Ice," I repeat. "I can get it from that food stand. Might help your knees. Paper towels, clean them up. It'll feel better."

He nods silently.

I hop up and hurry to the food stand. When I return with a wax-paper cup full of ice and a handful of paper towels, he and his dad are gone. My eyes fly to my backpack and drawing supplies. They're still on the bench. I glance around, frustrated, looking for the kid in the throngs of tourists. A bright metallic glimmer flutters through the crowd. I peer between people, straining for a look.

There. That girl.

That's weird. Her hair is an unusual shade of bright auburn, but that isn't the source of the glittery copper that captivates me. She radiates it; it seeps from her silhouette as surely as this couple's red and blue.

I've never seen copper, or any metallic aura for that matter.

I shove my sketchbook into my backpack. I push through the lunch mob outside the tavern and think I've lost her when the auburn hair flutters again, disappearing into the house I've just been sitting in front of.

Legs like scissors, I hurry back to the black house. There isn't usually a line for the wax museum and today is no different. The lobby area is decorated with intentionally dusty, serial-killer charm.

"This way, please," a girl with zombie makeup in a wedding dress says.

I duck into the Ghosts of Texas Past room, which is filled with newspaper articles and life-sized wax statues of famous murderers. Behind me, the zombie bride warns a family with small children that this house is meant for ages ten and up.

The girl with the auburn hair stands with hands folded in front of a wax statue of a middle-aged woman knitting in a rocking chair. I'm familiar with this display. It commemorates Deadly Annie, a female arsonist and murderer famous for setting house fires all over Fort Worth until she was caught in the seventies and sentenced to death.

The girl is a little younger than me, maybe a senior in college. Her upturned nose has a pointy tip and her cheeks are soft and smooth, golden tan and stippled liberally with mouse-brown freckles. Her complexion is part redhead, part brunette; she's all over shades of auburn and bronze. Tendrils of copper roll off her like a fog, and close up something shadowy and elusive lurks behind them. It's not a color but a darkness, as though the area immediately behind her is in shade.

The girl notices me looking at her. She gives me a polite smile.

She is beautiful. She glows with an incandescent planetary light, and for a moment I am paralyzed. Pure, clean and fresh, innocence leaking from her like a fragrance, she stares up at me for one, two, three heartbeats while my stomach turns to ice. I drag my eyes down and pretend to read Deadly Annie's biography on the informational placard.

"They think she killed over twenty people," the girl says. Her voice is a soft soprano.

"Twenty-eight," I correct her.

She scans the placard. "How do you know that? It doesn't say that here."

"They say it on the tour they do during Halloween season."

"Oh." She keeps her eyes on the wax figure, which is made to look intentionally maternal. It increases the shock value when you read about her crimes.

She murmurs, "She was, like, sadistic. They say she intentionally picked houses with kids in them. You think that can be right?"

"I don't know…they probably just say that because it makes for a better story. How could anybody know that?"

"Well, I mean…almost all of the houses had kids in them. So she must have picked them on purpose."

I shove my hands into my pockets and shrug. "This is Texas. Every house has ten kids in it. Even if she were trying to keep away from children it'd be impossible."

She adjusts her backpack and looks uncomfortable. Does it sound like I'm defending a child-killing arsonist? How long has it been since I had an actual conversation with another human being besides my mom and my psychiatrist? A year? More?

She says, "Didn't I see you here yesterday? At the fountain with the dolphins?"

I'm so shocked, I can't reply. I just stare at her.

She raises her eyebrows. "So…"

"I… I don't know."

"Well, *were* you at the dolphin fountain yesterday?" In the dim light her eyes are a catlike orange-brown, strange and beautiful.

A wave of medicated confusion washes over me. I lose my train of thought. My hands itch like crazy and I look down at my palms. The sight of them open like that makes my heart beat faster. What am I doing?

"Hello?" she says, her voice piercing through the fog.

"Huh?"

"Weren't you at the fountain yesterday?"

I swallow a mouthful of spit. Do I always have so much spit in my mouth?

I try to remember. What had I done yesterday? "I think so. Yes. I guess," I reply at last.

"So I did see you there. Why are you here two days in a row?"

"Why are *you* here two days in a row?"

She doesn't answer; her eyes are boring into the very core of me. I can't hide. Like an idiot, with no explanation, I make a break for the door. I pass through the other rooms without seeing the holograms and costumed staff and am back outside in the heat again. I'm claustrophobic. My heart is pounding drugs into my veins. I need to get away from people. All the tourists are closing in on me, their auras dirty and invasive, compressing me on all sides.

I make a run for the service alley behind the tavern and tuck myself up against the back wall, hidden between empty beverage crates. I breathe deeply for a minute, relieved to be out of the crowds.

I pull out my sketchbook. I have to draw the girl.

Why copper? What does it mean?

Once I've gotten her face right, I write down all the words I remember from our conversation. I sit there, surrounded by dirty asphalt, trash cans and old wooden pallets, and stare at her. She looks up at me and I can hear her voice in my ear. I feel the fog abating, the drugs like an ocean haze burning off in the afternoon sun.

I should go home. I should get as far away from this girl as possible.

I can't leave, though. I just…can't.

I get out a Magic Marker and set my headphones on my head. I listen to an old mixtape and scrawl little black designs onto the nails of my left hand. The first one looks like an eye so I make them all into eyes with Egyptian-looking eyeliner. I expand the pattern, creating an intricately patterned half glove.

I get some cassettes out of my backpack and inspect the ribbon of tape inside. I use my pinkie finger to wind them nice and tight. Just for fun, I rewind one completely and then fast-forward it all the way back, watching the tape loosen and tighten through the little plastic window.

I can't sit here forever.

My tape runs out with a hiss and a click. I have to stand up to dig the Walkman out of my pocket if I want to change sides.

What would I do at home all day and night? The idea of sitting in my mother's sterile house, staring at the television for twenty-four hours, is nauseating.

Fine. On with my day.

I extricate myself from my hiding place and walk my usual route through Future Land and Jungle Land. The Tarzan area has a good climbing area that I like to sneak into after dark. I decide to do that later. As I approach the entrance to Marine Land, I see her again at the fountain. She's leaning forward and looking into the turquoise water. Copper blooms like underwater flames from around her shoulders.

Dr. Shandra would say it's all right to talk to people. She would say it's healthy. She'd say I'm making progress.

Dr. Shandra doesn't know what she's talking about, I remind myself as I close the distance. I hover near the girl, half thinking I should back away, not sure how close to get. She looks up, not surprised to see me. Her eyes flicker down to the artwork I've done on my hand.

I gesture with it stiffly. "Here's the fountain." It's a good thing I'm not hitting on her. I clearly do not have what it takes to hit on a girl.

She nods.

I say, "But…I have to know. Why are you here two days in a row? Are you from out of town? And why are you alone?"

She shoots back, "Why are *you* here two days in a row? And why are *you* alone?"

I look at my shoes. "I don't know."

"Well, I don't know, either." After a beat, she laughs at my crestfallen face. "I'm just messing with you. You want to know why I'm here? You won't tell anyone?"

Fascinated, I put a hand to my heart. "I'll take it to the grave, ma'am," I say in my best imitation of a Texas accent.

She giggles. Her eyes light up when she does it, and it makes me want to be a total goofball so she'll do it again. "Okay. Well…I'm here to do something illegal," she says.

"Really? Seriously?"

"Sort of."

"Like what?" With my drawn-on hand, I play with the earring in my left ear. My head spins. I lose a moment; reality folds in on itself and I forget I'm anywhere.

"Hello?" She frowns. "Hello? Are you all right?"

I'm shoved back into the moment. "Sorry, what was that?" I blink a few times, hard, trying to clear my vision.

"I said, I'm Annabelle."

Annabelle.

I don't know if I would have expected her to be an Annabelle. I had imagined her as a Kristine, or a Stephanie. Annabelle seems old-fashioned in a way that doesn't quite fit.

She looks at me with raised eyebrows. I'm doing something wrong.

"What is your name?" she asks as though I'm slow.

"It's… I'm… It's Sean."

"Are you okay? You seem out of it." She pushes away from the fountain. Her turquoise backpack almost throws her off balance. Is it heavy?

"No, no, I'm fine." *"I'm doped up on antipsychotics"* is not something I plan on confessing to a beautiful woman no matter how out of practice I am. "So, what are your illegal activities? Are you a drug dealer or something?"

"I'm obviously not a drug dealer."

I have to smile. Her expression is so withering. "Well, what, then? You're killing me."

She presses her pink lips together and looks around sneakily. "I'm trying to find a place where I can do something without getting caught."

"What kind of something?"

"Well, I'm trying to find somewhere I can…disperse something."

"Like a toxic gas? Are you a terrorist?" That would be incredible.

"No!" She takes a deep breath. "I'm supposed to scatter my grandma's ashes here. I'm trying to find somewhere to do it. There. Happy?"

I mull that over and decide I like it. I ask, "Any particular reason your grandmother's ashes are supposed to go in Four Corners?"

"She liked it here. And I don't have any other ideas."

The ashes must be in her backpack. That's why it looks so heavy.

She has human remains in her backpack. This is the best day of my life.

"W-would you like me to help you find a spot?" I stammer through my excitement.

"I can do it. Unless you know some secret back area where no one will catch me. You know it's a felony to scatter ash without permission? I can't get caught."

"I know *all* the back areas. What kind of area would she like? I mean, you could do it right over there in the stream if you want. Is that why you're down here at the fountain?"

"I was thinking about it."

"But they come through the stream on those little canoes like fifty times a day, so keep in mind she'll get rowed through by a bunch of teenagers spitting into the water all day long."

"Great." She starts back toward the Tarzan area. "Any other ideas?"

I fall into step beside her. "What about the area behind Marine Land? There's a kind of park back there where they store all the equipment from the lake rides."

"I don't know," she says doubtfully. We make our way through crowds of kids and parents. "How often do you

come here? You really know your way around; you weren't
kidding."

I sigh. This will be the end of our conversation. "I'm here
pretty much every day."

"Since when?"

I fidget, crack my knuckles, rub my palms on my jeans. "A
couple of years, I guess."

"A couple of *years*? Why?"

"I don't know."

"What about weekends?"

"Um…" I look up at the hazy blue sky. "Not always."

In my peripheral, I see she looks up at me for a moment,
then resumes her pace quietly beside me. She seems to be
deep in thought.

Coming to Four Corners doesn't feel like a decision. I always just end up here, even when I've sworn I'll stay away.
It's been my home since I was released from the institution
and my mom dragged me to Austin. In a life where I haven't
made any meaningful adult decisions for myself, it's my own.
It's chaotic and strange, hot and messy, full of people and yet
lonelier than the most abandoned ghost town, and it's mine.

The institution—well, really it was a psychiatric prison—
in which I served my time had a library. I was so doped up in
those days, worse even than I am now, and I got fixated on
books about the Wild West for some reason. I read about ghost
towns in Colorado, old mining towns in Oregon, haunted
saloons in the California desert not far from the institution.
I fantasized about escaping and making my way with great
valor through the heat-stricken desert, taking shelter in one
of those old towns and becoming one of the ghosts. The fantasies became so real to me that sometimes I woke up in my

cell and cried because I wasn't out there, sleeping under the broken, wood-slatted roof of a ruined brothel.

Sometimes, on hot, dry days, I come to the Four Corners Wild West Alley and remember those days in the institution. Now, with Annabelle by my side, a glimpse of some other life twinkles, teasing me. Is this how all the subjects of my portraits feel, like they're a part of something, some encompassing culture of humanity, connected to and safe from the people around them? Walking around with Annabelle, I can almost imagine how wonderful that would be.

By sunset, we've discarded a hundred grandma-dispersal ideas. We end up back at the Marine Land Lake, which is a big, shallow, man-made lake where they have the fireworks show every night during the summer. I take her down to the side farthest from all the people and we stake out a couple of rocks that let us dangle our feet in the air above the water. We're both tired and hungry, and this is my last idea.

She settles onto her rock, smooth legs tan and lean as they dangle above the murky lake. A pair of discarded Coke cans float by and wedge themselves in the bank, joining a cluster of cigarette butts and plastic bags. The air is like steam around us, her copper aura melting into the heat, bright against its surreptitious backdrop of shadow.

"How do you feel about this place?" I ask solicitously, willing to search all day and night if it will make her happy.

"It's not windy, so that's good. The ashes won't fly back into my mouth. I read that can happen."

I try not to laugh and fail. It comes out as a snorting sound, and Annabelle narrows her eyes at me. "Stop laughing at me."

"I'm not."

"Yes, you are. Ugh. It's so hot." She pulls the hair off her neck.

"Wait till July."

She chuckles. "I know. Then in August the flying cockroaches come out. Gotta love Texas summers."

I run my hand over the shaved side of my head. It's sweaty.
Since I was released, I haven't cut my hair. It's an act of lib-
eration. I buzzed my head every few weeks in the institution. I was always claustrophobic in my cell, and my mop
of hair was too much to bear. I'd made a pact with myself:
when I was free, I'd have hair again. Weirdly, though, when
I was released and started growing it, I missed running my
hand over the prickly scalp, so I started shaving some of it so
I could run my hand over the prickles without losing my re-
bellion. I like to think it looks sort of punk, not that I've had
anyone to impress.

Annabelle is pawing around in her backpack. She's talking,
but I've missed it. I'm losing time again. I try to concentrate,
pull myself back into the moment. "Can you repeat that last
part?" I ask.

"What do you do all day, here at Four Corners? Don't you
get bored all by yourself?" She takes out a beige jar made out
of some kind of hard ceramic.

"Um… I don't know."

She shoots me a frustrated glare. "If you say 'I don't know'
again, I'm pouring these ashes into your mouth."

"I'm sorry." I try to gather my thoughts. I think I've forgotten how to have a conversation. I rub my palms on my
jeans to stop the itching. This rolls up some of my jelly bracelets in a weird way and I have to spend a second fixing them.
"Well, I people-watch. Draw stuff. Walk around. Find little
corners and hang out there."

"Why?" She does not take her eyes from the jar.

"I don't know why."

"Seriously. Tell me. Why?"

I sigh. "To practice my drawing, I suppose. That's the main thing I do. I… Honestly, I don't know what else to do."

"You're an artist?"

"Not a real artist. I just draw. I don't paint or sculpt anything." It's very strange to have someone asking me questions who is not my psychiatrist. It's extra strange because the person asking is beautiful, with a glowing copper innocence and a soft and pretty voice. It's strange because I'm very much alone with this person, which I probably shouldn't be. It would be better if I could draw her. I could be busy. She could stop asking me questions. My hands could stop itching and reminding me of all the terrible things they're capable of doing.

"Do you live alone?" she asks.

"No. With my mother. I moved with her when she got a job here. We're from San Francisco. She's a doctor. A neurosurgeon, actually."

"San Francisco—really? I went to undergrad in San Francisco!"

"Seriously?"

She grins, as excited as I am about the coincidence. "I loved it there. So beautiful. Cold, though. I came back here for med school. I was premed at USF. Now I'm a first year med student at UT."

"Wait. You're going to be a *doctor*?"

"Why are you so surprised? Don't I seem the type?"

"No, no, it's just—I hate doctors," I confess.

"Oh, I see. You're one of those." She smiles faintly, her attention moving to the jar in her hands. She turns it over and over.

I ask, "So, why'd you leave? Why not do med school at

UCSF? It's a great school, or so I hear. My mom worked at the teaching hospital."

"I was on a scholarship for undergrad only. My family doesn't have money, so I had to decide how much debt I wanted to be in when I graduated." She looks strained as she says this, as though it's something she's ashamed of. "Anyway," she continues. "Your mother is a neurosurgeon?"

I nod.

"There are only, what, like, ten female neurosurgeons in the country! What's her name?"

"Nancy Suh."

"I don't think I've heard of her. Wow. That's incredible. You must be so proud."

"I am." I'm not very convincing; she shoots me a look, so I have to elaborate. "She's so conceited about it that it makes me want to…I guess…minimize it somehow. Now that I say it out loud, it's probably mean of me."

She seems to have stopped listening to my babbling. Her eyes are fixated on the jar in her hands.

"I'm sorry," I say, embarrassed. "I should be giving you some privacy, not chattering away like this."

She turns her eyes on me and gives me a warm smile. She takes a deep breath and unscrews the top. "Might as well get this over with anyway. She's not really in this jar. She's dead and gone. And no one cares but me." Without ceremony, she upturns the jar and gray ash sprinkle-chunks down onto the lake's surface below. The ash clouds the top of the water. I'm surprised. No prayers. She must not be religious.

"Why are you doing this alone?" I ask gently, worried the question will upset her.

"There's no one else to do it. Almost my whole family is dead. And it's my grandma's birthday tomorrow, and…it just seemed like I should do this on her birthday." She screws the jar shut and returns it to her backpack.

I watch the large chunks gather water. The greasy, gravelly ash floats across the surface and then sinks down into the mire. Some ash is fine and clings to the surface of the water, and I follow the invisible, sluggish currents until they dissipate.

I'm like the ash. Every day I feel like I've lost another grain of myself, like I'm a mist settling over the ground and getting burned off by it. How much more of me is left?

Enough. My hands need to be busy. I'm halfway through unzipping my bag when she asks, "What are you doing?"

It occurs to me that I should have asked permission. "Oh. Um… I'm sorry. Can I draw you right now?"

"Draw me doing what?"

"Just keep looking down at the lake." I get out my book and graphite and start sketching.

She's lost in thought and so am I. I lose track of time and don't realize that now I'm colorizing, which takes forever and I should have done it later, until she says, "You don't have a job, or school, or anything at all?"

"No. I don't have anything." The sun is setting behind the trees that surround the lake, and she's glimmering in the orange light.

"Why?"

I ignore the question and return to my drawing. She gets up, obviously stiff from sitting for so long, and comes around behind me to look. I almost shut the sketchbook but stop myself. She sucks air in. "Oh my god."

I look up, worried. She covers her mouth with a hand.

"I didn't mean…"

She shakes her head. "I just didn't expect it to be so good."

"Oh." I look down at it. I'm making a background in this

one; I don't usually do landscapes, but something about the split complementary color palette is compelling.

"You are a real artist. Not just some guy who does drawings. Why did you make it sound so casual? Do you have shows? In galleries?"

"No." I darken the shading on the trees behind her. She crouches down so she can watch over my shoulder.

"You make it look beautiful. Like a beautiful moment. But it really wasn't. I was just sitting there."

"Maybe it was beautiful, but only from the outside. It's like that sometimes."

She sits down at my elbow and watches my hand. "My grandma was crazy. I was the only person who would take her ashes."

I consider that. It will probably be like that when I die.

"You shouldn't have made it so colorful. It looks too perfect."

"Can't help it. You are *really* colorful." I look sideways at her face, which is much too close for comfort. It's acting on me like a truth serum. "You're the most colorful person I've ever met. You're actually metallic. You have this glimmer about you."

She kisses my cheek, which shocks me into complete stillness. "That's a lovely thing to say," she whispers.

I try to say something, but the only thing that happens is a little croak from my throat and a sudden onslaught of sexual images. I hadn't realized I'd been cataloging the exact shape of her breasts, but now I can clearly imagine what they would look like if I were to set them free. Up till now, I had been operating under the assumption that she had no sexual interest in me. That had made me feel sort of safe. I'm no rapist. This one cheek kiss changes everything, though, and while my stomach fills with helium, my heart plummets down onto the ground beneath me.

Instead of throwing my pencils into my backpack and running for the park exit, which is exactly what I should do, I turn my face to hers and look directly into her eyes. They are close and mysterious behind their maple syrup gleaming. I wait for her to recoil but she doesn't. A wave of electricity passes between us. I kiss her, and she kisses me back.

For a moment I want to cry because I know I should stop, but then I can't care enough to think about anything but her soft, sweet lips and her clean-smelling hair that tickles my cheeks. I clench my hands into fists so they can't hurt her, and that clenching gives me hope. I don't want to hurt her. I mean, I do, but then, at the core of my being, I don't.

Her lips open against mine again, harder, her tongue delicious, slippery soft. Her fingers rake up my neck and grip the roots of my hair. A jolt shocks me and my arms wrap around her.

Mine.

The word slithers through me, ice-cold. I pull back.

Am I at the crossroads? Or have I already chosen a path?

CHAPTER TWO

I grunt a hello upon entering the air-conditioned office. "Good morning, Sean," Dr. Shandra says in her smoothest doctor voice. She stands by the window, a white, shoulder-padded suit jacket unbuttoned over a pale yellow blouse. Her last name is Beck, but she likes me to call her Dr. Shandra. The first-name doctor thing is supposed to make me realize how cool she is, how safe I should feel talking to her, and above all, how much my mom should continue to pay her top-of-the-line, went-to-a-fancy-school psychiatrist rate for these twice-weekly sessions.

I take my place in the armchair near the window. She's positioned it here because she knows it makes me more comfortable to look out at the traffic below. A Coke awaits me on the table, as does a box of Kleenex. This is a little symbol of hope on her part, of faith that someday her methods will work and my wall of reserve will come crumbling down, leaving a sobbing pile of Sean blubbering in her armchair and (apparently) chugging Coke to soothe his newly realized psychological torment.

She settles into her chair across the coffee table from me. Her black hair is organized into tiny braids wound into a maze of perfect neatness and piled into a decorative bun on the left side of her head, revealing diamond earrings that sparkle against the rich umber skin of her earlobes.

She awards me her talk-to-me smile. "What's goin' on, Sean?"

"Not much." I hook my index finger under the rubber of one of my black jelly bracelets and twist, hard. The coil of anxiety in my gut relaxes a notch.

She brushes an invisible piece of lint from her knee. "How is your week going so far?"

"It's fine."

"What did you do last night?"

"Just watched TV."

"Anything special on?"

"*Cheers. Three's Company* reruns."

"And how is Four Corners this week?" Dr. Shandra asks.

I hesitate, just barely. "It's fine."

"Any particular reason you wanted to reschedule this appointment for so early a time slot? That's unusual for us. I don't think we've ever met at eight a.m." She smiles.

I try to keep my face neutral. "I just didn't want to miss so much of my day at Four Corners. There's…some…stuff I want to sketch."

"Have you drawn any interesting portraits since I saw you last?"

"Not really."

"Are you still experiencing the…visual phenomenon?"

She wants to say *hallucination* but doesn't want to upset me. *Phenomenon* is the word she's settled on and she seems proud of having come up with it, as though she invented the word just to please me and is happy it has succeeded.

"Yep," I say.

"Well, that's all right. We are a work in progress."

I look out the window and twist my bracelet a little tighter.

"Have you spoken with anybody this week?"

I will not mention Annabelle. I shake my head vehemently. My hair falls down over my right eye and I let it stay there, more comfortable with part of my face covered. I let my gaze wander up to the painting of geometric shapes in black, white and primary colors. A trail of yellow polka dots runs through the middle of it like an asteroid belt. I often look at it during my sessions, trying to make it become something concrete: a deconstructed pizza, a bin of child's blocks hurled into space, a rabbit with triangles for ears.

Dr. Shandra is talking. I try to give her my attention. "What was that?"

"Maybe you can give it a try today?"

"Maybe."

"I want you to try. Just try. Can we agree on that?"

I shrug.

"Are you never lonely?"

I study the ripped knees of my faded black jeans. "I dunno." *"What the hell do you think?"* I want to scream.

"You're rehabilitated. It's time to start—"

I open my mouth to argue and then snap it shut. The Bible says, "Whoever guards his mouth preserves his life; he who opens wide his lips comes to ruin." I remember sitting on the hard folding chairs in Sunday School while the teacher rambled about the power of words and the need to use them wisely. One time when I was around eight, I remember answering my mother's usual "What did you learn today, Sean?"

with "I think the Devil talks a lot. Like a salesman. But then why do church people talk so much?" She'd stared at me for a moment, her eyes narrowing. She herself is not a woman of unnecessary words, so she didn't ask me to elaborate. She turned away, her hand tightening on mine, and continued our march toward the car. Our life is just that: an eternal purposeful march toward my mother's planned destination, her steps firm and single-minded, my gait bumbling as I try to catch up, knees knocking together, head scattered and restless.

Dr. Shandra clears her throat. I've missed a good portion of her speech.

"Are you feeling all right?" she asks.

"A little fuzzy," I admit.

She frowns. "Is this typical for you?"

"Just since the new, you know." I think about it for a minute. "Whatever new meds." My tongue is heavy.

"The change in your antidepressant?"

"I dunno. I just take whatever my mom puts in the pillbox."

She speaks to me for a little while but I'm in a vacuum. I play with my jelly bracelets, fashioning some of them into a ring-bracelet combination thing that's going to be very difficult to remove later.

Then I get blurry for a while, I don't know how long, and I find myself outside again on the sidewalk in front of the building, like time is a ribbon that has folded itself together and offered me a shortcut from then to now. The air is muggy and smells of exhaust. Overhead, the sun shines hot through an overcast sky, diffusing the light and sending heat waves into foggy rainbows off the grimy windshields of the parked cars that line the busy four-way street. I hold perfectly still for a long moment, racking my brain for memories of the last part of the session, but they won't come. I hate this, losing time.

I'm so tired of this. I can't remember what it was like before the meds, but I remember feeling like my head was clear, not full of bees and smog.

I don't have time for this. I haul myself back into reality. I have to hurry. Annabelle is picking me up in an hour.

At home, too nervous to eat breakfast, I hover around the kitchen near the answering machine. I rewind the squeaky tape and listen to a message over and over again, waiting for the doorbell to ring. The message is from my grandmother. It's in Korean so all I catch is my mom's Korean name, Min-Jung, and a few basic words like *hello* and *goodbye*, but the sound of my grandma's voice reminds me of my extended family in San Francisco. She only leaves messages in Korean so I'll know they're not for me. She won't even utter my name.

When my mom relocated here, she did so because she was being offered a position at the medical center in Austin. I wish we could have stayed in San Francisco. I had envisioned leaving the asylum and returning to all the things I'd missed so badly. I think I had even harbored hope that I could see my family again someday. I didn't yet know I'd been disowned.

My grandmother will never forgive me. I understand that now. The rest of my family always does whatever she says; she's the matriarch. Once she's made up her mind, there's no changing it, and she says I've brought disgrace on the entire family. I'd never been that close to them anyway, I suppose. My mom has an older brother who is obviously the preferred sibling. We only saw them for holidays and the occasional church event—my grandparents became Christians after World War II and are extremely religious—and even then, it felt strained and obligatory. My uncle and his family are always at my grandparents', and my cousins speak fluent Korean. After a childhood filled with Hispanic nannies, I know more words in Spanish than Korean.

When my last nanny took the stand at my trial, she'd broken down in tears. "Sean is a good boy," she'd insisted in trembling, accented English that still sounded like Spanish no matter how hard she and I worked on her pronunciation.

It had made me cry, too, right there with all those people watching me. I'd hidden my face in my arm and had struggled desperately and unsuccessfully to suck the tears back into my face.

I am *a good boy*, I'd thought desperately, sobs quaking my bony shoulders.

Afterward, when the judge dismissed us for lunch, my lawyer had squeezed my shoulder and whispered in my ear, *"Well done, Sean. Well done,"* and even my inner monologue felt like a manipulative, well-planned lie.

The doorbell rings.

I push Stop on the answering machine. My grandmother's voice is cut off with a screech and a click. I inch toward the front door, sliding my feet grudgingly on the slick white tile. Through the foggy glass blocks that surround the front door, I see a person-sized shadow.

The doorbell rings again. I breathe slowly, in through my nose, out through my mouth the way Dr. Shandra taught me, the way that is supposed to calm me down when I'm feeling anxious.

The bell rings one more time. If I don't answer it now, she'll surely leave.

Okay, then. I grip the handle and swing it open, swathed in surrealism when Annabelle appears in all her colorful spotlessness, standing shyly on my porch with copper and shadows flickering all around her like propane flames on a windy day.

"Hi," she says.

I nod. I can't speak.

"Am I…is this the right day?"

"Of course. I'll just get my stuff and be right there." I turn around.

"Can I come in?"

"Oh." My heart beats faster. It hadn't occurred to me that she'd want to come in. "Sure," I say, lingering on the *sh* sound. She steps in and I close the door behind her.

She stuffs her keys into the pocket of her pleated shorts. She looks at the white leather couch, the plush peach carpet, the spotless white walls. "Stylin'," she says.

"My mother," I explain, wondering if it makes me sound immature.

I make my way across the living room to the stairs. "I'm just gonna grab my backpack and stuff. Be right back."

"Is that where your room is? Upstairs?" She's following me. My heart pounds harder. This is not good—my mom would freak out—but what am I supposed to do?

"Your room is upstairs?" Annabelle repeats.

"Yeah. But…" I pause, awkward. We're not supposed to wear shoes in here, but she clearly doesn't take her shoes off in her own house. I don't feel right making her do it in mine.

"What?" Annabelle asks.

"Nothing. It's this way." She follows me up the carpeted steps.

"No siblings?" she asks. "Just you and your mom?" Her voice echoes in the stairwell.

"Just us."

"No dad? I'm sorry, it's just—my parents were divorced and I'm an only child, so…"

I turn around and smile, afraid she feels rebuked. "It's okay. No. No dad."

"Divorced?"

"Yeah. He moved back to Korea when I was a little kid. I don't remember him at all."

She makes a little sympathetic noise.

"Don't worry about it. Honestly." I lead her the rest of the way upstairs. In my room, I hurry away from her, relieved to put some distance between us. "I'll just be a second. Let me get my stuff." I start organizing my pencils and then stop. Is it safe to carry pencils around when I'm with her? I study the sharp tips. I used them yesterday and it was fine. Could I...would I? I don't think so. I pack them into my backpack.

Annabelle interrupts my paranoid train of thought. "Did you just move in or something?"

"What? No. Why?"

"It's so empty."

I look around, surprised. Bed, desk, dresser, bookshelf, shelf with stereo, all with the same reflective black finish. "What do you mean?"

"There's furniture but no decorations, nothing extra."

"It just...never occurred to me to decorate."

"But you're an artist."

I consider, looking at the white walls. "I guess this doesn't seem like my space to decorate. It's my mom's house. I never planned to stay here so long."

She spots the intercom panel by the door. "Shut up," she gasps. "You have one of these?" She pounces on it and presses the talk button. "Mission control here, what is your status?" she says in a mock-NASA voice like the one that broadcasted on all the networks a few months ago when the *Challenger* exploded.

I can't help but laugh. "I don't even know if it works," I confess. "My mom won't let me use it."

"Oh my god. You'd have to disconnect it if you lived with me. My roommate would kill me." She moves to the shelf above my bed; it's full of matching sketchbooks bound in black leather, the regular kind you buy at Aaron Brothers. There are about twenty lined up on the right side of the shelf; the left side is full of mismatched sketchbooks from my younger days.

"What are these?" she asks.

"My sketchbooks."

"May I?"

I hesitate. "Sure, I guess. That one on the end is fine. That fat black one."

She rests a knee on the black-and-white bedspread and tips the one I'd indicated off the shelf with a delicate finger. She opens it to a place in the middle. "You draw people at Four Corners all day? These are all tourists?"

I shrug.

She frowns down at the page. "You write things about them here. Do you interview them?"

"No. I guess I…kind of make up life stories for them."

"You're incredibly talented." She puts the book back onto the shelf and reaches for one of the smaller volumes. "Are these from—"

I leap across the room and take the book from her. I return it to the shelf. "Sorry. It's just…those are from when I was younger. They're more private."

"I'm so sorry." She's red in the face.

"No, it's fine. *I'm* sorry."

I return to packing my backpack and she moves to my closet. She slides it open and flips through the clothes. "Do you wear all these? They don't really look like you."

I zip up my bag and join her. Her shampoo smells fresh and summery. It's all I can do to keep from kissing the back of her neck.

She gives me an inquisitive look and I remember her question. "Oh. No. My mother buys me all of those. Hoping I'll wear them. Which I won't." There's a row of button-down shirts and slacks, clean blue jeans and polo shirts shoved to the side. In the middle are all my faded, ripped black shirts and jeans.

She touches an old black shirt. "She doesn't like what you wear?"

I smile with one side of my mouth. "That's putting it mildly."

"She wants you to be preppy?"

"Collegiate," I correct her, using my mom's favorite word.

"But you don't go to college. Or, wait. Did you already graduate?"

"I didn't go. She's hoping I will. My cousins are in college," I say in my best imitation of her bossiest voice, and Annabelle laughs.

"Your mom seems controlling," she says.

It's such a relief to hear her say that. "She is."

"I mean, you're, how old?"

"Twenty-three."

"Right. She shouldn't be buying you clothes."

"I'll tell her you said that." I smile to myself. While I think this is partly cultural, it's nice to hear someone agree with me.

She wanders to the tightly made bed and sits on the edge with her tan legs crossed, one sneaker tapping in midair, her Keds bright white against fluffy, hot-pink socks. She looks like some fairy-tale princess who wandered in here by mistake.

I shove my hands in my pockets to stop the itching. "Can I ask you something?"

"Sure."

"Why…why…" I feel my cheeks burning, which says a lot. I don't blush easily. Finally I spit out, "I guess I don't understand why you're here."

She pauses and then says, "I thought we were going to hang out today. You promised to show me all the secret passageways."

"That's not what I mean." Embarrassment crawls around inside my gut.

"What do you mean, then?"

I look into her eyes. "I mean, why do you want to hang out with *me*? You're—" I gesture to her metallic beauty. As though to illustrate my point, copper flames flicker through her hair like a fiery halo.

The corners of her eyes crease, like she's trying not to smile. "I like you. You're…interesting. I don't know. Why does anyone hang out with anyone else?"

"I'm Korean, for one. White girls in Texas never like Asian guys."

She feigns a gasp. "You're *Asian*? I hadn't noticed."

I can't help but laugh. "Shut up."

"Actually, I had guessed Filipino."

"I'm just tan from the sun." I lift up a corner of my shirt to show her my pale stomach.

"Ah. Well, that's going to be a problem. I only date certain *types* of Asians." Her grin is wide now, dimpling her cheeks.

Date. She'd said date.

"Is there any other reason I shouldn't want to hang out with you today?" she teases. "Any other physical traits you think I should, you know, really take heed of?"

"I dress weird. Especially for Texas."

She laughs, stands up, and runs a hand along the shorn side of my head and then down the long hair that covers my eye. Her touch sets off all kinds of little alarm bells and prickles inside me. "I figured you were just really bad at shaving. Or were recovering from brain surgery." Quickly she gets up on tiptoes and kisses my cheek. "Stop being stupid. You're a handsome, weird guy and I like you. Can we go climb buildings now?" Playfully she pinches my feather earring and tickles my ear with it. "Come *on*, Sean, I need a day off. You have to take my mind off the corpse I've been dissecting."

Handsome. She said *handsome.*

Unable to resist the giddiness that rises up in my stomach, I grin, bashful. "If you promise to tell me more about the corpse."

"I'll tell you everything." She excuses herself to use my bathroom, and I look around my room with my hands buried in my pockets. She's right. There are no posters on my wall, nothing decorative.

She comes out of the bathroom and squeezes my arm. "All right. You promised to show me secret passageways and you're not getting out of it." She pushes past me and trots down the stairs, leaving me to follow her with my heart and stomach and hands all tied up, itching and filled with ice and butterflies.

CHAPTER THREE

Against all my instincts, I decide to try to enjoy the day. When will I get a chance like this again? How can I not be a little bit happy?

By now I'm fascinated by Annabelle. I learn things about her: first, she wants to be a doctor because she loves helping people. She volunteers at the campus women's crisis line and talks passionately about the increase in sexual violence and correlation with underage drinking. She lives with a roommate in an apartment off campus. She works part-time in a restaurant called Duke's, which is known for its employment of young waitresses who are forced into a uniform of short shorts and skimpy tank tops.

I'm surprised by this. "That doesn't bother you? You don't seem the type. Med student and all."

She shrugs. "I don't know. The men can be creepy, but the tips are way better than anywhere else I've worked. My family... I don't have any money coming in from them."

She loves horses and grew up in a small town outside Dallas. She says it's a hick town and seems a little ashamed of it. She is an insane climber and beats me to a few roofs, which is impressive. I'm trying so hard to focus and keep time flowing forward at a normal pace. It's exhausting, not being able to retreat into my medicated stupor, but I don't want lose a moment of this day.

I show her all the rooftops and all the secret passageways I can, sneaking her into the paths between rides that look more like tunnels tucked between Hollywood-style building facades. We explore the secret areas where the actors' changing rooms are and where the ambulance docks are hidden. I lead her to the service stairs that run up the back of the three-stories-high fake skyscraper in Future Land I call the High Tower, making sure no one is watching, which is just a formality. This is shift change time and the rides are manned by a skeleton crew while a new shift of workers takes over for the night.

The roof is minimally slanted and I take her to my favorite spot, tucked next to vents on the southwest side. From up here, people are nothing but little crawling creatures, creeping along the paths in pairs and groups. Far ahead, where the blinding sun is beginning to sink into the hazy, indistinct horizon, the theme park ends and the city begins. The freeway curves along the south toward downtown and the skyscrapers poke up in a cluster.

We settle down on the gently sloping roof to watch the sunset, tired and arguing playfully. She wants me to take her to the basement of the wax museum where they store all their Halloween stuff. I've been down there a couple of times during chaotic shift changes when so many people are coming and going that they never noticed me, but I'm not about to go now on a slow weekday. I can't get kicked out of Four Corners; where would I go instead?

She kisses me and I forget all about our little spat. For such a sweet girl, she kisses like a goddess. Her lips and skin are so soft; my fingertips and lips aren't gentle enough to kiss and touch her properly. I trail kisses down her neck and she shivers, one hand clutching the back of my hair. I think she likes my hair; she keeps running her hands through it. I want to tear her shirt off and rip the buttons off her shorts but I restrain myself. She doesn't seem like the getting-naked-on-dirty-rooftops type of girl. Besides, I don't even know if I could have sex. How long has it been since I tried to masturbate? I try to remember and fail. Despair and grief flood me like another wave of drugs, always drugs.

I kiss her once more and pull back. Her eyes are half-closed and the setting sun is turning her into a copper glitter fairy. I brush the hair back from her forehead and try to memorize every inch of her face. "Let me draw you right now."

"Draw me doing what?"

"Nothing. Just laying there." I sit up to get my sketchbook from my backpack. She shifts on the rough tarpaper, trying to find a comfortable position, so I take my shirt off and wad it up for a pillow for her.

She wiggles her eyebrows at my torso. "Not bad. Except for the farmer's tan." The compliment embarrasses and pleases me so much that I feel the unfamiliar blush creeping up my neck again. I hadn't even thought to feel shy about taking my shirt off. My body has been a strictly clinical thing for as long as I can remember.

I sit cross-legged with my sketchbook on my lap. The light is perfect. Her expression is open and her waves of copper and shadows are sweeping through me. I'll get this one right, I know it.

"Why are you doing that?" she asks after a few minutes.

"Drawing?"

"Mmm–hmm."

I'm working on the line of her jaw; I've made it too an-
gular and I'm pissed off at myself. I erase, draw, erase, draw,
squint, draw.

"Sean?"

"Oh." I blink at her. Despite my efforts, I've lost a minute.
"Because… I guess because I want to remember this. Capture it."

"For yourself for later?"

I nod.

"We could do this again. Then you wouldn't have to draw
it."

"I have the feeling we won't be doing this again."

"Why not? We could."

I set my book aside. I lie on my bare stomach and take her
hand, press my lips to it. The beast and my conscience and
my mom and Dr. Shandra and the institution and even my
own self seem far away from this moment. The only thing I
feel and see and smell is her, and I want to immerse myself
in her and forget all those other things. I can almost believe
it's possible.

One day. That was the deal.

My lips against her hand, gravel grinding into my elbow, I
say, "You're going to be a doctor, Annabelle. I'm, like, Korean
Quasimodo. We both know nothing's going to come of this."

That last sentence lingers precariously, pinned to the air
between us.

She takes the hand I've been kissing and runs it through
my hair. "I think you'll change your mind. I think you'll be
calling me by…Saturday." Her tone is playful.

I lift myself onto a forearm and kiss her lips. I don't know what to say, and the second I kiss her, I forget I was planning to say anything at all. Am I falling in love with her? Is that what this is? Can I know her well enough for that? Maybe I can. I've been in love once before. It felt like this, or at least I think it did. It's been a long time. If anything, this feels stronger, more intense, more visceral. Is it because my memories of Elise are dulled by the drugs I've been taking ever since?

The name twists through me.

Elise. It's been so long since I let myself think about her. I remember tangling my fingers in her shiny black ponytail and pulling her face sideways to kiss her on the cheek. She'd giggled, something that had annoyed me at the time but feels precious and poignant now.

Guilt and horror pour down on me like rain, and the images attack me without warning. I see myself picking Annabelle up and hurling her over the roof. It's so sudden and vivid that I jump away from her, pressing my back to the roof, hands sweaty against the rough tar paper.

She sits up. "Sean? What's wrong?"

"We need to get down," I stammer.

"Are you okay?"

"Get down. Start climbing down!" My heart is pounding.

She looks me over for a minute and says, "Okay. Sure."

"You first. I'll see you down there."

I cling to the gritty tar paper and close my eyes. It's better if I don't know where she is. Safer.

I feel my shirt land softly on my chest. "Are you okay?" she asks.

"I'm fine. I just need a minute. I'll see you down there."

"I'll be right at the bottom."

I wait a minute, two minutes, three minutes, counting the

seconds by my pounding heart. When I open my eyes she's gone and I breathe relief out through my nose.

That was close.

This is what I was afraid of.

I'm so stupid. I'd thought of the pencils but hadn't thought it might be dangerous up on this roof? I'm distracted. I'm not being vigilant enough. This was sloppy, careless, irresponsible.

Enough. The day is over. I had my fun. If I care about Annabelle, I'll walk away now.

Back on land, humiliation setting fire to my every extremity, I walk beside Annabelle through the forest behind Marine Land that borders the whole back end of the park and the two-lane highway beyond. It's dusk and the forest is alive with the buzzing of cicadas. Somewhere not too far away a family is laughing. Their proximity makes me feel safer. We're not really alone in the woods. It just seems that way.

"I'm sorry about that," I say at last.

She laces her fingers through mine. "You're scared of heights?"

"I guess so."

"My roommate's afraid of heights." She tells me about a time they got stuck at the top of a skyscraper downtown because her roommate wouldn't get on the windowed elevator. I try to laugh but it comes out wrong. I'm full of misery. Right now all I want is to be like her, a normal, healthy twenty-something with friends, roommates, a job… All at once, I am acutely aware of how far from the world I am, how outside of and irrelevant to it, and it spears me through the stomach with loneliness and rage.

We're walking through the forest about fifty feet from the chain-link fence that separates Four Corners from the road when she tosses me a sad smile. "It's funny that you brought

me to this place. This was my grandma's favorite part of the
park. She took me here a million times."

"Here?" I glance around in surprise.

"She liked to escape the crowds. Every time I come back,
I walk through these trees and think about her."

"I didn't realize you came here that much."

"Every year on her birthday."

"We should have scattered her ashes here, then."

She shrugs. "It seemed too obvious. I figured you'd have
some more interesting ideas. And you did." She stops walking and looks up at me. "What happens now, Sean?"

"Now?"

"Will you call me?"

"I don't have your phone number. I don't actually know
your last name."

She holds a hand out. "Pen?"

I get out my sketchbook and turn to the most recent drawing, then flip to the next page and hand it to her with a colored pencil. She pages back and looks at her own face for a
long moment. "Do I really look like that?"

"You do."

She tilts the book. "I look different in my mind."

"Like what?"

"I don't know. I guess older. And not as...not as all-American,
I guess. Not as goody-goody."

I flip the page for her. "Write down your phone number
and stop being silly."

She writes "Annabelle Callaghan" with an Austin phone
number.

"Irish?"

She points to her hair.

"It's not really red."

"Close enough." She closes the book and hands it to me. "Don't give me yours. I won't call you. You can call me if you want to see me."

I put the book into my bag and decide I'm going to have to burn that page. I'm not going to be able to stay away from her otherwise.

She glances toward the road as though startled.

"What?" I ask. I look in that direction but don't see anything.

"I guess it's nothing." She shakes her head. "Okay, then. Well, Sean, thanks for showing me your secret passageways."

She's going to leave. She's going to walk away. All of the reasons not to stop her seem very small and stupid.

I can't resist kissing her one last time, my hands tight on her little waist and then soft in her hair. As they pass her neck, I get a wave of fear and an urge to squeeze, and I have to snap them open and take a step back, my heart pounding. I want to cry. I want to do violent things. I take another step back and confine my hands to my pockets.

She takes that as her cue and turns to walk away. I watch her go until I can't bear it anymore, and then I hurry off in the opposite direction. The cicadas, having seemed to quiet for a few minutes, start up their eerie buzzing. The noise grates on my nerves. I cram my hands to my ears, but the sound is echoing inside my head.

I have to stop and lean against a tree. The forest blurs around me, wavering like I've gone underwater. Somewhere closer to the park a child screams, probably having fun with a warm and happy family. What does it really matter if Annabelle has just walked away, vanished as though she had never been? Maybe she's been a dream. That's how it is going to be. I'm going to go back to my routine and it will be as though she never existed. She'll tell her roommate about this strange and creepy guy she made out with at the amusement park one time and how glad she is never to see me again.

The child screams again and I pull my hands off my face. I'm not sure that was a playful scream. I don't hear any responding cries from adults, or anything else, for that matter.

I turn and walk back the way I came, going on instinct, not really worried, just wanting to hear more and make sure all is well. The scream rises up again, and I realize it's not far from me; it's actually back the way Annabelle walked. Another scream slices through the trees, and the scream comes in the form of a name:

"*SEAN!*" the scream roars, and I tear forward through the forest because it *is* Annabelle.

Branches hit my face. My backpack is back on the ground somewhere behind me. The scream comes again, closer now, but it's choked and it cuts off. My heart pounds, stops, pounds again. To my right, red lights flicker through the semidark. I rush toward them. A person-sized hole has been cut in the six-foot chain-link fence that borders the highway. Against the hole, on the shoulder of the road, a white truck's rear tires churn up a plume of gravel. A blur of motion—a human body, legs flailing—someone being shoved across the front seat.

The passenger door bucks, kicked out—Annabelle's white sneakers, recognizable for an instant before they disappear with another terrified scream. "Sean—" Annabelle's voice chokes as the driver's door slams shut. A last scream makes its muffled way through the glass. Taillights flash and the tires make contact with the asphalt. It bumps onto the road and is gone around the corner. I'm right behind the truck, climbing through the hole in the fence, but I'm too late.

"Annabelle!" I scream.

I wait. Blood roars in my ears.

"*ANNABE*—" My voice cuts out; my throat's too dry. I dart into the street and almost get hit by a passing car. I run along the shoulder in the direction the white truck had gone, thoughts popping through the panicked fuzz inside my brain.

Where's the nearest pay phone? I have no idea. I can't think of a single time I've had to use the phone here. What is wrong with me that I've never had anyone to call?

I keep running. The woods are fuzzy through a psychotropic haze. My breath is hot, the cedar trees blurry around me, the dry forest floor puffing tumbleweeds of dust up around my ankles. I stumble, slam my shoulder into a tree trunk and fall backward on my ass. I realize my backpack is gone. I dropped it somewhere in the woods. I push myself up, keep running, brain spun with panic and throbbing with drugs.

The road takes me to a countrified intersection with horse fencing along one side of the highway and a ramshackle gas station on the other. I falter, hands on knees, hair falling over my face, sweat plastering my T-shirt to my back.

She's gone.

CHAPTER FOUR

Four cops surround me in a semicircle, their flashlights lighting up the trees. It's night, the buzz of cicadas having given way to the chirping crickets, humidity rising from the heat-packed earth like steam. Two cop cars are cruising the streets, their lights blinding passersby as they search driveways and alleyways.

I show them the hole in the fence. I tell them the same things over and over again. "Annabelle Callaghan. This was our first date. She goes to UT. We met here at Four Corners. She's *gone*. Can't you guys do something?"

The cops find my backpack among the trees, and I carefully rip the drawing of Annabelle from my sketchbook, the first one I'd drawn to capture her auburn eyes. They take turns staring at it with their flashlights trained on her face, passing it around and communicating silently with their eyebrows.

"I need that back when you're done with it," I say, nervous about them having it.

I know I look weird to them. I know they don't trust me. Am I wearing the feather earring today? I reach up to check.

Yeah. The feather. That's not good. This captures one officer's attention. He squints at the earring and gives me a look that is part disgust, part humor. Stinging shame burns through me. I yank the earring out and toss it aside when no one's looking.

They have a lot of questions. Why had we been wandering around all the way out here away from the park so close to the road? What's my name, they want to know, and when they hear my last name is Suh, which is how they pronounce *sir* in the sacred US Army or Marines or whatever, they raise their eyebrows at each other again as though I've blasphemed their great military culture with my offensively homophonic Korean surname.

Time does its fuzzy thing again and I'm at the police station, sitting in a waiting room on a goldenrod plastic chair against a puke-orange wall that probably hasn't been cleaned since the sixties. My heart is beating fast but regular: pound-pound-pound-pound-pound like I'm still running along the highway with my throat in my mouth. It syncs up with the click-clack of typewriters that echoes around the linoleum, creating an asynchronous rhythm like an indoor thunderstorm. My hair tickles my nose and I reach up with a shaking hand to push it back. It's wet with sweat. My whole body is damp and I bet I smell.

For a muddled minute, I watch a weathered-looking man in a chair nearby smoke a cigarette and contemplate the whorls of smoke that haze mysteriously through his navy-blue aura, and then I jump, remembering where I am and what I'm doing here. I put a hand out to search the floor around me for my backpack. It's not there.

I don't know who to ask. I'm in a big room with desks and there are cops behind the desks. Some other people in street clothes are sitting in chairs here and there, waiting like me.

I close my eyes and concentrate. I haven't taken my meds. I feel weird. You'd think it would make me feel clearer, but withdrawal from psych meds is no joke. "Come on, come on," I whisper. I hate it when I go blank like this. I need to remember where I put my backpack. My sketchbook is in there. Annabelle's sketches. I need them.

Where are the cops? Are they looking for Annabelle? Why am I here? I've told them everything already.

A flurry of motion makes me open my eyes and there's my mom, hurrying toward me with an officer at her side. "Oh no," I whisper. She makes a beeline for me, all efficiency and polished, suited authority. Her face is masked as always, skin stretched tight across her cheekbones, eyes sharp and darting. Her jaw is prominent, a feature that is more flattering on me than her. It makes her mouth look even smaller, her cheekbones wider. She is pretty in a geometric way, her face wrought with diamonds and hard edges, the point of her nose perfectly symmetrical.

She's berating the police officer when she gets to me, and he's actually apologizing. "Ma'am, I'm sorry, but he's an adult and we didn't know—"

"A mentally ill *young* adult, being questioned in the dark with no legal counsel, under what conditions do you suppose—"

"Ma'am, please, you can direct your questions to me," says a plainclothes detective who has appeared out of nowhere to rescue the young cop from my commanding mother. He's tall and athletic with bronzed skin and a thick golden mustache. His cheeks are pocked with acne scars.

She turns on him, the lower-ranking officer forgotten like he never existed, and begins her spiel again. I raise my hand like I'm in school. "Where's my backpack?" I ask the younger

officer but he just hurries away. The plainclothes officer trans-
fers us to a small room with a table and some chairs—is this an
interrogation room?—and my mom and I are alone for a minute while he goes to get his "colleague" to "take some notes."

My mom turns to me. "Sit down."

I sit.

She remains standing. Turquoise tendrils flicker around her
silhouette and fade into the space behind her.

I am afraid.

I smooth my hair with a damp palm and fold my hands
on the worn honey-brown table. "It smells weird in here,"
I whisper.

Her eyes flicker over my hair, my clothes, and then she dis-
cards me with her gaze. She looks around the room, examining the corners of the ceiling and then, weirdly, the underside
of the table. She comes to stand near me.

"What did you tell the police?" she asks in a voice so low
it's almost a whisper.

I look up at her uncomprehendingly.

She snaps her fingers in my face. "Sean. What did you tell
the police?"

"What do you mean? I told them what happened."

"And what is that?"

"They didn't tell you? But I thought—how did you know
to come here?"

"You told them to call me."

"I did?" I try to remember. "I need my backpack."

"Your backpack? Where is it?"

"I don't *know*."

"What do you mean? Does it have your meds in it?"

"I—no. Of course not. It has my sketchbook in it. My
pencils."

"Well, when did they take it from you?"

"I don't remember!" I instantly regret the admission.

"You're losing time." She sighs and smooths an imaginary wrinkle from the arm of her plum-colored, tapered-legged suit. She's straight from the hospital. I can smell it. Her hair is a perfect A-line bob, its lines even in every way.

One interesting fact about my mom that you'd never guess: she's very religious, just like my grandparents. It's weird on her, like a dress that doesn't fit, but it's how she's always been. I don't know how she reconciles her completely scientific approach to all problem-solving with her obsessive memorization of the Bible. I've never seen her pray in a moment of weakness or call a friend from church to solicit advice or company. It's more like a second job to her. She goes to church twice a week, studies whatever they tell her to study, and believes rigorously in good and evil and the importance of atonement for sin. She's really, really into sin. I mean, she's opposed to sin. Not *into* it. To be clear, she's interested in people *not* sinning, namely me.

The plainclothes detective returns with a woman also in a suit, albeit a less expensive one than my mom's. It has a boyish look, with rolled sleeves and a roomy fit that emphasizes her athletic build. Both are blond fortysomethings; a matched set. They have that Texas suntanned look that comes from going to sporting events and doing water sports in the six-month summer. The woman's bangs are teased into a style that tells you she's a professional but also a sporty, fun lady. Her eyebrows are thick and bold, darker than I'd expect on a natural blonde. The man is seeping maroon, an aggressive, thrusting color; the woman leaks a bluish violet. Both of them have their personalities in check and contained; their auras are faint, the tendrils delicate around them. They have a tape recorder and warn us that they're going to use it, only to aid their investigation or something since I'm not a suspect.

The woman has a story, I decide. I'd like to draw her. I want to capture the expression on her face. She's professional and this is work time so she's all business, but behind it there's a heavy, searching expression. She's carrying a burden. My mom has that same feeling about her; it's because of me.

"Mrs....Soo?" the female detective tries, unsure about the pronunciation.

"Dr. Suh," my mother corrects her. She leans forward in her most doctoral way. "Before we get you too worried, detectives, I should let you know that I have power of attorney. My son is mentally ill."

She's such a liar. "Mom—" I protest but she skewers me with a glare that sends my balls shrinking up into my body.

"I understand he claims to have witnessed an abduction," she goes on. "But I want you to take his statement with a grain of salt. He's a schizophrenic and can sometimes mistake his visual hallucinations for reality."

"Mom!" I yell. All three of them stare at me.

The detectives move their stares back to my mom.

The woman says, "Ma'am, your son claims to have witnessed an abduction of a young lady he was on a date with." She has been designated as the woman-to-woman conversationalist by some unspoken code of police telepathy.

My mom is unmoved by the show of sisterhood. Coldly she says, "My son doesn't date. He is extremely shy and reclusive by nature and really wishes nothing more than to be left alone. However, he does get easily confused. It could be that he witnessed an argument between a couple and internalized it inaccurately. These things happen. Many schizophrenic hallucinations are extrapolated from real events."

I have to take a deep breath and close my eyes or I'm going to yell at her. A lot.

"Mom," I say through clenched teeth. "I *was* on a date, and she *was* abducted." I hate the word. It's too clinical. She was taken screaming. There shouldn't be an easy word for it.

She stares at me for a long moment. "Let's call Dr. Beck. We'll get you in for an emergency session tomorrow. You need your evening meds. I'm sure you're experiencing disorientation—"

I appeal to the cops. "Her name is Annabelle Callaghan. Did you look her up? She's a real person. She goes to UT. She's a med student."

The woman tells my mom, "She *is* a real person, ma'am. We have made inquiries. We spoke with her roommate. She lives in an apartment off campus."

I seize onto that. "You see? Finally."

The male cop says, "She told her roommate she would be out of town for a week or two, visiting family."

I frown. Annabelle hadn't mentioned anything about that to me. Actually, I remember her telling me to call her on Saturday. Right? Why would she suggest I call her on a day she knew she wouldn't be home?

He continues. "What time exactly did you say this happened, Sean?"

"I don't know. It was dusk. I remember that the light was dimming."

"Dusk." He glances at his partner. "When did we get the call?"

"I'll have to look," she says. She starts paging through her notebook.

"How long did you wait before you called us?" he asks me.

My hands fly up in a gesture of helplessness. "However

long it took me to run around, look for the truck, then head across the street to the gas station. Five, ten minutes?"

"Eight forty-five," the lady detective says, reading from her notebook. "That's when he called. He called 911 and was transferred to the station by the dispatcher."

They share a quick look. "What time would you say dusk would have been?" he asks her.

"Eight?" she guesses. "At this time of year, maybe seven forty-five? We can easily check."

They look at me. I look back and forth between them. "What?" I ask.

"Are you sure it was dusk when she was abducted?" the woman asks. "Think carefully. You said there were taillights."

"I'm pretty sure," I say, becoming less sure the more they look at me like that.

I feel my mom open her mouth to speak, but the male detective beats her to the punch. "Well, I think we've got what we need for now," he says. "We'll be in touch."

"So how will you look for her?" I ask them. "Will you start with the white truck? You can access DMV records, right? You can look up all the white trucks in the area, see if—"

"Sean," he says, "why don't you get a good night's sleep? Go home and take your medication, like your mother says. We'll touch base with you tomorrow."

"Sleep? Seriously? That's what you're telling me to do?"

"There's nothin' here for you to do, buddy. I promise you we're takin' your report seriously. Just leave it in our hands." He displays his manly palms. I look down at my own hands; they're covered in faded Magic Marker drawings and black jelly bracelets that have been twisted into weird rings and chains. The cops and my mom are looking at my hands, too. I can imagine them thinking the word *freak*. I know it's not normal for guys to wear jelly bracelets. I know nothing about me is normal. The man's maroon aura turns slightly redder and flares out from his head. He stares at me in a smart, searching way that contradicts his football-and-beer exterior. "You had any problems like this before, Sean?"

"Like what?"

My mom answers for me. "We'll be available to help in any way we can," she says. She stands. I follow suit. The cops' eyes follow me and my stomach executes a slow, unstable somersault.

Then my mom and I are in her Audi, speeding along the highway, headlights flashing past us silently. The car is like a soundproofed tank, blocking out all road noise and vibrations until it seems like we're in a tiny room and the windshield and windows are just televisions with no sound.

"I need my backpack," I say into the silence.

She opens her mouth and closes it again. It makes a little smacking sound, almost like a kiss. I look at her, surprised by the hesitation of the gesture, and her aura is a sickly, putrescent brownish aqua. Unconsciously I reach out, wanting to touch the vapors, and she flinches away from my hand. I pull my hand back into my lap and look out the window, stung, feeling like a little boy.

"This is not good," she says in a voice that is rough and low. "What have you done?"

"I haven't done anything." My voice is weak. The words falter. I don't sound like I'm telling the truth; I sound afraid.

She presses a hand to her mouth. Is she going to cry? Is it that bad, being the mother of a monster? Her hand is beautiful, sinewy and delicate like the hand of a pianist. She wears no jewelry at all, and I always wish I could give her a ring to wear. Her hands were made to wield gemstones, maybe emeralds. My mother is beautiful in her own way, not quite feminine enough for current fashion ideals but smooth and catlike with long, slender arms and neck, aggressive jawline and stubborn brows.

I've upset her with this. I feel bad. I've upset her enough over the years. This is the last thing she needs. My stomach fills up with nauseous guilt, something I've felt so many times before but always with good reason. After the nausea always comes a barrage of memories, visual and visceral; usually these memories are of horrible things that make the guilt worse and worse until I have to run to the bathroom and throw up, but this time the memories are just of Annabelle, clean and simple: her hair, her collarbones and shoulders, the line of her jaw.

My mom draws in her breath. "You're losing time," she says, her voice shaky. "You're losing more time than you know."

"It's the drugs," I say. "What do you expect? They've always messed me up like this."

She shakes her head. She won't say anything else. Without understanding why, my body brims over with shame and self-hatred, like these feelings are overflowing out of her and into me. Outside the window, the dark Texas night flies by. Everything still looks foreign to me here. The billboards are too high, the buildings too far apart.

At home, in my bedroom where Annabelle stood just twelve hours earlier, I close the door softly and slide down to the floor in front of it. I bury my face in my knees. From the hallway, my mom's voice calls out, "Take your meds!"

If I were better, manlier, I would punch a hole in the wall and roar at her to go shove it. I would go out into the night and hunt for Annabelle until I fell down with exhaustion. Instead, I head into the bathroom. I take a piss and turn to the sink, reaching automatically for the place where the pillbox always, always is. My hand grasps nothing but air.

I snap my eyes down. The pillbox is off to the side, at least six inches from its usual spot at a forty-five degree angle to the sink, just next to the soap dish on the right-hand side of the faucet. Tentatively, as though the box has become a dangerous, alien object, I stretch out a hand for the cool plastic. I scoot it into its usual spot.

Had I put it back wrong after taking my morning meds? Doubtful. Had my mother moved it? She always leaves it in the same spot on Sunday nights, in the extreme middle of the counter where I can't miss it, as though she's afraid I won't see it and will stop taking my medication altogether. As far as I know, she's never messed with the pills except on Sundays.

I pick up the box and look inside. I count the pills. Nothing is missing.

In a flash, I remember Annabelle. She'd used the bathroom this morning. Had she moved this while she was washing her hands? That has to be it. She must have been worried about getting soap on the box and had scooted it away. Embarrassment flashes through me. Had she thought it was weird that I had this? Had she wondered what was wrong with me? Maybe she thought I had some incurable disease. Maybe that's why she was so nice to me. What if it was a pity date? What if—

Shut up, Sean, it doesn't matter if she likes you or not. She's probably dead, attacked, raped, God knows what, my conscience screams, and I'm instantly filled with horror and agony and, for some reason, guilt.

I take my meds and stay up all night drawing picture after picture of her, trying to recapture the moments I'd already drawn and lost, tearing up one after another in frustration as they fail to properly capture her sweetness, her wholesomeness, and her glittering bronze eyes. I fall asleep in the early morning on the bed where she'd sat the day before, dangling a white sneaker and running her fingertips lightly across my cheek.

I'm awakened a few hours later by my mom banging on my door. "We have to go to Dr. Beck's. Get dressed. I have preop at noon."

I stare at the popcorn ceiling.

Thoughts pop into my head, unwelcome but as clear as spoken words: it's been well over twelve hours since she was taken. She could be dead by now. Surely she's been raped.

The second thought takes hold of me as an image. Beneath me, Annabelle's eyes are closed and she's kissing me with her hands in my hair. Then, like the souring of a fairy tale, the image changes and her face goes terrified. I'm still on top of her, but now I'm raping her and she's screaming, crying, but there's no one anywhere close to hear her.

I slap my cheek so hard my ears ring. I'm awake now.

I hurry to the bathroom. I can't sit still another moment.

My mom is at the kitchen table with the cordless phone, the silver antenna jutting up from her profile like a spindly unicorn horn. It sounds like she's juggling her schedule, moving meetings to tomorrow and asking another surgeon to take one of them off her hands. When she shoves the telescoping antenna back in and sets the phone aside, I ask her, "What are you doing home?"

She looks me over. "Have you showered?"

"No. Why?"

"Don't you want to?"

"Stop, Mom, it's not a symptom. I'm just worried about Annabelle."

"Poor hygiene is a symptom of schizophrenia," she reminds me.

"I know. God. I know."

My mom is even shorter than Annabelle, who was—is—at least four inches shorter than me, but my mom always makes me feel like *I'm* looking up at *her*. Her color today is purple; it's because she's in a dominant mood. Red is mixing with her usual blue like it always does when she's in the mood to control me. Brown swirls through it occasionally, like the edges of a rotting eggplant.

"Have you taken your meds?" she asks, which always pisses me off.

"Yes, Mother."

She leads me out to her car. "Why are you home? Why are you doing this?" I ask as she starts the engine.

"I'm going with you to see Dr. Beck." That's all she'll say on the ride over.

The Texas sky is blue and hot. I wonder in passing what Four Corners is like today.

Dr. Shandra is waiting for us in her arctic office. She smiles at my mom. "Hello, Dr. Suh." She holds out a hand.

"Dr. Beck." My mom shakes the hand with considerably less warmth and takes a seat on the sofa.

I sit on the opposite side of the couch. I cross my legs and one foot taps nervously in the air. I shouldn't be here. I should be at the police station doing...doing what? What can I do?

Dr. Shandra sits across from us. "What brings you both to see me this morning?" She leans onto her elbow in her best I'm-here-to-help posture. Her lipstick is an interesting shade of orange-red today, made richer by the dark brown of her lips underneath.

My mom's voice is matter-of-fact. "Sean had an incident

yesterday. He called the police from Four Corners because he believed a young woman he'd been on a date with had been abducted."

I have to hand it to Dr. Shandra; she absorbs this coolly. "Okay," she says, and she looks at me as if to say it's my turn to speak. Her smooth forehead reveals not a hint of trepidation, as though these are the most natural words that have ever been spoken in her office. It's impressive.

My foot jiggles. I stare at it.

"Would you like to add to that?" she prompts. "Are you comfortable discussing this with your mother present?"

My mom's aura flashes fluorescent magenta. She's pissed.

I clear my throat. "I guess it's fine. She already heard everything anyway, yesterday at the police station. She doesn't believe me."

"You say this girl was abducted. Can you go into more detail?"

I recite my story for the twentieth time.

All she says is, "I see."

"I want to go see the police today. It doesn't sound like they're really taking it as seriously as they should."

My mom says, "I think we should conference about possible interactions between the haloperidol and the lithium given this recent hallucinatory episode."

"I'm not hallucinating," I protest, and Dr. Shandra gives me an *I hear you* look.

I ask my mom, "You think I hallucinated the entire date? Or what? How would I know her name, know where she goes to school?"

She turns to Dr. Shandra. The brown swirls through her aura again and her mouth quavers. I've never seen it do that. As the truth dawns on me, I say it out loud: "You're afraid.

You're worried I'm *not* hallucinating. You're more afraid of me dating."

Her eyes snap onto mine. "Do you blame me?"

Shame crunches tight inside my chest like aluminum foil.

A long discussion commences, during which Dr. Shandra fights for me to keep my antidepressants, which she feels are helping me and possibly contributing to my newfound desire to socialize. However, my mom feels they may be interacting poorly with the antipsychotic, which is the most important link in my chain of drugs.

I make a move to stand up. "Why don't I leave you guys to duke it out about the lithium and I'll catch the bus down to the police station, try to see what they're doing for Annabelle."

My mom says, "I spoke with the detectives this morning. They're doing everything they think is necessary, but given the fact that this girl told her roommate she was going to visit family, it seems clear that your account is unreliable at best."

"Then I should go down there and speak with them."

"Unreliable at *best*. At *worst*, you're suspicious. Do you want to give them cause to call California?"

"Call California?" I repeat stupidly.

"All they have to do is call the Department of Justice in California and request that they mail a copy of your record. It's 1986; they don't have to send a carrier pigeon. They can have it in a matter of days. Is that what you want?"

"No," I whisper.

"Then leave them alone."

I remember Annabelle dangling her legs over the lake and upturning the ashes into the water. She had looked so beautiful in the setting sun. My hands itch. She'd told me she was sure I'd call her by Saturday. That doesn't necessarily mean she planned on being home on Saturday. She was just saying that she was confident I'd be calling her soon. *Had* she been planning to visit family? Or is her roommate lying for some reason?

I tug at the bracelets on my wrists. My mom and Dr. Shandra are debating my dosages. Dr. Shandra's voice swells and she says, "Look at him. He's clearly overmedicated," at which point I am pinned by four sharp, dark eyes and two glowing fuchsia auras. I slump down in my seat and yank harder on my bracelets. The conversation between them turns into a debate about whether or not my mom should hire a nurse to babysit me. I know she won't. We've been through this before. Dr. Shandra keeps trying, but thankfully my mom is a stubborn rock of a woman who won't allow any strangers into our home or admit that we need help in any way. My hair falls over my face and I close my eyes. I feel like I'm floating.

I register that I am sad about Annabelle's disappearance. It's horrible. I can see that it is horrible and I can see that I am sad, but it is from a distance. The emotion doesn't register in my body at all; it's like I'm watching a movie where the main character is sad but I can't quite relate. Maybe Dr. Shandra is right; maybe my meds are too strong.

I *want* Annabelle, though. I want her so badly. I miss her presence. I want to know things about her and to study the shadows behind her copper radiation. That emotion looms large, the wanting, and it's all I can see through the medicine fog that shoves me down into myself.

Can I have hallucinated the whole thing?

Her scream echoes in my memory. I know what I heard and saw. No one has ever said I've hallucinated anything other than colors. I know what happened. Whether anyone believes me or not, I *know*.

CHAPTER FIVE

The apartment building is near the UT campus and is remarkable only because it is a slightly darker shade of beige than the neighboring complexes. It's a bit run-down, not more than ten years old but carrying the impression that college kids live here. Three mismatched vinyl-strapped lawn chairs recline drunkenly on the front lawn, surrounded by empty plastic cups. The dirty glass front door hangs halfway open and one of the front-facing apartments emits muffled Van Halen. I check the address scrawled on my hand. This is the place.

I lock my bike to the railing in front of the building and find apartment 214 on the second floor overlooking a central courtyard housing more lawn chairs and discarded cups. I knock, the sound quiet and hollow.

After a minute, the door swings open and a pair of wide blue eyes regards me from within. The girl standing in the doorway is only a couple of inches shorter than I and stares at me with eyes that are two sizes too large for her face. She pulls a length of honey-colored hair out from behind her back and lays it over her shoulder, stroking it. Its length pulls it flat over her head and shoulders, like a hippie. Her jeans are baggy in weird places, her shirt tucked in unselfconsciously. Around her silhouette, yellow-green coils unfurl peacefully.

I clear my throat. "Are you Annabelle Callaghan's roommate?"

She cocks her head from one side to the other. "Hmm... yes." Her voice is breathy and high.

"I'm Sean. I called the police last night. About Annabelle. They told me they'd called you while I was at the station."

"*Oh,*" she breathes. Her eyes widen further. They belong on a doll; they're too round, too glassy.

"I found your address in the white pages. I thought...well... I guess I thought I could talk to you, ask you a couple of questions." She's not responding, so I try again. "I'm Sean," I repeat. I remember Annabelle doing this to me.

"I'm Jenny."

"Nice to meet you. So, the police told me you said Annabelle is out of town?"

"They called me last night. I told them she's visiting family. Why did you tell them she was, like, attacked?"

"Because she was!" Her eyebrows shoot up and I take a breath. "I'm sorry. I was with her and she was, like, snatched out from underneath me screaming and all they can say is that *you* say she's out of town so they assume everything is fine. I don't know what to do. I guess I was hoping you were mistaken. You're *sure* she said she was going out of town? You couldn't be wrong about the timing?"

"The timing? No. I spoke with her the night before she was planning to leave, the night before last. How could I make a mistake?"

Two jock-looking guys in polo shirts and Members Only jackets walk past me in the hallway. One of them does a double take at the sight of me and cries, "Hey! What's up! Long Duck Dong!" The other glances at me and chuckles.

"What?" I ask, confused.

Jenny pulls her door open wider. "Sorry about that. Come on in," she says. She steps back and ushers me through the door.

"What is Long Dong?" I ask.

"From *Sixteen Candles*, you know, the Chinese guy," Jenny explains.

"Is that a TV show?"

"It's a movie. You haven't seen it? Molly Ringwald?"

"I'm not really a movie guy." Inside, I close the door behind me and hover near it. I haven't been in anyone's house in years, not since I was...sixteen, maybe? The apartment is neat and homey, the beige carpet freshly vacuumed, the furniture nondescript but clean and functional. A collection of pristine *Star Wars* posters lines the living room walls, and a bookshelf full of corresponding action figures sits prominently near the little aging television with crooked, foil-covered antennae. She walks toward the kitchen and opens the fridge, a beige sixties model with a rusting metal handle. I bet she can sit on her hair, that's how long it is. The ends look sort of frayed. She's slim and smooth, her features delicate, but something about her is completely asexual.

She pulls out a can of New Coke and turns toward me. As an afterthought, she says, "Oh...do you want one?"

"Um...sure. If it's not any trouble."

She returns to the fridge, opens the door and stares in again as though she's forgotten where the Coke is. By the time she hands me the frosty can, I'm craning toward her, awkward and frustrated. In the moment of waiting, I feel time start to unfurl and slide away from me, pulling me into my own head, blurring the world around me. I resist, forcing myself to focus. *I'm here. Annabelle needs me. Keep it together.*

"Are you *sure* she was going out of town?" I ask again.

She cracks the Coke open in a deliberate, careful way. She takes a sip. At last, she says, "She was leaving yesterday. I watched her pack the night before."

I consider this for a long moment. I crack open my Coke and take a swallow. I kind of like the New Coke flavor. It's a little sweeter. The can is cold and hurts my fingers a little. I ask, "Did she tell you what time she meant to leave? We were together all day, and we had it planned. It wasn't like we were supposed to wrap up sooner and stayed late."

"She didn't tell me what time she was leaving, but she didn't mention going to Four Corners with you either. I knew she was going the prior day, but not yesterday. I thought she had—" She cuts off. "There was something she wanted to do."

"Her grandma."

"Yes. So she told you." She frowns. "So you're telling the truth. She was with you."

"Of course I am. Why would I make this up?"

Her eyes are fixed on me in a new and focused way. Lemon yellow flickers through the air around her like electricity. "Why didn't the police make a bigger deal of this? They seemed to think it was a false report, a mistake."

"They didn't take my report seriously."

"Why?"

"I guess because you told them she's out of town and they figured I was making it up or something." I gesture to my clothes. "I didn't exactly inspire the faith of the cops. Maybe if you spoke with them we'd have more luck."

"Are you absolutely positive she was... I mean, maybe it was some kids playing around, or maybe it was someone else? It just seems impossible. Why would someone just come along and kidnap her out of nowhere? Who would do that?"

"She was screaming my name. You should have heard her. She sounded—" My voice chokes off. "Besides, there was a hole cut in the fence. I saw her get shoved into the truck." I put my Coke down a little too hard and a drop flies out, speckling the wood.

We both stare at the drop.

She rubs her eyes with her fingertips; tears escape and ooze onto her cheeks. "I'm sorry," she squeaks. "I just don't understand. It makes no sense. *No sense*. It seems so random. Are you *sure* it was her screaming? Do you know her well enough to be sure about it being her voice? You just met her. You could be mistaken."

"It was her." I look down at my hands. "I... I really liked her. A lot. I could tell." *Liked*. Past tense. My stomach twists into a knot. "Can you think of anyone who might have done this? That's really why I came here. I thought, being her roommate, you'd know if there was a guy she knew, an ex-boyfriend or something? Anyone?"

She shakes her head. "No. Nothing."

"Maybe a date she went on that didn't work out? Someone from work or school?"

"Not at all. Not that she told me."

I rack my brain. "Someone from her hometown?"

She shakes her head. "I don't think so. She never mentioned anyone."

"Does she go home a lot? I didn't get the impression—"

"She *never* goes back. That's why I thought it was weird, and that's why I was so sure when the police asked about it. I specifically asked her, 'You're going home? Now? Why?' and she just said she thought it was time. She never goes home to see her mom for Christmas, not even when she lived out of state—she told me that specifically when I was worried about her being here all alone last year. Plus she's been so busy lately. She's working with her abnormal psych professor on an article for a scientific journal; I'm working on a research paper. We're both slammed. It's just a weird time for her to go."

"Abnormal psych? Like psychology? Why?"

"Yeah, well, psych's her major."

I stare at her stupidly.

"What?" she asks.

"I thought she was in med school."

"Yes…a psychiatrist is a doctor." She's looking at me like I'm crazy.

You've got to be fucking kidding me. I try to pull it together. "How long did she say she'd be gone?"

"About a week."

"She was driving there? Is her hometown far away?"

"Yeah, she was driving, it's some little town outside of Dallas. A *really* small town."

An idea hits me like a ton of bricks. "Oh my God. Jenny. Her car."

"Her car?"

"She drove me to Four Corners yesterday. She picked me up. If she *didn't* get kidnapped, if she drove home, then her car should be gone. You know? If her car *is* there, then…well…"

She jumps up. "I'm calling the police."

I follow her into the kitchen and hover around while she places the call from a graying, heavyset wall phone, cranking the dial in circles while referring to a piece of paper stuck onto the fridge with an Ewok magnet. We're silent as the dial catches up, click-clacking like a wind-up toy car. She holds the receiver tucked against her cheek and plays with the curly cord while she waits on hold.

After five minutes, Jenny starts speaking. She explains our idea about the car. She's asked to hold again. We wait, both of us jittery. Then she cocks her head, listening, and makes eye contact with me. "Oh. Okay. Yeah. Oh." She cups her hand over the mouthpiece. "They already checked. Her car isn't there."

"Ask if they checked her mom's house."

Into the receiver, she asks, "Have you checked with—wait, what?" She pauses. "Sean. The guy who reported the kidnapping. Yes, at my apartment." A pause. "I was saying, have you checked with her family? I can't remember the exact name of her hometown but it's—yeah. Her mom. No, I don't think she has any family besides her mom, and they're not close." She listens, then shakes her head at me. "They checked with her mom," she whispers. "She's not there yet. But this isn't the detective on her case. This is just an officer who's been helping them. I'm back on hold." She moves out of the kitchen, stretching the cord as she stands outside the doorway. She pulls the cord to its max as she reaches for her Coke.

My eyes fall on a knife block. It's full of twelve different knives, their black-and-silver handles sticking up at an ominous angle. My gut is all at once filled with ice water.

I don't like knives. I don't trust myself with them. If I wanted to, I *could* take the knife and plunge it into someone. The idea goes so deep, it gives me a full-body shiver. The images of blood and broken bone flood me and I'm abruptly sure that's exactly what I'll do if I take a knife out. I can see it so clearly, see myself stabbing the knife into Jenny over and over—

My eyes go to the doorway where I know she has moved

to just around the corner. She is vulnerable, slender, an easy target. I could snatch any of the knives up and be on her in an instant. I can feel the crunch of knife through bone.

I sidle up to the knives.

The images come faster than I can repel them. I could throw a knife into her back and she'd fall to the ground. I could finish her quickly there. I don't want to; the idea is repellant, terrifying, horrifying, but the images come just the same. *No no no no no*, I scream inside my brain, clutching my head. I don't want to touch them, but I have to touch them. My hand pulls toward them like steel to a magnet. I try to hold on to my hair, try to pull my hand away from the knives, but the pull is too strong. I touch the handle of one, pull it out. It's small, a paring knife. Could I kill someone with this? Would I? How silky soft it would feel to draw a sharp knife through layers of human skin, how buttery.

I shove the knife back into the block. My hand is drawn upward, toward the largest one, a heavy butcher knife. I withdraw it a bit before pushing it back in. Blood roars in my ears. I'm about to lose it.

"No," I whisper. I force my fingers open, off the knife. I grip the countertop behind me. I feel my knuckles whitening, the bracelets cutting into my fingers where I've wrapped them around and around.

Jenny comes back into the kitchen. She settles the phone into its cradle. "As far as they're concerned, they think you're mistaken and Annabelle is on her way to visit family. There's a hole in the fence, obviously, so they're checking around and seeing if maybe someone else might have gone missing; maybe you misheard and maybe it was someone else screaming, or kids playing, causing trouble, vandalizing, something like that. Detective Ridgeway is supposed to call me back in a few minutes, when she gets out of a meeting. Maybe she'll have more to say than the regular officer." She plays with the ends of her hair, her face clouded. We look at each other for a minute.

"Did you meet Annabelle at school?" I ask.

She nods. "Different majors but we both started out in biochem. She moved into psychiatry and I moved into molecular biology."

The presence of the knives is heavy behind me. I grip the counter harder. My fingertips go numb.

She rattles on. "I want to do research. I'm interested in genetics. I'm working with one of my professors; he's researching the implications and potential uses for PCR—sorry. This is boring for people."

"What's PCR?" I'm frantic to distract myself from the knives.

"Polymerase chain reaction. Used to…well…how do I explain this…" Her hands make fluttering gestures. "It's a new technology used to make copies of a specific DNA sequence. It relies on thermal cycling. It's a very intricate process. My professor is studying the potential future uses of the technology and the potential barriers… I'm sorry. Anyway. Annabelle and I have both been on campus more than home lately. I feel like her professor has seen more of her than I have all semester, and probably vice versa."

The phone rings and she snatches it off the cradle. "Hello?" A pause. "Hi, Detective Ridgeway. I think I spoke with you last night." She curls the cord around her fingertips, listening. "Okay. Yeah, Sean gave me the idea to ask about the car." Another pause. This time, as she's listening, her eyes snap onto me, a new alertness in them. "Okay," she says. She waits.

"Yes." Another pause. "I don't know." Then, "Okay, sure." She holds the phone out to me. "She wants to talk to you."

I take the phone from her. It's heavy and warm from her hand. "Hello?" I say into the receiver.

"Sean. What are you doing in the girls' apartment?" I recognize the sporty female voice of Detective Ridgeway.

"What am I doing here? I thought I'd come by and check in about Annabelle."

"Check in? What were you hoping Jenny could do for you?"

I'm reminded of the days before my trial and my lawyer's constant warnings to never talk to any police officers. *This is different*, I tell myself, but I'm not totally sure it is. "Well, I thought I'd ask about the car, for one," I say carefully.

"I need you to do me a favor. Can you do that, Sean?"

"Sure." She's using my name a lot. That means she's trying to keep me calm. Why?

"I need you to leave the girls' apartment right now. Can you do that for me?"

"But why?"

"Sean, it's my job to look into these things. I need you to let me do my job. Can you do that?"

I feel stung. "Okay," I manage to say.

"All right, then. Please go home, Sean. I promise we'll be in touch."

I set the phone down back onto the receiver with a click and stare at it.

I wonder if they've gotten their hands on my records from California. How long would it take the records to arrive in the mail? A few days? A week?

"What'd she say?" Jenny asks.

I try to pull myself together. "They're working on it." I

sigh. "All right. Look, can I give you my number? Will you tell me if you hear anything?"

Outside, I unlock my bike from the lamppost outside the apartment building. The heat is alive, crawling up my shirt-sleeves and down my pants, collecting around my ankles and inside my hair. There's no shaking it, no escaping it.

Annabelle is studying to be a psychiatrist. What the hell is wrong with this world? Why was she attracted to me? I suppose she liked crazy people. Likes. She *likes* crazy people.

I push hard on the pedals and make my way home. I need to take my meds.

CHAPTER SIX

I'm sprawled out on the white leather couch with a bag of the new Cool Ranch Doritos, flipping back and forth between the Beastie Boys incoherently hosting MTV's Spring Break in Daytona Beach and a Michael Jackson interview on CBS when the kitchen door to the garage makes its metallic jiggling sound. I freeze, a chip halfway to my lips. On screen, Michael Jackson mumbles about Quincy Jones in a high-pitched whine that makes me realize—he's on drugs, like, really, really on drugs. I recognize the muddle-mouthed incoherence, the rambling way of talking that fades into silence without ever having come to a point. Is it prescription drugs he's on? I'm guessing opioids. And what's up with the nose? It looks smaller, pointier. Did he get another nose job?

My eyes focus on the mirrored wall behind the TV in which I can see the kitchen and the windows to the backyard. The kitchen door opens and my mother steps through in a puddle of navy blue. It hadn't occurred to me that my mom could possibly come back at any point today, not after going to work so late this morning. My stomach churns and grinds; I slide a finger under the bracelets on my left hand and twist. In the mirror, I see her set a pile of bags on the kitchen table and head for the far cabinet. She always drinks a cup of tea when she comes home. I rarely see her eat and when she does, it's always the same: rice and a small piece of meat or egg. I think she sees eating as a sign of weakness.

The cabinet shuts softly and the faucet turns on, then off. I hear the clank of the teapot lid, the click of the stove burner, a scrape, then silence. My eyes are glued resolutely to the set but I sense her closing the distance between us. I remember the television in Annabelle's apartment with its foil-covered rabbit ears, and I feel ashamed of our top-of-the-line Magnavox with its sleek wood sides and matching wood-tone cable box. In a second, my mother is standing above me, having arrived on silent ghost feet. Shadows hollow her cheekbones out, making her look gaunt and frail.

She says, "I'm going to begin weaning you off the antidepressants. I'll update your pillboxes with a lower dosage."

"'Kay."

"Don't take your meds until I do. In a few weeks, we'll be able to take you off the lithium altogether."

"Fine."

She walks to the set and switches it off manually. The picture implodes, sucking itself into a tiny dot of light, Michael Jackson's sunglasses disappearing last. I keep my eyes on the blank screen, the sharp edges of the rectangular TV remote cutting into my palm. "Is that your dinner—just chips?" she demands.

"I dunno."

"There's food in the fridge. I left you meat, vegetables, rice; why are you eating that junk?" There's no right answer to this question. She takes a seat on the armchair. Acutely aware of my lazy, slouching sprawl, I pull myself into a sitting position and set the Doritos and remote aside. I catch a glimpse of my own reflection looking scared and small.

"You went to Four Corners after our session with Dr. Beck, I assume," she says.

"Yes," I lie. I tighten the bracelets. My thumb turns red, then purple.

"Stop." She points to my bracelets. I shove my hands under my butt. She steeples her hands and presses the tips of her fingers to her lips in an uncharacteristic gesture of fatigue. "Sean, you need to understand that this incident is a major setback. Not just a setback, but an indicator that we aren't in any way successfully treating the symptoms of your schizo-phrenia. Do you understand?"

"I guess," I say, not sure that I do. "Isn't it normal to have to adjust medication, though? Dr. Shandra is always talking about how it's a work in progress."

"This is beyond the boundaries of normal. This is the third antipsychotic we've tried in the last two years with no im-provement in your symptoms, and now it seems that we're looking at an escalation, which indicates that the haloperidol is not only not resolving the hallucinations but—"

"I *didn't* hallucinate this. How can you seriously think I'd go from seeing auras to imagining an entire kidnapping? I spent the whole day with Annabelle. Do you want me to tell you all the things we did, all the things we talked about? My whole day was not a hallucination. That's crazy."

She steeples her hands again and looks at me over her fin-gertips. She opens her mouth as though to speak and then closes it. She wipes her eyes. They're bloodshot. Her hair falls clean and straight across her cheek, brushing it gently, and it makes me want to reach out and touch it to see if it's as soft as it looks. I've never seen her like this. Or maybe I have.

Something is familiar. Maybe she was like this in the weeks around my trial, back in California. It's been a long time and there were a lot of meds, but yeah, I kind of remember this.

She takes a breath. "Sean, we need to get your symptoms under control if we're going to continue to meet your needs in an outpatient capacity."

"What do you mean, outpatient?"

"We're being naive to think it's safe to…to…send you out into the world with your symptoms unchecked. It could be dangerous for you, dangerous for other people."

"You want to send me back to inpatient? To the institution?"

She says nothing.

"I'm *not hallucinating*." The words come out too loud. I clamp my jaw shut.

"If we say we have no sin, we deceive ourselves, and the truth is not in us." It's a Bible verse.

My blood is hot and cold at the same time. I bite hard on my lip and count the white tiles on the floor, beginning at the couch and moving toward the dining room doorway. I gather myself together. "If the meds aren't doing what you want them to do, maybe you're treating me for the wrong condition."

"Sean, no. We've been through this."

"Hear me out. I've never hallucinated anything but colors. Why would I suddenly be hallucinating entire—"

"What about the coffee shop girl?"

Her words stop me cold.

Silently, we stare at each other.

"That was different," I say.

"No, it wasn't."

"I wasn't hallucinating. You just didn't like the way I was behaving. That's a totally separate issue."

She leans so far forward that, for one frozen moment, I thinks she's going to reach out and touch me. Instead, she penetrates me with a direct stare. "It wasn't different. This is an amplification of that behavior, and it is very, very worrisome. I can see it. Dr. Beck can see it. You can't see it, because you're unwell. That is why you need help. You need to let us help you." Her voice is direct and firm; she's trying hard to make me understand.

"That coffee shop thing had nothing to do with my meds, though, or even my diagnosis," I argue. "I didn't even *do* anything to that girl. It was fine. It wasn't a problem. She didn't even know I was there! And it totally didn't have to do with any hallucinations. I don't even know if I do hallucinate. What if the aura thing is just—some other thing? Not a hallucination, just something else?"

"Thirty percent of schizophrenics disagree with their diagnoses. You have to trust your doctors."

"My doctors? You mean, you?" I ask bitterly. "You're not my doctor, *Mom*. Right? Because that would be unethical. Why am I hearing this from you and not Dr. Shandra?"

She slashes a hand through the air. "Enough. I won't open this up for debate. Dr. Beck and I are going to review your medication plan again next week. We'll try one other antipsychotic once you detox from the lithium."

"And then what? What if you don't see whatever results you're hoping for?"

"We'll discuss other treatment options."

My voice rises. "I'm an adult. You can't just *institutionalize* me. How is that legal? Has Dr. Shandra even agreed to this?"

The teakettle whistles and she stands. The space around

her seems to conform to her frame, fitting the house to her. Dark blue tendrils mist into the atmosphere around her and trail behind as she rounds the corner, leaving me on the couch by myself.

Fury rolls over me. "Yeah, walk away," I call after her. "Just like usual. Just do what you want. That's what matters, right? What you want?"

She turns. "Don't speak to me that way."

"Why, because you're a neurosurgeon?"

"Because I'm your mother."

"You're not a mother. You don't mother me. You just *manage* me."

She puffs herself up to her full size and converges upon me. Her face is tight with anger. "You don't speak to me like that. You are my son. Who do you think you are?"

"Stop ordering me around. I'm a grown man; you can't control me. You don't have power of attorney. Do you think I'm stupid? I was released. They didn't waive my rights."

She snaps back like I've slapped her. "You—"

I jump to my feet and now *I'm* towering over *her.* "You just like saying that because it makes me look weak, and you want to control me. That makes *you* weak, not me." I'm mean now, hissing like a snake, bending down to say the words hatefully into her stubborn face. I'm tired of going along with her, ceding to her authority, allowing her to take the reins in every area of my life. It's enough. I won't be bullied. I won't be silenced. A tear of rage trickles down one of my cheeks, and she tracks it with her glittering eyes.

Disgust twists her mouth into a sneer. "You can't control yourself. Obviously. Someone has to." The words slap me sideways and leave me reeling. Her eyes glitter and sparkle, her aura blanketing us in a cool purple haze.

I take the stairs to my room three at a time. I slam the door and stand there helplessly, surrounded by empty space. Annabelle was right. It's like no one lives here.

That's because no one does live here. I'm not a real person, just an empty shell, full of drugs and connected to nothing and nobody. Who will care if my mom does bury me in some asylum for the rest of my life where they'll give me enough drugs to make me drool and shit my pants? No one. No one will care.

I'm hyperventilating. The walls are crushing down on me, plastering me into myself.

I can't go back. I won't go back. I won't be a prisoner, never again. I'll never let myself be that powerless, never again.

I have to be smarter. I've been dumb, a complete idiot. From now on, with this change in medication, I'm going to pretend they've fixed me. No more talking about auras. I'll pretend. Whatever it takes.

My heart twists.

I miss Annabelle.

Maybe I could have been good for her. Maybe I could have been safe for her. I remember the moment on the roof. I'd been able to stop myself from hurting her. It had been okay. Maybe I'm not as bad as I think I am.

She might still be alive. It could be.

"I'm sorry, Annabelle," I whisper. Somehow this is my fault. I know it.

I let myself fall face-first down onto my bed. I slide my hands under the pillow and press it upward into my face, so tight I can barely breathe. "Annabelle," I moan into the pillow, and hot tears soak into the crisp cotton. My hands clutch the pillowcase so tight I almost can't unclench them. Darkness fills my eyes and sinuses. I picture the truck's red taillights and hear Annabelle's screams from within. I see her legs kicking out the passenger side door. It was no hallucination. It was real. I'm not crazy. I'm *not*.

Under the pillow, one of my hands encounters what feels like a piece of paper. I pull it out from under the pillow and roll onto my side to examine it with half-hearted curiosity. It's plain white, folded up into a messy two-inch square. I pull the edges apart. Unfolded, it's about eight inches wide, and across the middle, a handwritten message is neatly printed in all caps.

SHE'S MINE NOW.

I shoot to a sitting position and fling the page away from me, shaking my hand out violently like the paper had set it on fire.

Why did I touch it? I'm such an idiot. My heart threatens to pound its way straight through my ribs. The piece of paper looks so innocuous, white against the rumpled white cotton bedspread where it had fallen.

I let out a breath, unaware that I had been holding it. I inhale, and oxygen sweeps through my lungs. It burns. Someone's been in my house, my room. I jump up, run to the window, examine it. It's locked as always, covered by an airtight screen with intact glue around all the edges. I slide my fingernail around the seal, examine the window from above and below.

I step back, frustrated. No one broke in this way. So they came through the house. We rarely lock the back door; this is a safe neighborhood. Would the kidnapper just come in like that, for the sole purpose of leaving me this note? Why would he do that?

I return to my bed, shivering, adrenaline numbing my limbs, loosening my bowels. I stare down at the note.

I should take this to the police.

They'll think…what will they think? I remember my mother's warning and Detective Ridgeway's voice on the phone today. The detectives already think I'm crazy. They think I'm making this whole kidnapping up. What if this piece of paper has some sort of evidence that could help them find Annabelle? What if it has the kidnapper's fingerprints on it? It could prove that I'm not crazy; I didn't hallucinate the abduction. I pick up the note again, flip it over, look for anything that could provide a clue. The letters are printed carefully, as though someone's copying a typewriter font.

Paper pinched in front of me between finger and thumb, I hurry out of my room and downstairs, where I find my mom sipping a cup of green tea at the kitchen table, a pile of case files open in front of her. "Mom," I gasp, and toss the paper down in front of her, on top of what looks like an X-ray of someone's brain.

She looks at me, confused, reading glasses perched on her nose. They make her look severe and literary. "Look," I say, gesturing at the paper. She unfolds it, scans it through her glasses.

"What is this?" she asks.

"I just found that in my room. Under my pillow."

She takes another look at it, examining it closer this time, flipping it over and studying every inch of the paper.

Shakily, I ask, "What do I do—do I call the detectives?"

Face pale, she turns the paper over and over, neat, unpainted fingernails against the clean white page. At last, she sets it down. She takes her glasses off and wipes the back of her hand across her forehead. "No," she says at last.

I fall into a chair across the table from her. "You don't think I'll get into trouble? What if they need this? What if there's some evidence on it? I could get in trouble for withholding it. But then if I give it to them, I think that makes me look suspicious."

"What evidence? Someone's obviously disguising their handwriting. It's plain white paper."

"Fingerprints?"

"I can't imagine anyone would be that careless. They'll only find yours and mine." She folds it up and holds it out for me. "Hide this away somewhere. If you get any more of these, we'll turn them in to the police."

I meet her direct brown gaze. "You really don't think we should call the cops?"

Her gaze drops from me to the brain image in front of her. "What good have the police ever done us? We don't owe them anything."

I take the folded paper back from her and stand up. Halfway back to the staircase, I turn around and try my voice again. "Mom?"

She looks up. A black lock of hair clings to the earpiece of her reading glasses, sticking out sideways.

I say, "I really didn't hallucinate this. You can see that now. This is proof." I hold the paper out like a talisman.

She scans me from head to toe, dark eyes inscrutable. At last, she says, "Yes. I see, Sean." She watches me turn and head back upstairs. In my room, numb and unsteady, I tuck the note into my nightstand drawer and sink onto my bed.

CHAPTER SEVEN

My eyes fly open. Something is wrong. I stare at the pop-corn ceiling, trying to make sense of the fingers of shadow between the bumps in the texture. All is silent. Outside the blinds, the gray half light of dawn pokes its way inside.

My stomach lurches. Pain stabs my gut. I roll out of bed and make a hobbling run for the bathroom, where I barely make it to the toilet before the vomit explodes from my mouth. I retch pathetically, clinging to the porcelain bowl. My guts are going to come up next, I'm sure of it. I'm barely done throw-ing up when I have to yank my pajama pants down and switch positions, plunking my ass down on the toilet seat so hard it hurts. Chills shiver through me and I clench my teeth until my body has been cleared of everything it could have possibly been storing in my intestines. The peach-and-green wall-paper swims around me like a seaweed reef come alive. At last I flop forward onto my knees. I reach around to flush. Sweat has soaked through my T-shirt and I fumble it off weakly.

Back in bed, I pull the covers to my chin and wait for sleep to take me. My arms prickle with invisible pins and needles, like the skin has fallen asleep, leaving the muscles intact underneath.

When I wake up again, it's light outside and I feel almost normal, if a bit edgy. I sit up and run a hand across my stomach. I can feel my ribs and abdominal muscles, like all the fat and water has been cleared out of me, leaving behind only the leanest trappings of a human body. I push myself up and swing my legs over the edge of the bed. I still feel nauseous and food sounds disgusting, but I don't feel like I have the flu. In the shower, I begin to feel even more normal, and I decide I must have eaten something bad.

At eleven o'clock I find Professor Johannsen's office, which is tucked into the School of Medicine's East Wing. Apparently he's the only professor of abnormal psychology on the UT campus, so this has to be the professor Jenny described. The girl in the office had smiled. "He goes by Professor Spike," she'd said.

"Why?"

"I don't know. We all just call him that."

I approach the office door. What is he, some crazy wrestler-turned-professor?

He has a fancy desk, a throne-like chair, and walls full of degrees, and he sits behind an electric typewriter, fingers clacking rapidly on the keys. I clear my throat and tap a knuckle on the open doorway.

He looks up and the illusion of toughness is shattered. Sitting in front of me is a shaggy-haired aging hippie, diminutive and almost pretty with light blue eyes and a pink, sensitive mouth. He's about forty and sports a loose white button-down shirt.

"Can I help you?" he asks. "You're one of my students?"

"No. Um…may I come in?"

"These are my office hours."

I step through the doorway. "My name is Sean. I'm wondering if you have any idea where Annabelle Callaghan might be. Nobody seems to know where she's gotten off to and her roommate says she's been spending most of her time these days working on an article with you."

"Where she's gotten off to? What do you mean?"

"She's supposed to be visiting family but hasn't shown up there. We're concerned." I'm not going to mention the kidnapping. I don't need more people thinking I'm crazy. This seems like a good enough story.

He frowns, sets down the paper he'd been grading, and twirls the red pen between two fingers. "She seemed fine last week. May I ask who you are?"

"I'm just a friend. Her friends noticed she didn't make it to see the family and when we started asking each other, nobody could figure out where she went. So I told everyone I'd come ask you if you had any idea."

The implication that I am the mouthpiece for a supportive group of friends has a positive effect. Professor Spike's expression moves from suspicious to thoughtful and he taps the pen on the desk. "Have you mentioned your concerns to the police?"

"Yes. They don't seem very worried since she told everyone she was going out of town."

"But you're worried."

"Well, yeah. We're all worried."

His eyes are penetrating. "You say 'we,' but I get the impression that *you* are especially worried. Since you are the only one here."

I forgot this is a professor of fucking psychiatry. God, I hate doctors.

"I *am* worried," I say. It's always best to speak the partial truth so they can hear the honesty in my voice. "I saw her last and she didn't say anything about going out of town, but then

I found out she's packed her bags and no one knows where she went. That's kind of weird, right?"

It seems like he's hiding a smile. "You think she may have taken a little vacation with another boy?"

I consider. "I guess that's possible. But I hadn't thought of it. Do you know who that might be? We just want to make sure she's all right."

He chuckles. "I'll put your mind at ease. I don't think that's really Annabelle's style. She's a bright girl, not one to take time off work without good reason. If she hasn't told her friends where she is, I'm sure there's an excellent reason. I'd trust the police. If they're not worried, I'm not worried."

At once I notice the halo surrounding him. It's fire-engine red and unfurls into the air like a poisonous gas.

"Is there anything else I can help you with?" he asks.

"Has she mentioned anyone bothering her? Any ex-boyfriends, anything like that?"

He frowns, leans forward onto his elbows. Something is off. He's considering too long, as though weighing his options.

"But I'm not sure that's an appropriate question for you to be asking." His aura fades from red into a neon orange. He glances at the clock. "Now, unless there's anything else…"

I thank him and leave, and once I'm outside the building, I stand in the middle of a grassy lawn and stare into space.

I need to draw him. I need to capture him. It will help me think. I'm so naked without my sketchbook. I put a hand out to a passing girl with a fluffy mane of permed red hair. "Excuse me, is there a bookstore, a student store, something like that around here?" I ask.

She takes a step away from me. "Back toward the main entrance of campus." She gives me turn-by-turn directions and I hurry to follow them. The student store has a wall of art supplies for the art students. I grab a plain black backpack, a sketchbook of the right size and with the hard binding I need, a few pencils, a sharpener, and a box of colored pencils. I pay for these things with some of the cash I always carry around courtesy of Dr. Suh and rush outside, where I find a bench and get to work on Professor Spike. Why Spike? Who came up with the nickname?

I contemplate his aura. Fire engine red. Interesting. I wonder why it switched to orange when he answered that one question. Was he lying? Hiding something? Often, people's auras will change when they're lying. It's not an exact science; people's auras can change to match their emotion, no matter what the emotion is.

The colors I see don't work like a mood ring, not exactly. Blue isn't sadness, yellow isn't happiness, and pink isn't longing. It's nowhere near that literal. Rather, colors seem to indicate what people do to the world and how they affect the people around them.

For example, red is popularly considered the color of anger. I don't experience red like that. It seems to indicate a pushing or forcing of their personality onto the world and others. Whatever their emotion is, they tend to push that emotion outward and take up space with it. Red is usually a large aura; it occupies an entire area around a person if I really look.

Blue is the opposite. It indicates a retreating inward. Blue usually shows up as subtly as steam off a hot drink on a cold day. It wafts away from people and evaporates almost as soon as it hits the air. Red immediately overpowers it; if someone leaks blue near a red person, the blue will all but disappear.

Yellow is neither out nor in. It's the hardest color for me to describe. The best way to think about it is this: there are two worlds that we humans experience. There's the world around us and the world inside us. Yellow is neither. It indicates that a person's energy is going into an entirely other world; sideways, as it were. Kids are often yellow, as are mentally ill and old people. It makes me wonder if the sideways place their energy gravitates toward is the dimension we come from and where we'll eventually return; the afterlife, or the beforelife, as it were.

People will often emanate two colors at once. For example, a brash young man might push red into all the air around him, but something might happen to knock him off his feet and that might make him pulse blue for a moment. The blue will keep leaking out of him after the red comes back, and that will combine into purple-magenta swirls that both draw and repel people around him until he regains his confidence. A blue person might experience a momentary bout of anger, which draws them out of their usual interior-centeredness, and this red flare-up takes a minute to fade, turning the air around him fuchsia and confusing all the passersby until the mood passes. Yellow people might experience something that yanks them into reality, especially with children. It's not uncommon for me to see a two-year-old flashing shades of apricot and tangerine during a tantrum which pulls him half out of his sideways world.

Red. I think about that. Why red? Not just red, but a pure, hot, lipstick-bright red.

In my sketch, Spike's eyes are watchful. He makes me nervous. I feel like I may have somehow given life to this drawing.

My new backpack is sitting on the bench next to me, graphite and colored pencils tossed onto it in a disordered pile of pencils and shavings. I grab a yellow and brown, check the points on them, and start in on his stringy hippie hair. I meditate on his eyes as I colorize them. They are the answer.

I stare down at them. He gazes up at me with a contented smugness that frustrates and intrigues me. He knows something. Or rather, there's something I don't know. Why would he be so smug and so...so...red? I look down into his eyes. So arrogant, so knowing.

What kind of car do you drive? I want to ask.

Someone's poking me with their nearness. Four people are standing nearby in a semicircle, two girls and two guys in coordinated pastel shirts-and-shorts ensembles—preppies. The girl closest to me is peeking over her friend's shoulder at my sketchbook.

I snatch the sketchbook up and shove it into my backpack along with the pencils. As I'm packing up, it occurs to me that it's already long past noon and I haven't felt fuzzy once today. The lithium must have been slowing me down more than I'd realized. I'm surprised that I already feel this big a difference. My skin is tingling again. I rub my arms, which stops the pins and needles only until I remove my hands, and then the prickling picks up again, stronger than before. *Do I have a fever? Am I sick?* I feel my forehead, but it seems normal. I don't know what's wrong with me.

I wait outside the School of Medicine for the rest of the afternoon. I watch the building lights go on as the sky turns grayish blue. I know his office hours. I know when he will leave. I'm happy to wait as long as it takes. If there's one thing I learned in the institution, it's patience.

When the light goes off in his office, I am hiding in a spot that allows me to view both exit doors, one on each side of his hallway. I release my pent-up breath when the left entrance door opens and his small frame emerges. Back straight, he heads away from me toward the parking lot. I follow at a distance.

He approaches a silver VW Bug, shoves his briefcase into the passenger side and inserts himself neatly behind the wheel.

I hop on my bike and follow him at a careful distance as he puts the car in first gear and navigates slowly through the parking lot. He turns right onto the small drive that winds through the campus and I tail him, keeping to the shadows along the side of the road. We pass by benches filled with students and stop at a pedestrian walkway to allow people to pass. He never looks my way.

I follow him out onto the street, worried about losing him on a highway or busy road, but he keeps his speed down, probably limited by his ancient car. I barely struggle to pace him along midsized streets and through residential neighborhoods. I'm a fast bicyclist, having relied on my legs for transportation my entire life, but a couple of times he gets his speed up high enough that he disappears around a corner, outpacing me until the next red light. I almost lose him as he turns right into a nondescript suburban neighborhood populated with beige houses and half-mown lawns. He surprises me by turning into one of the driveways and turning his car off; I don't have time to stop far enough away so that he doesn't see me, so I speed up, turning my head aside so he won't recognize me if he should happen to glance back.

I park my bike around the corner and wait a few minutes to give him time to get into his house. It's pretty much dark now; the streetlights leave golden puddles on the asphalt and sidewalks around me. I shove my hands into my pockets and keep my head down, slouching down the sidewalk in the direction of his house without looking up. The neighborhood is featureless with almost no trees or distinguishing differences between the houses. They seem to have been built recently in a modern Spanish style by an architect with only enough time to plan one house. If not for the silver Bug parked in the driveway, I'd never have been able to figure out which one was his.

The fact that he'd parked in the driveway makes me wonder if there could be another car parked in the garage. A white truck, maybe? I try to picture Professor Spike abducting Annabelle and dragging her through the fence. The image doesn't come, but I know better than most that people can be more dangerous than they appear.

I check around for nosy neighbors and slip around the side of the tan-colored garage toward the backyard, dry grass crunching under my Converse. My black hair and clothes turn me into just another shadow in the dim evening. Crickets pipe up around me. Above, a couple of cicadas compete with them, their buzzing more eerie and otherworldly than the crickets' melodic chirping. One millimeter at a time, I raise the metal latch on the chain-link gate and ease it open. It barely creaks. I slink through it and close it behind me, taking a thousand years to slip the latch back into place. The backyard is small and square, ill-lit and bordered by waist-high chain-link. I find a door in the stucco garage and try it. It's locked.

I lean against the wall and ponder the situation.

So, here I am, in Professor Spike's backyard. My heart is pounding and my head is full of buzzing, but I'm crystal clear. It's the first time I can remember feeling adrenaline without the immediate rush of drugs behind it. It's intoxicating, invigorating. I feel powerful and in complete control, like I'm breathing fresh air after being indoors for years. Was my mom right? Was the lithium slowing me down that much? I'd thought it was the antipsychotics. I hate it when she's right, but I can't even be mad at her. I feel amazing.

I try the garage door again. It's still locked. I run through my choices.

I could leave.

No. I need to know if he has a truck in there.

Okay, then. So I need to get into the garage.

I could go get some sort of tool to unscrew this doorknob, I suppose. I bend down to inspect it and don't see any screws or anything that would allow me to do that. I check for hinges, but there aren't any screws on this side of the door. There's a lock on the handle of the door, but I have not the first clue how to pick a lock. I wonder if the garage door operates on an opener. I've heard stories about people being able to open other people's garage doors before.

Right. My chances of picking the lock are better than that.

I remember the letter, the sheer cockiness of whoever wrote it and broke into my house to stuff it under my pillow. I remember Annabelle screaming my name. She'd screamed to *me* for help. If this is the guy...

To hell with it.

I tiptoe back along the side of the house and cross the lawn to the front door. I shrug my backpack off and leave it in the shadowy bushes. I stand in the light of the porch and ring the doorbell.

He answers it with an irritated look on his face. He's even shorter now that he's taken his shoes off. When he recognizes me, annoyance passes into fury that flashes indignantly through his eyes and sends his aura spewing red all over the hallway. I don't wait to get yelled at. I push forward into the house, knocking him back onto his ass, and I kick the door shut behind me.

CHAPTER EIGHT

Before he can run, I'm on top of him with a knee in his stomach. He won't stop squirming. I press down hard with the knee and pin his hands to the floor with mine. He squiggles like a dying fish. My new clearheadedness is exhilarating. "Do you have her?" I demand.

He stops resisting. "What? Who? Annabelle?"

"Of course Annabelle, you dick. Do you have her?"

"No!" He huffs a laugh and I crush his stomach, knocking the air out of him. "Let me look in your garage," I say. He wants to say something but his face is turning purple, his hair a mess around his head. I let up a little.

"Why do you want to look in my garage?" he gasps. Yeah, he's going to throw up if I don't stop it with the knee.

I look around the hallway. There's nothing in the immediate vicinity to tie him up with. His legs start kicking and his body starts bucking, but I have at least thirty pounds and five inches on him, and I'm half his age.

He starts screaming like a little girl, and I reach back and punch him in the face. He screams harder, now with one hand free to clutch and scratch at me. I'm getting sick of this. I pull his button-down shirt up and over his head like I'm taking it off him, but instead I kind of capture his annoying, squirmy arms inside it. "Stop screaming," I grunt, struggling to hold my grip on him. Frustration takes hold of me and I punch him in the gut, which turns his screams into quiet retching sounds while I tie off the shirt above his head with his arms trapped inside. It's really funny-looking.

I pull my belt off and tie his ankles together with it, punching him in the gut a few more times to keep him quiet and still. I contemplate elbowing him in the neck and shutting him up for good, but I'm not trying to critically injure him. I just want to look inside his goddamned garage. Through this, he curses and retches and finally throws up a little inside the shirt. The cotton darkens in a sickly splotch. I smell the vomit and my stomach lurches sympathetically, sore from throwing up and achingly empty. I'm sweating profusely; my armpit sweat is soaking through my shirt.

I stand up, my chest heaving. "You better hope there's no white truck in your motherfucking garage," I pant.

He mutters things inside his shirt. His stomach and chest are pitifully pale and bony, red spots blossoming where I'd punched him. I leave him there and head through the hall, through a living room/dining room combo, and through a small, white-tiled kitchen to the garage door. I pull it open.

There is no truck. There are a few piles of boxes and bins and nothing else. It's just a normal, half-empty garage.

I curse the room.

I head back into the hallway. He's managed to inch a few feet toward the living room. I run over and kick him in the gut. He curls up, obviously unable to breathe. "Don't. Fucking. Move," I order.

I search the bedrooms and closets for trap doors, false floors, anything that might indicate some sort of hiding place. The place is spotlessly clean, like a monk's house. The only possessions seem to be shelves and shelves and shelves of books; the office is a mess of papers and bookshelves.

The office closet is filled with even more books, and it takes me a while to dig around and confirm that there are no trap doors in the ceiling or floor. I pull cardboard file boxes from the top shelf in my search, hurrying, certain he'll figure out a way to get up and call the cops before too long. Neat white labels say things like "'84 Taxes" and "Lesson Plans: Intro Abnormal Psych." Frustrated, I dump their contents out, making a messy pile of lined papers and dittos.

Behind the cardboard boxes, I find a heavy, unlabeled wooden chest, smaller than a file box but heavier when I lift it off the shelf. It's equipped with a built-in brass lock, and when I try unsuccessfully to lift the lid, something clattery rolls around inside.

I grab a pair of metal scissors from the desk. I kneel in front of the wooden box and wedge the point of one of the blades into the hinge. I use it like a lever, applying pressure so the metal separates from the wood. I strain against it with all my might and then fall forward when it rips off. The scissors slip and I crack a knuckle against the corner of the wood, bloodying it. I blot my hand on my shirt and open the box.

Plastic prescription bottles tumble around on top of a pile of cutouts from *Playboy* or *Penthouse* magazines. For a minute I'm confused. Porn and meds? Why would he keep his prescriptions in here with his porn?

Wait a minute. These aren't cutouts from magazines. The naked girls in front of me are all Polaroids.

I pull a few clear orange prescription bottles out of the box

and check the labels. They're his, all right, but I don't recognize the names of the drugs. I set them aside on the floor
and pull the snapshots out of the box. There are at least fifty
of them, maybe more; the stack is about double the width of
a standard envelope of photos. As I flip through them, I recognize this house. Each girl is photographed nude, lying supine on his bed, calm and peaceful with arms resting by their
sides. They look like they're sleeping, and they all look alike.
They're young, white, dark blonde or light brunette. None
of them is overweight at all; they're slim, girlish. I contemplate the size of the stack. Can he have really slept with all
these girls and—what? Taken photos of them sleeping after
sex? Weirdly, underneath their naked bodies, the bedspread is
perfectly smooth in every photo, like they've been laid there
carefully, not at all like they've fallen asleep after a moment
of passion. And why would all of them fall asleep afterward?
I'm no expert, but I've never heard of women falling asleep
immediately after sex. Also, these girls look really young.
Not one of them looks older than Annabelle. *What the fuck?*

I grab the photos, jump to my feet, and run back toward
the living room.

I find him near the wall where he'd managed to roll,
squirming against his bonds. His aura has soured into an
angry dried-blood rust color. I squat near him and untie the
shirt. His face is wet with puke and red with terror and fury.

"What the fuck is wrong with you?" he shriek-screams,
his pale eyes wild.

Silently, I hold the photos up for him to see.

His face grays. Even the white skin of his stomach pales.

I can't imagine what my face looks like. This is the closest
I've ever been to killing another man.

My voice is low. "Where is she?"

He shakes his head so quick it looks like a seizure. Blood splatters the bottom half of his face. I don't know if he's bleeding from his nose, his lips, or both; it's all gotten smeared with vomit into his straggly hippie beard.

I hop up, return to the office and grab the scissors. I carry them down by my side on my way back as though concerned with safety. It's almost funny.

I squat down in front of him and pinch the bottom of his beard. With the other hand, I brandish the scissors. His eyes widen. Roughly, I snip the bottom of his beard off. Little chunks of sticky hair cling to his chest.

"What are you doing?" he stammers, tongue thick with fear.

"I'm cutting things off until you tell me where Annabelle is. Next will be your mustache. I hope I don't miss and cut off a lip."

I pinch his mustache, hard, and he gasps. "N-n-no-no. What do you want? I'll tell you."

I open and close the scissors. *Snip snip.* "Where is she?"

"I don't have her!"

"Will I find her picture in that fucking stack?" I might lose control and start stabbing him any minute. My hands open and close the scissors five times in quick succession: *sni-nip-sni-nip-sni-nip-sni-nip-sni-nip.*

"No! I've never slept with her! She's just a student!" His aura flashes magenta.

"Huh." I reach out to touch the smoky tendrils. His eyes follow my hand. "Did you kidnap her?"

Back to dark-rust, his aura throbs in a terrified rhythm. "What is the matter with you?"

"You're the one with the stack of photos of girls you—are those your students? You, what, drug them?"

His aura flashes orange. "No."

"You're lying. You *fuck*." I raise the scissors. "Did you do anything do Annabelle?"

"No!" The air around him returns to a cool magenta.

"Hm." I sit back onto my heels and contemplate. The scissors dangle from my index finger. His breath comes in sharp, shuddering gasps.

"You wanted to," I guess. "You were planning to. You're just...you like to...to..." I wrinkle my nose. "You like to fuck them while they're asleep? *Why?*"

"No," he hisses, but the vapors go orange again. I trail my fingertips through them.

"I can see your lies. So you rape them in their sleep. That makes no sense. It's like hunting prey that's already dead." His eyes fill with tears; his mouth twists into a childish grimace. "You're embarrassed? You don't want to see their faces when you rape them? Or, what, you don't want them to see you?"

"What are you going to do to me?"

"Answer the question."

"I'm not a rapist." Orange throbs through the air and I run my fingers through the mist. I like how it tints my skin tangerine. "What are you looking at? What are you touching?" he squeaks.

Now what do I do? He's not the guy I'm looking for. The guy I want is bold and fearless. This guy is so ashamed of himself, he needs his victims to be unconscious. Plus, Annabelle is young, healthy, strong. There's no way he could haul her away so fast.

He struggles into a sitting position, arms tangled in his shirt. "Listen to me. You are not well. Your name is Sean? You're suffering from delusions. Do you understand? You're experiencing a psychotic break. I'm a doctor. I can understand what you're experiencing. You need help. Maybe medication. I can help you get the help you need."

My voice slams out, sharp and angry. "What's wrong with you doctors? Why do you think medication fixes every problem? Do they teach you that in med school? You *fuck*." I backhand him in the cheek, hard enough to knock him back down. His aura flashes red, a neon color we don't have on this earth. The stench of vomit floats by me, then recedes.

"I'm taking those photos with me. And your drugs. If you tell the cops I was here, you're going to jail with me." I begin untying his ankles. "If you start screaming or move at all, I'll turn around and give you an ass-kicking that will leave you unconscious. Got it?"

He nods.

"I'm going to check up on you. Don't do this shit. You hear me? I'm watching you. We're not done yet."

He nods again.

"You're a piece of shit."

He looks down at his own trembling stomach. "I know," he whispers.

Before I finish untying him, I make a quick run through the rooms and remove the receivers from the phones. I can't fit them in my pockets, so I run to the back door and hurl them out into the yard. I retrieve my belt and, with a little effort, my shoestring, leaving his wrists tied. I manage to fit the sheaf of photos into my back pocket and the prescriptions into the other one. If I get stopped by the cops while carrying these, I'm screwed.

"Scream and I kill you," I tell him as I leave. I close the front door behind me and hurry around the corner of the house, crunching dead grass underfoot. The night sky is a high celestial dome, echoing with a bruised violet light. It's beauti-

ful the way the nights always are here, close, the breeze running its whispery fingertips softly along my arms and cheeks.
The air is warm and heavy with a salty, woodsy aroma. I fill
up my lungs with it, deep down to my stomach, letting power
and clarity course through my veins. I haven't lost a moment
today, not one single second.

Maybe it's not the change in my lithium dosage after all.
Maybe violence is fuel for me; maybe I need it to feel alive.

CHAPTER NINE

It's nine o'clock by the time I'm back on the UT campus, heading through the darkened walkways to the social sciences wing and the office where the crisis line is housed. This must be a common release time for classes; droves of students make their way across the grass and along the paths, some ambling casually in groups and some hurrying along with heavy packs strapped to their backs. It occurs to me that I blend in here pretty well. I'm the same age as these people. I don't look that different from some of the more punk rock and New Wave students with their gelled, asymmetrical hair, heavy eye makeup and ultramodern, form-fitting clothes. There aren't many Asians, but there are a few. I wonder if my mom is right—maybe I should go to college. It hadn't occurred to me that I'd be more invisible here than anywhere else.

I feel clean like the night, as though some violence has been purged from me, leaving me calm and empty. It was so different, hurting Spike, so easy to stop. I hadn't felt any of that old intensity, the bloodlust and urgent, primal need to keep going at all costs. Have I grown out of it, maybe?

I find the social sciences building and knock on the door to room 129. Surreptitiously, I lift my shirt up and take a whiff. It smells faintly of Spike's vomit. My stomach turns around uneasily, but it doesn't feel like I'm going to throw up again. I'm still sweating and my arms are prickling like someone is poking them with tiny needles of electricity.

I hear murmuring voices behind the door. When it's opened, the murmurs overflow into the hallway. A pretty brunette in her midtwenties with a short, shaggy haircut and large red glasses gives me an inquiring look. Behind her, a girl sits at a desk against the far wall of the office. "Have you tried talking to your parents?" she's saying into the phone, coiling the cord around her index finger. "Sometimes it helps to have family support."

"Sorry to bother you," I tell the woman. "I think I'm supposed to start volunteering today?"

She frowns. "Excuse me?"

"This is the crisis line office, right?"

"Yes, but...you said you were here to volunteer?"

I smile in as friendly a way as I can muster, which, judging by her face, makes me look like a serial killer. "With my friend Annabelle. She told me I could start today? She said you needed volunteers."

The girl on the phone gasps. "Oh my God. Are you okay?"

The woman spins around and gestures toward a third figure, a slightly older girl, who takes the phone away from the brunette and starts talking in a low, soothing voice. The woman pulls the door shut, forcing me a step backward into the hallway. She squints through her glasses. "Annabelle is out of town and she didn't mention sending me any new volunteers."

"Oh." I feign surprise. "Well, I'm sure I told her I'd be by tonight. She said you guys start at seven o'clock but to give you a couple of hours to get rolling before I showed up. Is this the wrong time?" This is what the girl at the front desk had told me, actually, but whatever.

"No, it's the right time, we're open, but I'm sorry, she didn't tell me anything about your coming. And also, we only employ female volunteers."

"Oh." After a confused pause, I ask, "Why?"

She frowns. "We deal with victims of sexual assault, domestic violence. They need to feel like the person on the other end of the line understands what they've been through, like they might have gone through it, too. It's important to the process, to making them feel safe."

The words, delivered so bluntly, slap me back and send me into a captive reverie. Is she right? Do those things not happen to men? Men are supposed to be strong, to fight back. The thought makes me feel small, and the panic in my chest tightens into a ball of shame.

She leans forward. "It's okay, don't worry. We appreciate that you want to help. These women have experienced trauma. They've felt powerless—violated. You can't—"

And then the rage comes like a spark triggering a gas explosion. I want to slam her back into the wall, hit her like I hit Spike. I want to be strong, huge, terrifying. *I* want to be the threat.

I fall back a pace. No. *No. I don't. I don't want to.*

She smiles up at the horror on my face. "Please, don't worry about it. No harm done. I'm surprised Annabelle didn't mention you. We were just talking about needing new volunteers. It's really nice that you wanted to help out. I wish Annabelle had told me; I'd have saved you the trip. She's a great volunteer, probably our best."

I gather my thoughts, sick, disgusted; I focus on the memory of Annabelle's clear, shining auburn eyes. I remember the trusting way she'd lifted a hand to run it through my hair. I picture her laugh, her carefree voice calling into the intercom in my bedroom. I can do this. I can be better than this for her. I need to focus now. This isn't about me.

I find my voice. "Annabelle's very special," I say.

She accepts this easily, smiles wider. "Oh, she's great. We're glad to have her. She's amazing with the girls who call in. She takes the hard ones, too. She'll be a great psychiatrist. She's so good at making connections with them, really helping them work through these challenges. Half the work is getting them referred to the right agency, but it's not easy. Sometimes they're too scared to make a change." She blows her too-long bangs out of her eyes and smiles up at me shyly. She seems amenable to a conversation. I want to get her talking, get her telling me things about Annabelle's life.

"I bet some of the girls who call have pretty crazy boyfriends," I try.

She rolls her eyes. It's supposed to be a yes.

"Must be kind of scary for you guys working here. Those creepers never, you know, try to find out where you are? Maybe it wouldn't be a bad thing to have some guys volunteering here with you."

"No, it's not like that at all. I'm more concerned about the girlfriend in that scenario. She's usually the one who gets in trouble for calling."

"I wish there was something I could do to help."

She raises her eyebrows, excited. "Actually, we do have a petition going around right now. Make sure Annabelle has you sign it. Maybe you can help her get signatures. That would be really helpful."

"Sure, of course. What's the petition?"

"We want a separate crisis line open 24/7 for sex crimes only, with specially trained volunteers. It was Annabelle's idea, actually. She's right; it's no good, having these untrained college kids fielding calls like that. They need a professional. Right now, Annabelle and I are the only ones with the level of training needed to take those calls. Anyway, I need to get back in there. Thanks for the offer to help."

I resign myself to the fact that I'm not going to be able to ask anything more personal about Annabelle without seeming creepy. Maybe I can follow up with a phone call tomorrow, figure out a way to build a rapport with her.

"Thanks anyway. I'm sorry to waste your time. I'm Sean, by the way." I hold out a hand to shake.

"Meghan." We shake hands and she gives me a shy smile. "Hey, have I seen you before?"

"I don't think so."

"You look familiar. Do you go to the clubs with Annabelle?" I try to picture wholesome Annabelle dancing with the other college kids in the popular nightclubs on Austin's downtown strip.

"No, I've never been with her. Have you?"

She shakes her head. "Maybe we could go sometime." This comes out in a wobbly nervous voice. "Have you met her friend Summer? She knows all the bouncers. She could get us in free at a lot of the clubs. Annabelle says they never wait in line." She smiles hopefully.

"Yeah, maybe. Sounds good," I lie, my brain spinning from this new information. Annabelle in the clubs? Annabelle with a friend who knows all the bouncers?

As I turn to leave, I realize she's flirting with me. I guess I don't smell like vomit after all.

CHAPTER TEN

It's eleven o'clock and the inside of yet another nightclub makes me nauseous. Strobes illuminate the faces of twenty-somethings in cut-up jeans so tight they must hurt. Music pounds into my skull from speakers set into the ceiling. Against the far wall, a DJ spins records with headphones pressed to one ear. It's half-empty tonight, a tribute to the fact that it is a school night; this club seems to cater mostly to UT students.

I've already been to four different clubs on Sixth Street. The night air is warm and fragrant with the cooling smell of cedar trees. If nothing else, Texas has beautiful nights. It's a nice change from the bracing San Francisco nights where you always, always need a jacket.

I check my wallet. It's a good thing I stopped at home to grab cash; I've never been to a club before tonight, and I can't believe how much they charge at the door.

I stand at the bar for a minute, eyeing the people. Most seem to be on dates; some are moving on the dance floor, the rest clustered around the bar area, talking and laughing loudly over the music. A bartender approaches me, a blond ponytail bouncing straight out from the side of her head with the help of three fat scrunchies. Her frilly pink midriff-baring tank top marks a stark contrast to the fishnets and tattered T-shirts worn by her patrons. "Get you something?" she asks.

"No thanks. I'm actually looking for someone." I dig a crumpled drawing of Annabelle out of my pocket and unfold it for her. "Her name is Annabelle. I'm also looking for a girl named Summer, but I don't know what she looks like. They're friends." I've shown this to eight bartenders and an infinite number of club-goers tonight.

The bartender shakes her head. "Sorry!"

I move through the club, stopping people here and there. "Do you know this girl? What about a girl named Summer?" I ask again and again.

Nothing.

On my way out, I ask the bouncer if he can recommend any clubs in the area. I make a list of the ones he names and continue into the next club on Sixth.

Nothing. Nothing at all.

At the next one, yet another blonde, tan, ponytailed bartender looks at Annabelle's picture. I ask, "Have you seen her? Do you know her?"

"I don't know. I just started a couple of weeks ago. Johnny!" She waves an equally blond bartender of the male persuasion over. He has a fifties greaser look, with one lock of hair pomaded into a practiced curl over his left eyebrow.

He looks me up and down and smiles. "Hey," he says with one side of his mouth crooked into a practiced smirk.

"He's looking for this girl," the girl calls to Johnny.

He peers at me and then at the picture. "Your girlfriend?"

"No."

"Not your type?" I'm not sure what he means by this, so I just shrug. His smile gets even more crooked and he says, "I know her."

"You know Annabelle!" I'm so relieved and grateful after hours of frustration. "She's gone missing. I'm trying to find the friends she parties with, see if they know where she is."

"Wow, that's messed up. But sweet of you for looking for her." Sweet is an adjective that has never yet been used to describe me. I almost laugh. He unrolls one sleeve of his white T-shirt and extracts a soft pack of Camel Lights. He shakes one into his hand and grabs a matchbook out of a nearby ashtray. "I don't have a clue where she might be, though," he says, lighting up. "I only remember her as 'vodka cranberry without the vodka' girl." A group of girls tumbles up to the bar. They're sloppy drunk. Johnny tosses his cigarette into the ashtray and I watch the smoke unfurl from its cherry and join the fog that hovers overhead. Johnny fills the girls' order, demonstrating how to make each drink to his female sidekick, and returns to me with a dramatic sigh. He retrieves his cigarette, takes a hit and blows his bangs out of his eyes in an eye-rolling gesture, sending a plume of smoke up to mingle with his aqua-colored aura. "I hate these yuppie kids," he says. "They come in here, never partied before, get stupid wasted. Not cute."

His sidekick leans onto the bar next to him and grins. "They're pretty sloppy," she agrees.

"Was Annabelle like that when she came in here?" I ask.

"No, but her friends, God, the worst. I'm just saying, I'm sick of it. Sometimes these kids jack themselves up in the bathroom so much we have to call the paramedics."

"Great." The female bartender sighs. She looks downcast at the mention of cleaning up messes.

I interject, "But Annabelle didn't drink? Just cranberry?"

He nods. "She seemed cool. Head together. Her friends are total hosers, though. Total ass-clowns."

"Do you know them? Would you recognize them?"

"Naw. All these college kids, they all look the same."

"Do you know anyone named Summer?"

"No. Why?"

"Never mind." Dejected, I turn to leave.

Outside, on the way back to where I've locked up my bike, I think about Annabelle and her vodka cranberry without the vodka. I suppose she's not a drinker.

I finally strike gold around one o'clock in the morning, at a club called Blue just off the strip. The bouncers let a group of girls ahead of me in free but charge me five bucks. Inside, rainbow disco lighting blurs through a fog of cigarette smoke that hangs low over the clusters of dancers.

I make my way into a tertiary room with couches and slightly quieter speakers. I find the bar and go through my speech, and the bartender, a brunette with a nose ring, lights up. "Of course, yeah, Summer and Annabelle! They're here all the time!" she cries over The Pretenders, snapping a mouthful of bubble gum.

"Is Summer here tonight?"

"Yeah!"

"Where?"

The bartender searches around the room and points to a corner where a set of velour couches form a crooked L near a cluster of arcade games and pinball machines. "Over there! The one who looks like Madonna!"

I push my way through dancers and smokers; every club seems to be playing Van Halen. I approach a sprawling, drunk-looking group of girls with a few guys, all congregated around the couches. I notice Summer right away. She's wearing a cut-up-T-shirt-and-beads ensemble to go with her unnaturally bleached, stick-straight hair. I think the dark roots are on purpose.

I flag her down. "I'm Sean!" I yell. "I'm looking for Annabelle. Have you seen her?"

"Annabelle?" Summer looks me up and down. "Why?"

I explain again, for what seems the thousandth time, and her blue-shadowed eyes look thoughtful. "Wow. That's trippy. Let me think. Um…no, I can't think of anyone who might be a threat to her. But I mean, she's wild, that one. Honestly. She could have a lot of friends I don't know about."

I would never have thought Annabelle would be considered wild. "Is she dating anybody?" I ask. "Maybe someone her roommate and work friends don't know about?"

Summer shakes her head slowly. "Not really dating, no."

One of Summer's friends, a guy with a spiky brown mullet and stoned eyes, interjects, "Annabelle? I hate that bitch." I snap my head to face him and he steps backward. "Whoa, dude, what, is she your girlfriend or something?"

"No. But why would you say that?"

Summer is frowning at him, too. Defensive, he says, "Hey, man, everyone knows that bitch is a cock tease. Greg says so." He points to a black guy with a flattop as though producing evidence.

The guy—Greg, apparently—puts his hands up. "Don't look at me," he protests.

"Yeah, try and act innocent." Mullet guy laughs, punching him in the chest.

I look at Greg. "Is it true, though?" I ask. "Seriously?"

Mullet guy wiggles his eyebrows at me. "Why, you hoping to get in there? Good luck."

"Shut up, you're such an asshole," says Summer.

"What? This guy's like a Chinese Robert Smith."

I wonder if I could beat him up. I kind of want to. Summer screams at him again, and he puts his hands up in a conciliatory gesture. "Aw, c'mon. I'm just joking. Look, she's a tease. I never hooked up with her but a lot of guys I know did. They all say she gets them to second base and that's it. Junior high style." He grins and walks away.

Summer sees me eyeing his retreating back with disgust and laughs. She leans over and whispers in my ear, "Come on, let's do some blow."

I raise my eyebrows. "Really?"

"Yeah. I have some in my car."

I contemplate this. Is Annabelle into cocaine? "Yeah, sure," I say at last.

Summer takes my hand and leads me through groups of people flashing neon lights, their auras confusing the scene so I feel like I'm drowning in an ocean of color. Her hand is cool and holds tightly to mine. It stirs something up in me, and I find myself admiring the outline of her ass inside the tight leather leggings. What is wrong with me? I try not to look, but her butt cheeks are winking at me, the leather shiny under the colorful disco lights.

Outside, I breathe a sigh of relief in the clean, empty night. I follow her to a dusty Nissan and she unlocks it. "Get in the back," she instructs. Before joining me, she turns the car on and fiddles with the stereo. "Billie Jean" blares out of the speakers, filling me with an eerie, anxious excitement. In the leather back seat that smells like cigarettes, she gets comfortable and keeps up a steady stream of chatter as she cuts me a couple of lines on a hand mirror. I pretend I've done this a million times. It smells plasticky all the way up through my sinuses and I'm left with a dripping, chemical taste in the back of my throat.

I immediately feel amazing, like I have light rushing through my veins instead of blood. I've felt clear all day, but I feel twenty times clearer now, like I could do literally anything. For the first time in my life, I understand the word *high*. It's the right word for this in every possible way. This is nothing like the drugs I've been on all these years. Those have made me feel hollow and numb; this fills me up from my heart to my fingertips.

Summer sniffs up two lines of her own and sighs happily. "That's good shit." She grins at me, and something in her smile makes me laugh. It's so silly, and it doesn't make sense, but I'm not sad about Annabelle right now. I see that everything happens for a reason, and whatever happens to Annabelle, it's all part of the universe's master plan.

"Have another line," Summer tells me.

"I'm good," I say, but she won't take no for an answer. I've never done coke and don't know how much I should do, so when she's not looking, I cup my hand over my nose and blow some of the line away.

Her hands are a bit shaky as she takes the mirror back. "I hope Annabelle's okay. I love that girl. I've always worried about her."

"Yeah. She's great." I'm confused. I feel sad all of a sudden, horribly sad, and I want to cry even though I thought I just had some massive revelation about how everything was okay. I try to reclaim it.

Summer keeps yammering on, now with a long, slender cigarette dangling between two fingers, filling the car with menthol smoke. "She's a good girl, you know? She shouldn't be into all this." She leans back and takes a hit off the cigarette. She kicks off a jelly shoe and wiggles glittery toenails. The colored light filtering through her aura catches the glitter, and I'm reminded of Annabelle's copper shadows, exotic and mysterious. Summer's torn-up T-shirt falls off her shoulder, revealing the strap of a black lace push-up bra and a mound of cleavage.

I can't imagine Annabelle being friends with this girl or doing drugs or being promiscuous...none of this seems right. I suppose I'm biased. After all, how well do I really know her? In my mind, she looms brighter than life, like an angel.

Summer is still talking. "Anyway. So I told him...wait... what was I saying? Oh yeah. Annabelle. Anyway. What business is it of mine? It's just, you know, she's a nice girl at heart. She's from the tiniest little hick town. They don't have this shit out there. I'm from Dallas so I know what's up. I heard of her town growing up but never knew anyone from there. It's so hick you can't even believe it."

"Do you know the name of her hometown? I don't think anyone ever told me." I strain to remember if Jenny had mentioned it by name and come up short.

"Lone Herman. Can you believe that? Lone friggin' Herman. What kind of name is that?"

"Lone *Herman*?" I'm sure I've heard her wrong.

"Right?" She laughs hard. Her cleavage jiggles. "She's just a nice, small-town girl at heart. I worry she, like, gets in over her head. You know?"

My head is spinning; my heart pounds an irregular beat. I press a hand to my chest, not sure if I'm imagining the butterfly-fast pattering inside it. The drugs are doing crazy things to Summer's aura; it's spewing five different colors at me. I think I can see layers of color, like multitudinous pinwheels spinning in different directions, each a different facet of her personality, each a different way she's affecting her environment. I reach out to touch the colors and then hesitate, sure she's going to recoil. Instead she bites her lip and gives me a little smile. "I've never kissed a Chinese guy," she says.

Equal parts grossed out and turned on, I say, "Neither have I."

She laughs hard at this, exposing a mouth full of gums and teeth. I recoil from the sight, but then she closes her mouth and my eyes focus on her breasts again.

"You want to make out?" she asks.

"Wait, seriously?" My head spins.

"Seriously!" She sits up and leans forward. Our faces are six inches apart. Her shirt hangs open in front. Deep cleavage spills out over her black lace bra. *What is wrong with me? How can I be staring at this girl's tits while Annabelle is missing?* "What's wrong?" Summer asks, pulling back. When she does, her rough, bleached hair falls back from her shoulders, revealing a pristine white throat, exposed over her swelling cleavage.

A whoosh of adrenaline implodes in my head and my hands become claws. The muscles in my arms tense up, my shoulders burning. I need to hurt her. I need to hurt her *right now.* The monster inside me roars, pushing me, driving me forward.

I open the car door and topple out of the Nissan, spilling onto the pavement. I pull myself up and sprint away, heart racing, stomach heaving with revulsion. I have to get away from her. I can't let this happen again.

I ride my bike through the night for a long time, my brain exploding into different colors and ideas. I find a spot on the sidewalk of an underpass, get my new sketchbook out and start drawing. Drawing while on cocaine is something else.

I remember the moment with Summer in the car, and I promise myself that I must never do cocaine again. In the meantime, though, I use this fuel to draw some pictures of Annabelle. I'm angry with myself for getting so close to Summer. What is wrong with me? Annabelle is going through hell right now, surely. How could I have been so—I'm disgusted with myself, furious, horrified, and the only way I can think to cleanse myself of my sins is to draw Annabelle's portrait over and over again.

At some point I notice that the underpass smells like urine, that homeless guys are asleep in huddled blanket lumps nearby, that an elderly lady is yelling at an empty spot on the concrete wall, but I pay no attention. My only redeeming quality is my art, and I have to draw all night long, until I know that I've done everything I can to make up for my moment of weakness.

Would I have hurt her? Had Summer just brushed elbows with death? In an alternate reality, am I murdering Summer in her car right this moment?

My mother is right. I shouldn't be out in the world. I shouldn't be interacting with women. I should be staying far, far away from them, like I promised myself after Betty.

Betty...

I don't want to remember—can't—won't—and yet the cocaine tows me down into the riptide of my past, and I'm back at the asylum.

It wasn't a coed institution, not really; there were male and female wings. The only time we mixed was in the common areas and even that was seldom for prisoners like me, high-risk offenders. Betty took a liking to me, though, and sought me out whenever possible. She enjoyed being drawn. She was pretty—not beautiful, nothing like Annabelle—and she was from Los Angeles, some poverty-stricken neighborhood deep in the city. She spoke wildly of all the crimes she'd commit-

ted and some I'm sure she invented, and she had schizophrenia, too, so I was always comparing, wondering if I sounded
like her.

One day, we sneaked into a bathroom to make out, and I
had her up against the wall, her giant, gorgeous breasts pressed
up against me. I was eighteen. This was the first time I'd
kissed anyone besides Elise, and I was monitoring my reac-
tions, careful, watching myself...

Suddenly it swooped through me, the desire, the urge,
the totally overwhelming *need* to *hurt her* and my hands were
on her neck. It wasn't a decision; they were just there, and
I was squeezing, gripping, choking. Images flashed through
my mind: her breasts, her face gasping, the warmth draining
from her soft, pale skin. Once she was dead, she would be
mine. I'd own her. I'd have *collected* her. This was a moment
that no one would ever know about, not anyone but her and
me, and when she was dead, it would be *all mine*.

Her nails tore at my face. I slipped on the slick tile. We
crashed to the ground, me on top. Her face was purple. She
spat out flecks of foam and rolled panicked eyes back into
her head.

Someone banged on the door. "Who's in there?" The doorknob jiggled.

I tried to get my hands to let go of Betty's throat but they
wouldn't. *Stop, please, stop,* I begged myself, but my hands
wouldn't listen. I couldn't do this again, couldn't, wouldn't,
and yet I couldn't stop my hands from squeezing. I didn't want
this but I *needed* this. Outside the door, keys jingled. *Almost
done,* my hands seemed to cry.

The door burst open and two orderlies' shouts echoed
around me, sound waves bouncing off the tiled walls and
floor. Something clubbed me in the head. My hands released

Betty and I fell backward onto the cold tile. My head spun from the blow. I opened my eyes. The bathroom ceiling plaster was darkened and moldy.

Coughing sounded nearby. Betty was coming around. Through my relief, an earthquake of dread was rumbling to life.

I knew the truth. What had happened with Elise was not an anomaly. In some part of my brain I had hoped against hope that once I left the asylum, I'd go on to lead a normal life and would never want to hurt anyone again. I was hoping that once the meds kicked in, the desire to kill would be gone and I truly would be rehabilitated.

But no. If I was schizophrenic, that wasn't why I had killed Elise, and it wasn't why I had done this. I'd suffered no delusions, no hallucinations.

Apparently, at some cellular level, I simply wanted to kill women.

Betty's coughing got louder. I rolled my head to the left. She was looking at me. Her eyes were wide and blue, her face clammy with sweat and tears.

"I'm so sorry," I whispered. My eyes squeezed shut from shame and horror. *I can never be alone with a woman. I have to stay away from them. Forever.*

And I had. I had stayed completely away from them. Until now.

Dr. Shandra doesn't know about Betty. Betty never pressed charges. She was poor, and mentally ill, a product of the foster system and a ward of the state. The whole thing was swept under the rug, just another thing the asylum didn't care to deal with, like the thing that happened to me—an inconvenience—a hiccup in their operations.

The California records state that I am rehabilitated. But I

know. I'm not rehabilitated. I'm not safe. I'm not better. The therapy they gave me didn't work and neither did the meds because they're treating the wrong illness. What I have can't be treated. It's just what I am. I am a predator.

I am a beast.

The homeless woman near me lets out a low shriek, almost a wail, and I turn my head and look at her. She's doing a strange, slow shuffle down the sidewalk, one hand extended as though holding someone's arm.

She's worth drawing.

After all, what else is there except this moment, this capturing of the people to whom I'll never belong and who will never belong to me?

I reach into the front pocket of my backpack, searching around for a pencil I know is there, when my hand encounters a piece of paper. It's unusual—I don't remember putting a receipt or anything in here—so I pull it out and hold it up to the light. It swims in my gaze and then comes into sharp focus.

It's a folded up piece of white paper. It looks like the note I found under my pillow.

I stare at it stupidly for a few seconds. I must have put it in my backpack, I decide, and unfold it expecting to read the three words that are already carved across my brain. I really thought I tucked this into one of my old sketchbooks. I specifically remember picking one from high school, a really old one no one would have any reason to go through.

Unfolded, the note is the size and shape I expect, but an unfamiliar and longer message is written in those neat block letters across the middle:

THIS IS WHAT HAPPENS WHEN YOU LEAVE THE FISH IN THE CARE OF THE CAT.

I drop the paper onto the concrete. My hands stay open. They look like claws.

My heart races. *What does it mean?*

Fumbling and shaking, I ransack my backpack, turning it inside out, looking for anything else from the kidnapper. A handful of colored pencils rolls away from me toward the curb. They spill into the gutter.

I set the backpack aside and pick the note up again, pinching it from the absolute edge.

Is someone following me? How did they get this into my backpack? *Where has my backpack been today?* I ask and answer the question in one thought: *In my room and with me.*

He was in my house again, with me in there. While I was going to the bathroom and changing my shirt and digging cash out of my mom's nightstand, *he was there.*

Fury roars inside my chest, fueled by fear and shock and the last remnants of cocaine, and all I want is to find this person, this man, whoever he is, and kill him. I want to slice through his skin, peel him apart, pull his intestines out, cut his balls off. When the impotent, body-freezing rage departs, I'm left empty, staring at the note trembling between my pinched white fingertips.

I have to tell the police. This has gone too far. Tentatively, I place the note flat between two blank pages in my sketchbook and close the book around it.

I don't feel like drawing anymore. I just want to go home, but home doesn't seem safe, either. Could this psycho be planning to do something to me—to my mom?

By the time I get home, just before daybreak, the high has worn off, and I feel grainy and spent. I let myself in silently. My mom's car is in the garage but the lights are off. I check and recheck all the downstairs doors and windows, confirming that they're locked. I creep upstairs and peek into her bedroom. Under the white comforter, in a shaft of soft dawn light that sneaks in through the peach-colored curtains, her body forms a small lump no larger than a child. I watch the rise and fall of her breath for a long moment and then retreat to my room, shutting my bedroom door softly. Afraid to turn the light on and wake my mother, I find the sketchbook in which I'd hidden the original note and add this one to it. I tiptoe through the dark into the bathroom, where I start the shower. The small window lets in a little bit of streetlight, just enough for me to see the outlines of my face glowing in the mirror. My cheekbones look high and tight like my mother's, my jaw stubbornly set.

What does the note mean? Is it meant to bait me somehow? Why send the notes to me at all? I'm not Annabelle's steady boyfriend. No one knew we were on a date. I suppose the kidnapper must have been following her and by extension me, but it seems strange. Why wouldn't he taunt her roommate, her family, the police? What do I have to do with this?

I reach down for my medicine box and open today's little cap. Inside, the pills glow white against the opaque plastic. I shake them into my hand: one oblong and two round. I raise my hand to my mouth in a practiced gesture but stop and bring the pills up to my eyes.

Does the oblong one look different?

I set the round pills aside and pinch this one between my fingers. I lift it up to examine it. It seems smaller, the edges more square than I remember. Steam from the shower dances around me gracefully.

I shake my head. I'm either losing it or my mom switched pills again, maybe to the generic or something. I scoop all the pills into my mouth and swallow them with a gulp of water from the sink. I shower off in deliciously hot water and get in bed. My heart is racing, erratic like an old car idling too high. I can't get Annabelle's face out of my head.

Of all the things I had pictured Annabelle being into, drugs would have been the absolute last. I remember her pervasive air of innocence and her commitment to becoming a doctor. I remember the guys describing her as a cock tease.

Annabelle, you have some seriously messed-up taste in friends, and your taste in guys is even worse. I start laughing into my pil-. low because that means I'm part of her taste, and yeah, that's pretty real. The laughing turns into crying because it flashes into my brain: she could be dead by now. The note doesn't say anything about her being alive. Horrible things have happened to her, I know it. I moan into my pillow through my tears. *No. She's not dead, she's not dead, she's not dead,* I'm thinking, and then I'm chanting it: "She's not dead, she's not dead, she's not dead…"

Sleep takes me abruptly, like I've been drugged.

Inside my sleeping brain, all is dark and quiet for a long, long time. Underneath the quiet is chaos, like a blanket has been thrown over a fire, but the coals still burn, ready to burst back into flame.

A soft, sweet smell works its way into the darkness, creeping, creeping.

I try to open my eyes but everything's black as pitch.

"Shhhhh," someone says. The voice floats in the dizziness that rolls me around until I can't tell which way is up or down. I'm an astronaut in the space inside my own head.

"Who's there?" The voice I hear is my own.

A new voice is whispering in my ear now. "It's Annabelle," it says, and I feel my own tears soak into my hair.

"You're dead," I whisper.

"I'm not dead." Her voice echoes around and repeats. "Not dead, not dead." It trails off into silence.

Even in my sleep, I know I'm fooling myself. "You are," I whisper into the woozy dark, and more tears soak into my hair.

"Shhhhh." She's kissing me now, and it's so real, her lips on mine, her tongue on mine, her hands in my hair, that I'm almost sobbing. *I'm going to wake up* is all I can think and then I'll be crushed because this is so real.

"Why are you crying?" she whispers in the darkness.

"Because I know you're dead."

She kisses me again and pulls up my shirt, and I feel that her body is naked against mine, her breasts pressed into my chest, hot and soft. She kisses my collarbone and neck, kisses my lips, runs her fingers through the long side of my hair like she had on the High Tower. I run a hand down her back and the skin of her ass is silky smooth against my fingertips.

"Don't hurt me," she whispers.

This isn't real. This is wrong.

My imagination detaches, pulled apart by the animal lust and all-consuming need I feel for Annabelle, and I remember the white truck's red taillights, the wobbly tires on the gravel shoulder of the road, legs kicking out the passenger's side door. "Sean," Annabelle screams, but then all of a sudden she's screaming in my ear and I'm *inside* the truck, watching myself running in the half light of dusk. She's next to me, screaming my name, but she's not asking for help; she's screaming for me to stop, to let her go. Her wrists are tied and she's fighting me, legs kicking against the leather seat, but I'm a beast who feels no compassion. I reach back and punch her temple, quieting her. I crank the gearshift, tramping down hard on the gas. Her hair spills onto my lap; she's limp, legs splayed.

I look up at the rearview mirror and see a man, like me but different, younger, cleaner-cut, face clear and earnest, legs pumping as he chases the car. "Stop," he cries. He wants to save Annabelle. It infuriates me. I stomp my foot down on the accelerator and the truck bounces up off the shoulder and catches traction on the asphalt. The younger man in the mirror fades into the distance and then I lose him around a bend. I've won; I've outrun him, this better, nobler version of myself, and I have my prize.

"No," I moan, but now I'm moaning it into Annabelle's neck, and she's in my bed on top of me again, lips on mine, hair tickling my nose and my hands are on her breasts. The truck was just a nightmare. This is the real dream, and I welcome it now wholeheartedly. I fall into kissing her and down a long, dark well where there is only her and me and the rustling of sheets beneath us.

CHAPTER ELEVEN

"Sean!" My mom's voice echoes off the high ceilings and stairwell.

"Coming," I groan, closing my bedroom door behind me. I trudge downstairs miserably, a hand on my forehead, the worst hangover of my life pounding at my temples with hammers. I've thrown up twice—mostly bile—since waking up, and I've spent some quality time sitting on the porcelain throne, evacuating whatever remained in my gut. Apparently I do have some sort of stomach bug.

"Come on, Sean, get down here," my mom calls for the third time.

"I'm coming!"

New policy. No cocaine mixed with whatever psychotropic meds my mom has me on. Bad idea all around.

Shielding my eyes from the sun that streams in through the skylights, I get to the bottom of the stairs and come abruptly to a halt. In the dining room sit my mom, Detective Benton and the female detective whose name I can't remember. They're deep in conversation. My mom is wearing one of the expensive polyester pantsuits she reserves for off-work time, her A-line bob so perfectly neat and straight it looks like a wig. Her aura is turquoise today; the cops' combine into a tangerine-grapefruit fog. When she sees my pajamas, her eyes widen with shock and anger.

"Hey, buddy," Detective Benton says. He gives me a winning smile, his mustache lifting at the corners. "Why don't you come on over here and cop a squat."

I hike up my plaid pajama pants and find my way clumsily toward the table. I slide into a chair across from Benton, as far from my mom as possible. The female detective is paging through a sheaf of papers in a manila file folder. She glances up as I sit down, then returns her attention to whatever she's reading.

I rest my hands on my lap, avoiding leaving smears on my mom's glass table. The detectives are callously leaning on it with their forearms; both are wearing lightweight pleated slacks and short-sleeved button-downs, his green, hers baby blue with shoulder pads. I can see the oily fingerprints on the table where they've been touching it.

Ridgeway looks up after a moment. "These are from California," she says.

"California?" The fog in my head parts and a single, clear, horrible realization is left: The pictures and drugs I took from Professor Spike. They're up in my room, in my desk drawer.

They're looking at me. What were we just talking about? I race to pick up the thread. "What do you have from California?" I ask at last.

Ridgeway smiles. Can she read my mind, smell the sweat that beads up in my armpits? Can they search my room while they're here? What if my mom gives them permission?

Benton strokes his mustache. "Your California release papers. Still waiting on your juvenile record. You want to tell us about that, save us the trouble?"

My mom cuts in. "Sean, don't answer. Detective Benton, please explain your question."

"It's just interesting." He gestures and Ridgeway slides the file toward him. "I see here that Sean was incarcerated in a psychiatric corrections center. For three years. Seems like they sent you all the way out near Mojave. Maximum security, maybe? Tell me about that. What were you convicted of?"

My mom holds a hand up. "I'm sorry, Detectives. I thought you wanted to interview my son about this girl who was abducted."

"We do." He grants her a warm smile, not too broad, just a few straight white teeth. "Sean, tell me something. Can you help me out with something?"

"Sure," I reply, guarded.

"You saw the truck drive away at dusk. You said that. Correct?"

After a brief hesitation, I nod.

Detective Ridgeway cuts in. "You were very positive on the point. You said you remembered the way the light looked after sunset, that you were certain."

"I know. I am. I'm sure."

"We checked our records. Double-checked, actually. You called us forty-five minutes after dusk."

Silence reigns around the table. Even my mom is quiet, eyebrows threaded together, back stick-straight in her chair.

Detective Ridgeway says, "The phone booth you called us from is not far from the hole in the fence. I walked it myself today. Even with false starts and stops, it couldn't take longer than five minutes, and if you were running like you say, it should take much less than that."

I look back and forth between the three of them. I can't explain this. I try to remember, try to take myself back to the darkness in the woods, but I find a blank space where the information should be. I don't remember calling the police. I remember walking up to the phone booth, but the next thing I can picture is standing in the flashlight beams of the police officers, showing them the sketches I drew of Annabelle.

What saves me from the confusion is, unexpectedly, my mother. She reaches a protective hand toward me. It hovers over my arm, two inches from my skin. "Detectives, you need to understand my son's condition. Schizophrenia presents with classically disorganized thought processes. Sean doesn't experience the world the way you or I do. His brain doesn't process information in a linear fashion. What feels like five minutes for him could be forty-five minutes for us." She drops her hand to the table without making contact with my arm. I feel a sigh of relief escape my chest.

Benton has been following this with hooded eyes, one hand petting his mustache absent-mindedly. "He seems to be tracking pretty good right now," he observes. "Matter of fact, he seemed fine at the station, as well."

"The symptoms aren't any more linear than the thought processes," my mom explains. "You should consult with a mental health professional before you question my son again. In fact, I'm going to insist that future conversations with you be held in the presence of our attorney." She stands up.

They take the cue and stand up, too. "Yes, ma'am, if you like," says the male detective.

Oh shit, the note. It comes flooding back: the weird note in my backpack, discovered in the golden lamplight in my cocaine-fueled drawing frenzy last night.

They're leaving. Do I have to show them the notes? Of

course I do. They could contain a clue. If I don't show them now, if I wait until some later time, it will look suspicious, like I've been hiding something. I force my mouth open and push the words out. "Hang on," I croak, almost knocking my chair over as I stand up. "I have to show you something before you go. Don't leave."

My mom opens her mouth to protest, but I hurry toward the stairs. I trot upstairs and dig around in my backpack. When I come downstairs, the detectives are standing in the foyer, eyes flitting around the living room, examining things I can't begin to see. Their backs are to the mirrored wall, and I catch my reflection, chest heaving, eyes wide and wild.

"I've been getting these notes," I say, breathless. In front of Detective Benton, painfully aware of how much taller than me he is, I open the sketchbook and flip through pages. His hawk-quick eyes take in all the drawings he can, probably cataloging them in his detective brain. Ridgeway steps forward so she can see. I feel like a child who has found some precious thing on the beach.

I find the right page and pull the notes out with shaking fingers. They look innocuous, just squares of white paper, much like the unused leaves of my sketchbook. "See, here they are. I've been finding these. I found one the other day and one yesterday." My voice sounds high, eager. It's the hangover; I'm not myself. My heartbeat pounds in my head, a steady, solemn beat.

The detectives glance at each other and then frown at the papers. It's almost funny.

"What are these, exactly?" Benton asks.

"They're notes. One showed up under my pillow and one in my backpack. I think they're from the kidnapper."

They look at each other again. This time the look is more serious. "Did you read them?" Benton asks.

"Of course. I didn't know what they were at first. I didn't know if—I'm sorry. I realize now in retrospect I shouldn't have touched them. But I didn't know what they were until I'd already opened them." I sound defensive. I need to stop talking.

My mom has joined us. "What is this?" she asks.

"I got another note," I tell her.

Ridgeway unzips her black leather fanny pack and pulls out a pair of latex gloves. Slipping them onto her hands, she says, "Pass me the sketchbook." She takes the book, notes and all, to the kitchen, where she lays it out on the counter. She unfolds both notes and lays them out side by side. We all cluster around, eyes trained on the neatly printed black letters. SHE'S MINE NOW blares crudely next to THIS IS WHAT HAPPENS WHEN YOU LEAVE THE FISH IN THE CARE OF THE CAT.

"I don't know what the cat one means," I say uselessly.

"You didn't tell me about this," my mother murmurs.

"I didn't have a chance. I just found it last night."

"Which one came first?" asks Benton.

"This one." I point. "I found it under my pillow."

"When?"

I strain myself searching for the memory. "Two days ago? The day after Annabelle's kidnapping?"

"Is that a question, or do you know for a fact?"

"I know for a fact."

"And the next one?"

"Last night. I was…out, just walking, and I'd stopped to do some drawing. When I reached in my backpack, it was in the front pocket with my pencils."

"Where do you normally keep your backpack?"

"In my room or with me. I always take it with me every-where." My whole body is shivering.

Ridgeway frowns. "I thought you lost it at the station."

"Yeah. I got a new one."

Ridgeway rips two sheets out of my sketchbook and sand-wiches the notes between them. My mom fetches a manila envelope from her office, and Ridgeway makes the whole thing into a flat, neat package. She asks us a series of ques-tions. Have we left any doors or windows unlocked, noticed anything out of place, heard anything from the neighbors about any strangers loitering in the area? The answers to all these questions are no. When they leave, they take a moun-tain of anxiety with them, leaving me with my aching head and my burning gut.

Then comes the crushing remembrance: they're looking for my juvenile record. It's just a matter of time until they get their hands on it. It's not sealed; you can't really get a record sealed as easily as the movies make it seem, not one like mine. I was too old and my crime too violent. The idea of them reading it makes me nauseous, and this time it's shame that tears my stomach in half. I search my body for some feeling of drugs, looking for the comfort of numbness, but I come up short. My head hurts like hell but my brain is working fine. Guilt shoots through me sharp and clear. I close my eyes, shove my knuckles into the sockets, and Elise's terrified face flashes against the darkness. Every part of me cries out against this, the worst and most forbidden of memories, and I shake my head furiously, trying to clear my mind, trying to think of anything else. I rub my eyes with the heels of my hands and hear myself hyperventilating as though from far away.

My mom's voice jolts me out of my panic. "You're not well," she says.

I snatch my hands from my eyes. She's standing in front of me, her face clinical as she catalogs my behavior.

I wipe my eyes, try to smooth my hair. My skin prickles and the muscles in my legs ache. "I'm fine. Just the change in medication gives me a hangover for the first couple of weeks. It'll pass. I feel better, actually, with the new meds. Clearer. You were right about the lithium."

"You didn't tell me about the second note."

"I just found it last night."

She shakes her head. "You understand what's happening here, don't you?"

"What do you mean?" I look down at my hands. The jelly bracelets have cut red lines into my middle fingers from being wound too tightly.

"You are their prime suspect. And you just made it worse."

"But—I'm the one who called them in the first place. Why would I do that if I was the one who had kidnapped her? Why would I volunteer those notes? I didn't have to do that."

"You're mentally ill. No one expects you to make rational choices."

"I'm not ill," I hiss. "It's not as bad as you make it sound. I hate it when you tell them I'm schizophrenic. I don't know why you have to humiliate me like that."

She lets out an unrestrained, frustrated groan. "Sean, look at you. Look at you! It's past noon! You just conducted an interview with detectives who suspect you of a violent felony in *your pajamas*. What else do you want me to say? I have to explain your appearance, your behavior. It's better for them to know you're mentally ill. Otherwise they'll think you're—"

"Who cares that I'm wearing pajamas?" I cry. "That doesn't have anything to do with anything! You called me downstairs! How was I supposed to know the cops were here?"

"It's noon, Sean! How could I possibly know you'd still be in your pajamas?"

"I have a crazy hangover from the medication you keep giving me." My chest heaves, the accusation heavy between us.

"It's time to think seriously about readmitting you," she says. "Look at you. *Look at you.*"

"Nobody cares what I'm wearing, Mom. They never have. You're the only one who gives a shit. Out of all the things to worry about right now, my pajamas are not one of them."

"Don't swear at me! How can you even— What is wrong with—" She throws her hands down by her sides. "That's it." She whirls and marches toward the staircase.

"Where are you going?"

Her legs whisk up the stairs like a horse trotting. I watch her, kind of fascinated and almost enjoying seeing her lose her shit like this, and then I hear my bedroom door slam open.

"What are you doing?" I yell, taking the stairs three at a time. She's in my room in front of the closet, and she's taking all the black clothes out, throwing them violently into a pile on the white carpet. "Mom, what the hell?"

"Don't even—just don't," she snaps. She flips through the shirts. "You have normal clothes. You have been given everything you need to be presentable. Everything. Everything." She cuts me with a glare. "There isn't one thing I haven't provided for you. Do you realize that? This is all your choice. Your choice to look like this, to behave this way!"

I cross my arms across my chest, and I enjoy that I have muscles there that I didn't have when we used to have these fights during my preteen years. "A second ago I was ill. Now it's my choice?"

"Being sick is no excuse!" She's screaming now. Her face is red. "It is no excuse to do what you've done—it's no excuse to do any of this. Any of it! How much have I sacrificed for you? How much have I done for you?"

Stunned by this, I wail, "What have you sacrificed for me? I was locked up for three years, and before that, I was with nannies all the time, for my entire life. How exactly have you sacrificed?"

Her face is dark. "I sacrificed my career for you, moved to Austin so you could have a fresh start. I spent my savings on you, on your lawyers and your treatment. Do you think all this has been free? Do you think Dr. Beck is covered by insurance? I pay for all of it, give you the best, and this is how you thank me." She yanks a pair of old black jeans off a plastic hanger so hard the hanger breaks. She wrestles with them for a moment but they won't come off the broken hanger. Finally she throws them on top of the pile as hard as she can. The movement seems to deplete all her strength and she's left with her arms hanging by her sides. She keeps her eyes on the pile of clothes. "I cannot control you. I cannot protect—" She brings a hand up to her mouth, which twitches and pulls down at the corners like mine does when I'm trying not to cry.

Guilt and anguish are fighting a battle inside me. They're both winning. Through twisted lips, I whisper, "You think I killed Annabelle. You think they'll find her body and I'll be found guilty. You don't even wonder if I did it. You have no doubt."

"I *know you*." Her eyes meet mine as wide as day. Images flash through my mind: Elise, eyes wide and terrified; Spike, eyes rolling with fear; Rebecca, making coffee, chatting with a nearby coworker; Betty, face purple against the institutional white tiles; Annabelle, eyes bright, copper aura glimmering in the twilight under the trees.

It rears up invisibly, the thing between us, and we stand quietly for a long moment, eyes locked.

"They should never have let you out," she hisses.

I step forward, fireworks exploding in my temples. "Don't you think I know that?" I whisper, the words sharp like broken glass.

She presses her fingertips to her eyes and then runs them through her hair. She squats down and grabs the pile of clothes. Jeans and T-shirts hang down, straggly and threadbare. "These are going in the trash," she says.

She walks toward the door. A T-shirt detaches itself from the rest of the clothes and sticks to the door frame. The shirt crumples to the floor. She's gone around the corner.

My room is empty. I'm completely alone.

I move slowly toward the bathroom. I haven't taken my morning meds.

My mom is right. I'm not functioning. I'm sick, ill, messed up in the head. I'm not a normal person. Why do I keep fighting her? She's the expert, not me. What if she's right—what if it is safer for me to be locked up?

With violence born of desperation, I yank open the pillbox and shake the morning pills into my hand. I shove the pills into my mouth and swallow them with tap water. My fingertips are tremulous, my head spinning.

I can't go back to the institution. I'll do whatever it takes. I'll take any drugs, say whatever words need to be said.

I sit on the edge of my bed. I look at my hands, limp on the knees of my pajama pants. I can't go back. I won't. What can I do? Can I run away from my mom? Where would I go? How would I support myself? I have no high school diploma, no college degree, no skills. And what would I be capable of if I were off my meds? What would I do?

I take a moment to think about Annabelle. It centers me. It

makes me feel safe. It's like going home. I turn my attention to her disappearance, summon memories from the kidnapping, draw forth the image of her feet kicking out through the truck's passenger side door. I won't let it go. This memory is proof of my innocence, even if it's only myself I'm proving it to.

It's such a shame that Annabelle had been planning to go back home at this same, inconvenient time. Why *would* Annabelle go back home after so long, anyway? And why would she be abducted right before she was leaving? Are the two events connected, or was it just a weird coincidence?

A question pops into my head that feels like the question I should have asked before, like I've been wasting my time not asking it: *What was Annabelle planning to do in Lone Herman?* The question teases its way through my brain, erasing worries about my mom and my mental illness, leaving behind a tantalizing sense that I am on the precipice of a revelation.

Why was she going back? Why now? There had to be a reason. What was she up to? Was there something she planned to do, someone she really needed to see? She had to have planned to stay with someone, or maybe she booked herself a hotel room. The only family member I've heard mentioned is her mother, but she might have old friends she could look up if she didn't want to see family.

The police had likely called Annabelle's mother and had been told by her that Annabelle had never made it to Lone Herman. But they haven't been doing much of an investigation. Obviously they think I either hallucinated the kidnapping or abducted her myself, so I doubt they went into much detail with Annabelle's mother, or anyone else in Lone Herman, for that matter. It's not like someone has physically gone to Lone Herman and checked to see if she's there.

An entire cast list of suspects, previously unconsidered,

pops into my mind: possible cousins, aunts and uncles, family friends with old grudges, high school boyfriends, angry teachers...

No sooner has the thought crossed my mind than I'm throwing my sketchbook and pencils into the backpack I purchased at the student store, my mind flying through preparations. As I do it, my eyes are drawn to the drawer where I stashed the pictures and drugs from Spike's house. Should I bring them with me, try to get rid of them somewhere? No, that's crazy. What if the cops follow me, search me? Conversely, what if I leave them here? What if they search this house?

Would they?

I curse my stupidity. They could have searched me today. It's only luck that kept them from doing it. Only by the slimmest chance did I escape. In another reality, I could be in jail right now.

I can't just leave the photos in my drawer.

I whisper curses to myself, eyes flying around the room. Where is there to hide them that the cops won't search? Do we have an attic? I don't think so.

I open the desk drawer and peel up the corner of the envelope. They're still there. I push them further back in the drawer and then change my mind. I pull the envelope and medication bottles out of the drawer. I can't leave these here. I'll have to take them with me. I'll bury them somewhere in Lone Herman. They can't just stop me and search my backpack without a warrant, right? Besides, I'll be careful. I'll sneak out the back. To be safe, I wrap the photos in an old beanie and bury them deep in the bottom of the backpack, under my sketchbook and pencils. The beanie is from high school. It's tattered and worn, and I run a finger over the knitted fabric. I wore this when I first kissed Elise. She was so happy. I was her first boyfriend. We were going to go to the upcoming homecoming dance. I didn't want to, but she was excited. She didn't care about being cool and above everything like I did; she wanted to dance to the Bee Gees and wear the off-the-shoulder disco dress she had made her mother buy her. It was purple and sparkly. I remember seeing it on the hanger in her closet. She was so excited.

I close my eyes and bring the beanie to my lips. I inhale deeply through my nostrils, catching the scent of dusty yarn and long-ago hair gel. Instead of pushing the memories back, I welcome them. I strain to remember if any part of me had known what was coming. Had there been any warning signs, any little alarm bells? I force myself to run back through my time with Elise. I catch glimpses of our junior year of high school: riding Muni buses, laughing as we shared chips out of a bag during nutrition break, fighting at Pier 39 near the sea lions because I'd thought she'd flirted with another boy. Once we ditched school and spent the day wandering around Haight-Ashbury, a couple of upper-middle-class kids in department store bell-bottoms fascinated by the hippies squatting near their trays of jewelry, inhaling the unfamiliar aromas of patchouli and marijuana. I hadn't known what would happen any more than she, that six months later she would be dead and I'd be sentenced to twelve years in a psychiatric prison.

CHAPTER TWELVE

The bus smells like mildew and the earth stretches away from me in flat expanses of grass and dirt. This is what most of Texas is like: flat and empty. The hill country is beautiful, though, with low-clustered cedars hugging the ground like a dark blanket. It's early in the morning, barely sunrise, and the landscape is gray and green. California isn't like this. Even in the less populous regions there are mountains, hills, orchards, car accidents, police cars, fruit stands… Here, you can go hundreds of miles and see absolutely nothing. Texas is a huge, giant expanse, one you have to experience to understand. It should be four states instead of one. Texans love to say that everything is bigger in Texas. They're not wrong.

The first bus I take, from Austin to Dallas, is half-full; everyone seems like a low-level commuter. I imagine these guys selling insurance or something. As we blow through the wide, blue-skied emptiness, banks of cedars peeking over the horizons, I push my headphones on and click Play. Ministry fills my ears and I lean my forehead on the scratched window. Outside, billboards fly by, some covered in graffiti, some with peeling paper revealing older signs underneath. One from the American Cancer Society depicts a baseball player holding a bat with the slogan "Be a winner! Don't dip or chew!" Someone has spray painted a giant cigarette onto his lip with smoke curling up above him.

When the Dallas suburbs cluster around me, I push my headphones down around my neck and pull my sketchbook out of my backpack. I review my notes and the hasty map I'd drawn myself based on my mom's giant atlas of Texas. I'm going to transfer to another bus in Dallas that will take me to Lone Herman. I have no idea what to expect from Lone Herman, but it looks tiny on the map. It barely seems like it counts as a town; I'd counted no more than ten square blocks clustered around Route 66 about forty minutes from Dallas and twenty minutes from Greenville.

I'd driven myself crazy trying to figure out how to find Annabelle's mother's address without the Lone Herman white pages, and then it had occurred to me that if the town really were small, there might not be very many Callaghans. Sure enough, I called Information and there was just one: Barbara. She lived on County Road 3231, which in itself sounded insane. In all my years, I'd never imagined such roads existed.

I'm kind of proud of myself. For the first time in years, I have a plan. I feel like complete shit; my head is pounding, my stomach aching, my arms and legs sore like I've been exercising all night instead of tossing, turning and sweating through my sheets. I don't know what's wrong with me, but I don't have time to be sick. I'm on a mission. I have a plan.

The bus station in Dallas is busy and full of normal people, but the bus to Lone Herman is filled with people going to Greenville and I'm acutely aware that I am Korean. Every single person on the bus stares at me when I walk down the aisle. They're all white. Every single one. I suppose my hair and clothes aren't helping me much, either. I should have put on one of the outfits my mom picked out, I think, hindsight being twenty-twenty.

The highway out of Dallas dwindles to a two-lane road upon which our bus roars like the *Titanic*. On either side, long stretches of dirt and grass make way for abandoned-looking sheds and houses.

I'm dumped unceremoniously at a Chevron on the highway's access road. "I can get a bus back tonight, right?" I check with the driver.

"Eight p.m., give or take," he confirms. "Pick up right here at the Chevron. Be where we can see ya or we may not stop."

"Thanks." I sling on my backpack and trot down the metal steps. I'm the only one getting off here. I watch the bus swing out of the parking lot and up to the turnaround. It gets back on the access road and accelerates north. An older man in ironed jeans and a Western button-down is filling up his tank about fifty feet from me. I smile and nod. He gives me a grim stare and does not return the nod.

Okay, then.

I get out my sketchbook and consult my hand-drawn map. I stuff it back into my pack and head south on the access road of I-30. Trucks thunder past on the freeway overhead. I turn right onto FM 36, which stands for Farm to Market, which, like the term "County Road," is apparently a common way of naming streets here in Texas. I imagine it has something to do with the road that leads to town from the agricultural areas. I take up a position along the right shoulder and walk as fast as I can. The atmosphere is silent except for the hot rural sounds of insects and far-off farming equipment. It's at least ninety degrees and so humid my shirt is already sticking to my stomach. The smell of manure hangs heavy all around me. On either side of the road, horse fencing borders the asphalt and far beyond I catch glimpses of cattle and horses. The cattle have horns—or are they called antlers? Anyway, the horns mean they're male, so that means they're for beef, right? Or is that a different type of cow altogether?

After a couple of miles I walk over some train tracks and FM 36 turns into Main Street. As I pass slowly through downtown, I'm struck by how haphazard all the buildings look. Everything seems put together with plywood and shingles. The fire department building is made of corrugated aluminum. One building from the 1800s stands in a clearing; an antique sign out front declares it to be an opera house. "Downtown" is really just one block. I have to stop myself from passing the street I want, thinking it's an alley. I haven't yet encountered a single human.

I turn onto County Road 3231. I imagine that only one pickup can get down this lane at a time. It's thick with oak trees, which hang in picturesque lace over my head and around the neighboring houses. These houses are small, not like the modern ranch houses I'd passed on FM 36. They're old-fashioned with triangular porch roofs. Every porch has a rocking chair or two on it, and I pass by a gray-haired, hunch-backed lady in a muu-muu tending some flowers right alongside the road; there are no fences between the yards and they're all very close together. As I pass by, she stands up and gawks at me. She even drops the trowel she's holding.

"Hello, ma'am," I say politely, remembering my Texas manners. She nods.

"It's a hot one," I say.

She nods again and I pass by. My face is burning. Across the street, an old man is sanding something on his porch. He stares at me and I nod politely. *Why are there so many old people here?* As I pass another block full of small houses close together, I decide that the younger people must all be at work in Greenville. This is the middle of the workday, after all.

It hits me. I'm an idiot. A complete idiot. Annabelle's mom is probably working. It's noon—what am I thinking?

Well, I'll have to wait for her to get off work, then.

Where? Here on the little lane, surrounded by old people? Back on Main Street, in front of the opera house? I curse my lack of foresight.

I find the address: 824 County Road 3231. It's a graying house that used to be white. The rocking chair on the porch is ancient and missing the seat. In the driveway, a beat-up Chrysler from another age sits on flat tires. I have to study the brown grass to find the path to the porch.

An old man in golf pants hiked up over a T-shirt comes out of the house to my right as I pick my way across the weeds. "Hello," I say. I remind myself to smile but then remember that smiling makes me look like a serial killer.

"What you up to, son?"

"Just visiting." I indicate the house I'm carefully approaching.

"Are you expected?"

"No. I'm a friend of her daughter's."

His face barely changes but I sense this comes as a surprise. "Friend of Annabelle?"

"Yes, sir." I smile again, smaller this time, and continue toward the front door. The man continues to watch me from his porch.

On the wooden porch, I'm presented with a problem. There's no doorbell, but I feel it's intrusive to open the rusting screen door so I can knock. I squirm underneath the weight of my backpack and the humidity. *Okay, fine.* I sigh internally, and I open the screen door under the neighbor's watchful eye. It creaks. I knock hesitantly.

The door opens after a moment and a heavy woman with graying copper hair in a baggy floral housedress faces me across the threshold, cigarette in hand. Her face is cloudy and distant like the tarry, brownish-orange aura that oozes around her silhouette.

"Um…" I hadn't considered how to begin this conversation, and the cigarette smoke drifts straight into my nostrils and makes me want to puke. "Hello. I'm Sean. I'm a friend of Annabelle's. From Austin."

"Oh." Her eyes register surprise. They're bloodshot. She sucks on her cigarette. "What can I do for you, Sean?" She has a thick Texas drawl, as did the neighbor, more pronounced than any I've heard in Austin.

I clear my throat. "I'm sorry. I don't want to upset you at all, but have you gotten a call from the police in Austin asking if she was here?"

"Yes. I told them she wasn't." She takes a hit from her cigarette. "I guess there was some mix-up at her college. They thought she was coming to see family and were trying to reach her. I told them they were mistaken." She notices the ash is an inch long and reaches out through the door to tap it off onto the porch.

"Well, to be honest, I was a bit worried because her roommate seemed pretty certain she was coming here to visit you. I thought I'd just come out myself and make sure, maybe see if there's any other family she could be visiting that her friends don't know about. To be honest with you, ma'am, we're a little concerned."

She stares at me, cigarette forgotten. "The Austin police told me I shouldn't be worried."

I nod. "I thought maybe the police hadn't thought to ask about other family or friends. That was my theory, that there were family members or family friends, or even friends from high school and her roommate just misunderstood her. That's why I figured I'd come out here and just put everyone's mind at rest." I'm babbling, trying to fill the awkwardness with my assurances of goodwill.

"She had friends in high school, but I don't know if she's kept in touch with them. I have no idea. She's been gone for years." Her nose is red-veined and her face has a ruddy, sunburned look. "God, do you think she's all right?" Her hand shakes as she raises the cigarette to take another drag.

"I'm sure she's just visiting friends or something. Right? Can you think of anyone?"

"I don't even remember their names. It was so many years ago. I… I don't remember names too well." This seems like a deep admission of guilt.

The air out here is hot and steamy. I wish we could go inside. "Maybe someone at her high school would know who her friends were, or are? A teacher, a principal? A counselor?"

She considers this for a long moment. "There's a teacher there who knows all the girls. She teaches English, a young teacher. All the girls look up to her. Annabelle loved her. She might know. I really don't remember her name. I don't… I don't remember things well."

Yeah, you mentioned that.

"Something Burns," she says abruptly. "It's the daughter of that minister who moved here from Greenville to start a church. I remember now. The teacher. She's named Burns. Unless she's gotten married. I don't keep track."

"I'll check with her. Is there any other family I should check with, any cousins or in-laws or second cousins or anything? Grandparents?"

Nearby, the neighbor has been steadily inching his way closer to us under the guise of weeding some of the strip between his yard and Barbara's. She frowns at him, steps back and beckons me into a tiny, wood-paneled living room where a black-and-white TV flickers on a stand from the fifties. She closes the door firmly behind me. I sit on a rust-orange couch and she settles her rear into the tattered recliner that is obviously her favorite perch. Ancient, avocado-green shag carpeting squishes beneath our feet, faint plumes of dust rising up from every footstep.

She sips her beer. "There's no family to speak of. Just me and Annabelle are left. She has my last name, Callaghan. That's not a married name. That's my name I gave her. Didn't even put her daddy on her birth certificate. Didn't want nothing to do with him, but that didn't work out as I'd hoped. But he was the only child in his family as was I, and his parents are dead just as mine are. There can't be anyone else. No other family, not except me and Annabelle."

"Her father didn't remarry? There could be step-cousins or some other relatives you're not acquainted with."

"No."

"Annabelle mentioned a grandma who had passed," I venture. "Maybe the grandma had some family?"

Her face closes. "We won't talk about that woman."

"I'm sorry?"

She studies me with careful eyes, and for a fleeting moment, I can see Annabelle in her. "She didn't tell you about her grandma?"

I'm not sure what to say. "She mentioned her grandma wasn't...that she wasn't liked by others. Something like that."

She nods. "I understand. I think that's best. Well, if that's what she's shared with you, that's where I'll leave it."

"I'm just trying to figure out where she might be." Frustration pulls my voice up a couple of notes.

"I don't know how to help. Annabelle hasn't been home since the Christmas after she went to college. She doesn't call, doesn't write. She walked away and never came back." Tears well up in her eyes and she pinches her fingers against the eyelids. "There's no family. There's no one. Nothing for her here. I don't blame her for leaving. There's no reason she'd come back."

"I'm sorry."

She wipes her eyes. "It was her father. His family. He was the reason it was like this. I tried to keep him away. Didn't even give her his last name. Callaghan is my family name." She drinks deeply from her beer can and looks at me as though seeing me for the first time. "You seem nice. You're friends with Annabelle?"

"Yes. We go to UT together." God help me if she asks me questions about med school, but I think I'm safe. It seems like she knows less about Annabelle's life than I do. I notice the wood-paneled walls for the first time. The one behind her is covered in framed school photos of Annabelle.

Barbara says, "That's nice. You seem nice. I got no problem with the Chinese. They're fine people. Hard-working. Built the railroad, after all, right?"

I nod, willing myself to keep the neutral expression on my face.

"Annabelle deserves to have nice friends. She's a nice girl. My princess." She notices my attention to the wall behind her and her eyes widen excitedly. "You like the pictures? That's Annabelle. All the way up through school."

"May I?" I ask, standing to get a closer look. She gets up

and stands right next to me, close enough so I can smell the sweat and stale cigarettes in her hair.

"That's kindergarten. Ain't she just precious?" She points to the oldest of the photos in a cheap drugstore frame. Annabelle grins at the camera, gap-toothed and freckled, a vintage sixties pinafore tacked onto her, hair done in elaborate waxy curls. I'm led through an extensive tour of the wall of photos, and I watch Annabelle transform from a cherubic, ginger-haired child to a serious, wide-eyed teenager. In these later photos, she's not smiling. She's staring at the camera uncomfortably, hands clasped in front of her, collarbones protruding under cheap seventies blouses, hair ironed flat to her head. "She always hated to smile when she had braces," Barbara explains and returns to a long rant about how good Annabelle was in school, how sweet, how much smarter than both of her parents. "And I'll just tell you one thing," Barbara confesses once we've reached Annabelle's senior year and I'm inching toward the front door. "I had custody. I raised Annabelle by myself, with nothing, just me and her. But then her grandmother and father decided they wanted custody, and I knew that would be bad for her. But they won. But then her father killed himself right after the ruling, and she never did have to go, and I said good riddance."

"Wait." I stop backing away from her. "Her father committed suicide?"

She nods. "But he was a bastard. It was better for Annabelle, that's what I'm saying. She was able to finish school, she did well. She went to college. That's more than anyone else in her family. She's the first one."

"How old was she when her father died?"

"Let's see. She would have been...twelve?"

My heart wrenches in my chest. Twelve years old. My eyes

return to the photos. "Is that her at twelve?" I ask. It's the last photo in which she is smiling.

Barbara smiles mistily. "Yes. Such a pretty girl."

"Seventh grade?"

"Must have been."

I stare at the following photo, the one from eighth grade. Annabelle looks much different. She's gaunt, her eyes darkened by heavy shadows, her mouth clenched into an attempted half smile. Her round cheeks are gone, shadows carved into them by her cheekbones. She looks sallow, unkempt and utterly alone.

I wish I had known. I remember Annabelle asking me about my father, saying her parents were divorced. I wonder how many times she avoided that conversation with people she'd just met. For the first time, I feel lucky to have no idea where my father is, to have no face to put to the name.

Poor Annabelle. The more I see of her life, the worse I feel for her. She's like a diamond in a pile of horse shit.

The air in here is thick with the sour smell of Barbara's beer. I'm worried I might throw up. I thank her and head for the front door, leaving her in a state of muttering, empty can clutched in both hands like a baby's bottle. "Tell me when you find her," she says as I pull the door open. "Tell her I love her. Tell her to write."

CHAPTER THIRTEEN

The high school is located on the extreme outskirts of town, far down Route 66 where dirt sprawls out in all directions as far as the eye can see. It's a small building that lies flat against the flat dirt next to a disproportionately large parking lot; it reminds me of a strip mall. Next to the school, an endless grass field follows the highway to the faraway horizon. The front parking lot is half-full, mostly of trucks and Town & Country–style station wagons that have all seen better days. Half of them have Reagan Bush '84 stickers stuck to their bumpers. If I'm looking for a white truck, I'll definitely find plenty of them in this town. I see three in this parking lot alone.

As I enter the main office, I remember my private prep school in San Francisco. Where my school's buildings were historic gray brick and its front entrance opened into the heart of a courtyard that towered above a steep hill in Pacific Heights, this one feels short and low in every way, even inside. Are all ceilings this low? I can't remember now. It seems like they aren't.

The middle-aged office lady looks at me like I am Alice

Cooper. She has her hair teased into a beehive style I haven't seen since I was a kid. "Is Ms. Burns available?" I ask.

"The teacher?" She has the drawl, too. It must be a thing here. I wonder why Annabelle doesn't have it.

"Yes, ma'am, the teacher," I answer. "I was hoping to speak with her really briefly. Of course, I don't want to interrupt her when she's teaching."

"She's…um…" She tears her gaze away from me and shuffles some papers around. She finds one with a handwritten schedule on it and puts reading glasses on the tip of her nose to examine it. She consults a wall clock and says, "It's seventh period. She's got sophomores."

"What time does school let out?"

"Two forty-five."

"That's half an hour. Do you mind if I wait here?" I indicate the line of chairs near the wall.

"That's—that's fine." Her eyes are devouring me with curiosity.

"Thank you, ma'am." I sit straight up in one of the chairs with my backpack on the floor between my feet. I keep my hands folded in my lap, willing myself to look like a model citizen. A radio behind the counter plays "Now and Forever" through a cover of static. Students come and go, greeting the office staff with polite *ma'am*s. They peer at me, their faces young to my eyes. The fascination goes both ways. What is it like to grow up in such a small town, and how did Annabelle fit in here? Had her beauty been enough to gain the acceptance of her peers, or had it had the opposite effect? I see no place here for Annabelle's brand of clear-faced flawlessness. Even the pretty girls look sort of coarse. For a few minutes, I sit tight-lipped as the office lady has an intense conversation with a teacher about the recent instatement of

Martin Luther King Jr. Day and how they don't believe people should be forced to celebrate it. Sometimes I miss California so much it hurts.

After a while, the bell rings. The office lady picks up a phone on her desk and makes a call. Moments later, she hangs up and beckons to me. "Miss Burns is in room 12. She coaches girls' track and is supposed to be on the field in twenty minutes, but she says she'll meet you in her room if you can make it quick. I'll show you where it is."

She gets up and makes her way around the counter, widens her eyes as she gets a better look at my jelly bracelets and Magic-Markered hand, and leads me through the office into a linoleum hallway that is like a miniature version of all the public schools I've seen in movies. My own private school was much more pretentious. Everything was antique, even the wooden floors and restored plaster walls.

She stops in front of a peach door with a little window in it. I realize she's waiting for me to open it for her and I do; she leads me into a classroom with linoleum floors and a few small windows against the far wall. Again I'm struck by the lowness of the ceilings. The room is nicely kept with posters of Shakespearean plays lining one wall and prints of Renaissance paintings lining another. Miss Burns is grading essays and looks up as we enter. She is a pleasant-looking woman in her late twenties or early thirties with dust-colored hair and pale skin dotted with freckles.

"This is the young man who asked to speak with you," says the office lady.

I approach the desk and Miss Burns gestures to a chair next to it, which is clearly meant for students. "You're not one of my former students, are you?" she asks.

"No, ma'am."

"Have a seat. And thank you," she calls to the office lady, who is already hurrying out of the room and closing the door behind her. To me she says, "I didn't think so. I'd remember you."

"Yeah, I expect you would. I'm Sean."

"Miss Burns." We shake hands. Her faint turquoise aura is a springy, happy color. She makes nice eye contact with me. I understand why her students like her. She doesn't make me feel small or insignificant. "So, how can I help you?" she asks.

"Well, I'm friends with one of your former students. Annabelle Callaghan?"

"Oh sure, Annabelle." She smiles. "How's she doing?"

I find myself almost duplicating her accent as I answer. It's the kind of thing that seems contagious. "Well, that's the thing. She told everyone she was coming home to visit family and she never showed up. Her mom had no idea she was coming and I guess she hasn't been home in years. So I'm trying to figure out if there might be any old friends she'd be visiting in town, and maybe it was just a misunderstanding."

She frowns. "Are you telling me she's missing?"

"The police aren't worried. But her friends don't have any idea where she might be. I offered to take the bus here and just ask around."

"Did you check with her mother?"

"I just came from there. She recommended I ask you, said you might remember the names of some of her high school friends. She didn't remember anyone herself."

"Friends... Gosh, I don't know. How long has it been since she was my student? She'd be, what...finishing college by now, wouldn't she?"

"She's in medical school. Studying psychiatry."

"Psychiatry?" Her eyebrows hop up and she laughs. "Wow.

Well, med school sounds about right, although I remember her being more of a chemistry nut." She steeples her fingers and frowns. "Let's see. I had her during junior year. I teach all tenth and eleventh graders and sometimes fill in a period with home ec." She laughs. "It's a small town."

"That's what Annabelle said."

"You're from Austin?"

"San Francisco. Been in Austin a few years."

"Wow. Well, then this *really* seems like a hick town to you."

I don't know what to say. "It seems very nice," I finally manage.

Her eyes twinkle. "Sure."

I meet the eyes and risk a small smile. "I do feel a little out of place."

She cracks up. "Well, I can't blame you! God, Annabelle. I haven't thought about her in so long. That was a hard year, though, not one I can forget. One of my hardest and I'd only been teaching for a few years at that point. Her best friend was this girl named Stacey Hetzel. She's still in town. The two of them were really close. Other than that, I can't remember Annabelle being particularly close with any one girl. She was a little, you know, underdeveloped. She always seemed young for her age. She wrote like a thirty-year-old, though. Brilliant work. I loved her pieces on figurative language. I still use some of her essays to teach the SAT prep class."

"Stacey Hetzel?" I get my sketchbook out and scribble the name on a blank page. "Do you know where she lives? Maybe I could stop by."

"I don't think she'll mind. I don't know where she lives, though. She's in the book, I'm sure. I haven't heard from her in years, but I've seen her around town here and there." She rummages around in a drawer and pulls out a purse. "Is there anything else? I'm sure she'll turn up. Annabelle isn't the type of person to get involved in anything she shouldn't. Her roommate likely misunderstood, or she changed her plans. Or at least, I hope so. I hope to God nothing's really wrong."

On impulse, I ask, "What was hard about that year? You said it was one of your hardest."

"Oh." Surprised, she sits back down with the purse in her lap. "Well, that was the year Preston died."

"Preston?"

"You wouldn't know. I'm sorry. I'm so used to everybody knowing everybody. He was on the football team. Senior year. Drove his car into a wall. Died in the crash."

"Into a *wall*?"

"The other kids were devastated. In a school this small, only a few hundred kids, they've been together their whole lives."

"How do you even drive into a wall?"

"Alcohol. Drugs. We're a small community but we're near enough to Dallas that our students have access to all the same drugs they do down there. And kids get bored. You know how it goes." Her eyes are far away. "Annabelle had a harder time than most, what with her family and all. She handled it well but it was tough on her. I didn't blame her for leaving Lone Herman. The boy who died in the crash was dating her best friend, Stacey, like I said, and it was hardest on them, I think. Of course, no, it was hardest on the boy's family. I just meant that the girls took it very hard. I'm not sure Stacey ever recovered, but I shouldn't say that. What do I know?"

She makes her way around her desk, purse in hand. "I'll worry until I hear she's all right. Please, have her contact me when she turns up. I'd love to hear from her." We're halfway to

the door when it opens in front of us and the office lady steps
through, followed by a police officer in his fifties. He's completely monochromatic: brown hair, tan skin, his crisp uniform in shades of dark and light brown stretched tight across a
muscular frame, his brown hair crowned with a worn-looking
chocolate-brown felt sheriff's style hat. A dark red aura rolls off
of him in a thick fog. For a moment, I want to laugh. What
is up with these Tom Selleck mustaches? It's like all the Texas
cops watched one too many episodes of *Magnum, P.I.*

Miss Burns smiles. "Hi, Officer MacFarlane. What brings
you here today?"

"Hello." He nods politely in her direction and touches the
brim of his hat like a cowboy. His drawl is as thick as Annabelle's mother's. "You having any trouble here?"

"Trouble?" she echoes.

He looks at me pointedly. We're stuck near the doorway
in an awkward cluster. The office lady seems to be holding
her breath and hoping I don't notice she's the one who called
the cops. I wonder if there is a police code for this. I picture
a dispatcher yelling into a walkie-talkie, "We've got a seven-
twelve in progress! Unidentified goth kid in small town Texas!
All units please respond!"

Miss Burns is reassuring the cop. "Everything's fine. This
is Sean, he's from Austin, he's friends with Annabelle Callaghan."

"Annabelle *Callaghan*?" His brown, suspicious stare turns
on me in triple force.

"Yes, sir," I say, since I'm obviously supposed to say something.

"Why d'you need to speak with Miss Burns here?" He
puts a hand on the holster of his gun belt. He also carries a
night stick.

"I was just hoping she could help me with something," I tell the cop in my nicest, friendliest voice.

"What kind of something?"

I glance at Miss Burns, nervous about telling him the truth, not sure what else to tell him.

She senses my nervousness and speaks for me. "Annabelle told her friends she was coming home this week. Sean's just trying to figure out where she could be. She's not with Barb so they're worried."

He squints down at me. "Annabelle doesn't come home anymore. Who says she's here?"

"She told her roommate. I thought she might be staying with friends here in town."

"She has no friends here," he says with finality. "And if she's not at Barbara's house, that's the end of it."

"Okay."

"You drove into town?"

"No, sir. I took the bus."

"From Austin?"

"Yes, sir."

"You're taking the bus back then? Catching the 8:15 at the Chevron?"

"Yes, sir."

"I'll give you a ride over there. You can wait for the bus at the Chevron. C'mon." He beckons with a meaty hand and exchanges a glance with Miss Burns. "Sorry for troubling you, ma'am." To the office lady, he says, "Don't let anyone through next time without checking in with me." She nods, her face red.

He leads me through the hallways, through the office to the parking lot. I lag behind, feeling suffocated by his wine-colored aura and the aroma of Old Spice deodorant that pours off him. He must be a former football player, I decide, remembering the way the office lady had flushed and looked sideways at his muscular forearms.

The last time I was in the back of a police car, I was sixteen years old. The day I was arrested, I had drawn little lips all over my left hand so they covered it like a glove. I remember staring down at the lips-covered fingers and suddenly thinking the lips were insects, panicking because I wanted them off my hand, screaming and filled with primal terror.

"This kid is batshit crazy," said the officer in the passenger seat.

"Batshit," agreed the driver. They had loud voices. They said these words jokingly but did not laugh. Their faces were blank with horror from what they had seen, from what I had done.

This time, the drive happens in silence. After a few minutes of listening to Officer MacFarlane's breathing, I say through the screened partition, "I'm sorry to cause any trouble, sir. I certainly didn't mean to."

He grunts and casts a glance at me in the rearview mirror. "Don't know what kind of shit Annabelle is into now judging by the sight of you, but I'd recommend you keep as far away from her as you can. She's had enough trouble in her life."

"You must mean her father. I was sorry to hear he had committed suicide. That must be hard on a young girl."

He makes a right onto the two-lane freeway. "What's your name?"

"Sean Suh, sir." It sounds weird, like I'm saying the same word twice, wrong both times.

He pulls into the Chevron and puts the cruiser in Park. I only now notice that his radio is on; Dolly Parton wails in wavering tones through the aging speakers. Not showing any signs of letting me out, he pulls a notepad out of a front pocket and scribbles on it. "You got your ID with you?"

I hesitate, then decide I'm not in much of a position to argue. I pull my wallet out of my back pocket and hand over my Texas ID card.

"No driver's license?" he asks.

"No sir. I'm from San Francisco. Not used to needing a car."

He raises his eyes to me. "San *Francisco*?"

"Yes."

"How long you been in Texas?"

"Three years."

He snorts a half laugh and hands me my ID back. I can all but hear the derogatory jokes exploding in his head. He gets out and opens the back door. I hurry out gratefully, pulling my backpack with me.

He says, "Wait right here for the bus. Don't go bothering us anymore. Annabelle's not here. I'd have heard about it if she was."

"Yes, sir." I sling my backpack on and watch him get back in the car. He casts me one last glance and bumps out of the asphalt driveway. I'm left in the dusty parking lot, frustrated and hungry. *What a dick,* I think, and head for the gas station to get something to eat.

It hits me: the photos and pills from Spike. They're in my backpack. They've been in there this entire time. This is the second time I've gotten lucky. Something tells me there won't be a third.

What am I going to do with them? I need to get rid of them as soon as possible.

As I'm squatting on the curb near the air and water machines, trying and failing to eat a bag of Cheetos, I think about Stacey Hetzel. Cop or no cop, photos or no photos, I decide I won't be so easily discouraged. I can't. I've come this far. I have to keep going.

CHAPTER FOURTEEN

I study the well-worn envelope on which the gas station attendant drew me a map based on the address I'd gotten from Information. I know I haven't taken any wrong turns.

This can't be right. *Can* this be it?

I'm standing in front of a—house? compound?—on the outskirts of town, about four miles from the gas station. The sun is beginning to set over the limitless acres of golden-brown, knee-high grass alive with the skreaking of grasshoppers. Rusty chain-link fencing half hangs off the posts bordering the yard of the structure, which is surrounded by cars in varying states of decay. The actual house is guarded by sentry piles of plywood and discarded sheets of faded wooden fencing.

In front of the fence and a few feet to my right, two mailboxes lean on each other as though for support. I step forward to examine them. One of them has a handwritten name tag, bleached from the sun and rain, that reads Austin Jackson. The other's name tag is on the opposite side where I almost can't see it. It reads, Back House, Stacey Hetzel.

Back house? I don't see a back house.

There's no way I'm going onto this property without being invited. This is Texas. They could shoot me for putting a toe in their yard and never see the inside of a jail cell. I mutter obscenities under my breath and walk along the property line until I pass the piles of rubbish and cars. Sure enough, behind them lies what looks like a trailer. Its small, curtained windows are lit. Someone's home.

Well, shit.

I remember the photos. I don't know what's going to happen to me in there, but I'm sure as hell not going to be caught with this backpack full of rape pictures. I duck aside, find a patch of tall bushes along the fence and drop my backpack into it. I pat my pockets, checking. Wallet, keys. Fine.

Annabelle, this is how much I love you. The thought fills me with pain and rage, and I take a deep breath to calm my pounding heart. I return to the front gate and push it open. It creaks loudly.

As I pick my way through grass, which I'm sure contains biting insects and rattlesnakes and pit bulls, and wait for shotgun pellets to explode my guts open onto the side of this rusting 1950s truck, I realize that yeah, I do love Annabelle, maybe more than I've ever loved anyone in my life and despite only having known her for a few days. As clear as if she's here in front of me, images of her silky bronze hair and her smoothly freckled skin flood me, so familiar, like I'd just been kissing her yesterday. Love and pain well up inside me.

Then comes the rolling, sickening knowledge that she's gone. The empty space around me, the absolute absence of her hits me in the stomach like a fist. I don't care anymore if I get shot or bitten or stung.

I stop, wipe my eyes and push it away. Keep looking. Just

keep looking. Until I've given up, she's still out there somewhere, waiting for me to find her.

Why I feel so close to her here, in this crazy person's dump
of a yard, I don't know, but I don't have time for it now. *I'm
going to find her or die trying,* I vow, and I'm not used to feeling
so purposeful. It's invigorating and I feel stronger, smarter,
able to face down bigger threats than rattlesnakes and pit bulls
and hicks with shotguns.

I find a little path leading to the door of the trailer. I climb
the two steel-and-plastic steps and knock on it. When it opens,
the smell of cigarette smoke pours out of the little metal doorway and straight into my nostrils, and it takes a minute to see
the person who's opened it.

The first thing I notice is her aura; it's a pale blue, so light
it's almost invisible. I don't know if I've ever seen an aura this
faint before. It's almost like it wants to disappear. The next
thing I notice is her hair. I remember Summer's hair, which
had dark roots that had been allowed to grow in to mimic
Madonna's; this girl has roots down to her cheekbones. The
ends of her bleached hair are wispy and dry, her bangs shoved
behind ears that stick out just a little bit too much. She has
delicate, even features, her mouth a shade too thin, her eyebrows just a little too high. Her eyes are a dead shade of gray
in the lamplight pouring from the doorway behind her, where
I spy aging linoleum and yellowing walls. The trailer is a long,
thin structure, not more than one room wide, and it seems
like the front door opens into a living room.

"Stacey?" I say. "My name's Sean. I live in Austin; I'm
friends with Annabelle Callaghan."

She raises her eyebrows. "Annabelle?"

"Yeah. She said she was coming home for a visit but her

mom doesn't know where she is. I thought she might have come to visit you, or maybe one of her other friends."

"Other friends?" She makes a snorting noise. "She doesn't have other friends."

I look back over my shoulder. Long shadows are stretching the yard into a creepy horror movie set. She follows my gaze. "I know," she says. "My landlord is, like, a hoarder."

"It's super creepy out there," I agree with relief.

"Come in. If you don't mind a mess." She steps back.

We move into a kitchen. The trailer reminds me of a boat. Everything seems unsteady, plasticky, temporary. The kitchen is dirty, dishes piled in the sink, a yellow-and-brown refrigerator from the early seventies leaning drunkenly in a corner. She yanks it open with all her strength. "Beer?"

"Sure." I rub my arms, which are prickling again. She pulls out two Bud Lights. Her Jordache cutoffs are a size too small, her tied-up blue T-shirt leaking a roll of belly over the top button.

We both sip our beers. "So you're her boyfriend, then?" she asks after a minute. She hops up on the kitchen counter and dangles her legs over the edge. Her toenails are painted bright pink.

"No. Just a friend."

Baby blue billows out around her. "No friend comes all the way out here just to make sure she is where she says she is."

"I'm not being possessive. We…it's a group of friends. Most of her friends are girls. I just… I volunteered to be the one to come check things out."

Her eyebrows shoot up. "Most of her friends are *girls*? Well, that's new."

"It is?"

She shrugs, takes a long swallow from the can. "She didn't get along too much with girls when we were in high school."

"Why?"

"They thought she was a stuck-up bitch. Which she was."

"Oh." Shocked, I don't know what else to say.

"With a crazy family. Not the most popular setup. Y'know?"

I don't want to be distracted. "So, she's not staying with you, then, I assume."

"Not with me. Not in town, not that I can imagine. How could I not know if she was? She ain't got no one else to call. No one else would put her up, not except for her mom, but if you tried there... You tried there? You asked Barb?"

"Yes, I did."

Her aura flares out in a sudden bloom of purple. She shrugs. "She's not here, then. Simple as that."

What was that emotion, that purple? I study her. "Who else was she close with when you guys were younger? Anyone she might keep in touch with, even if it's only a little?"

"She don't talk to no one in Lone Herman anymore."

"You can't think of any reason at all she would be coming home? I can't imagine why she would lie to her roommate. She was coming home for something."

"Nothing comes to mind. I've barely spoken to her over the years. Only person I can imagine her talking to now is Rob Shiner, but he's in Austin, as well. Moved out there to go to UT, same as a lot of kids do. She called me up like a year ago, asked out of nowhere if I could get her Rob's number, wanted to go work at this restaurant he's running, some titty bar place. I still keep in touch with him. *I* keep in touch with a lot of people."

"Titty bar place? Do you mean Duke's? The restaurant?"

She nods.

"He's the manager there?"

"Yeah. He's a few years older than us."

I contemplate for a long minute. "Do you think Rob and Annabelle were dating?"

"Are you kidding?"

I shake my head, confused by her incredulity.

"Of course not. No. Rob don't want nothing to do with her. Not like that. He was just doin' a favor, felt sorry for her. Not that it was right of her to ask him. What is *wrong* with her?"

"What do you mean?"

"I dunno. Maybe she's different now. But she's from that messed-up family. They're...they're...like...cursed. Bad luck or something. And she don't even act as humble as you might expect coming from such...whatever. Such trash. She's always the one judging, holier than thou, prissy. You know. Can never let loose, always has to be the best, always has to be *good*. You know I've never seen her drunk? And how many parties did we go to together?"

I remember what the guys in the club had said. "Would you say she was a tease?"

"Hell yeah." She laughs. "You got her number."

"What's so bad about her family? Her father's suicide?"

She stares at me, her mouth hanging open a little. "What d'you mean, what's so bad? The fuck is wrong with you?"

"I mean, her mom seems... I don't know. Nice enough, I guess. What's so bad about her? She's poor? She drinks?" Stammering, I say, "I'm not trying to be rude. I'm just—"

"Her mom? I'm talking about her dad's family. Her grandma. Are you sick in the head?"

I hold my hands up. One still has the beer can, so it looks

like I'm toasting her. "I don't know anything about her family. She never talked about it."

She stares at me for five full seconds, her aura going cobalt around her. "That bitch," she says at last. "I mean, I figured she was ashamed and was all like, yeah, as you should be. But that bitch is pretending— Lying little bitch." I think she might throw something, she looks so angry.

"Stacey," I say in a conciliatory voice. "Please. I don't know what you're talking about."

Her voice goes quiet. "It's so messed up. How can you live your life like that? It's…it's not…it's not…*respectful*. And with Rob? How—what? He just pretends along with her?"

"Pretends what? Respectful to who?" I'm desperate to understand. "Is this about her grandma? Or about her dad? What is it?"

She huffs a breath, stops talking and looks me in the eye. "Her grandma was *Annie Ray*."

Everything is silent for a handful of pounding heartbeats.

"Holy shit," I whisper at last. "Deadly Annie? Deadly Annie was Annabelle's *grandmother*?"

"She's named after her. Named after a *serial killer*."

I stare at her, not seeing her or the kitchen around me. All I can see is Annabelle in front of me in the Black House. When I'd told her that Deadly Annie had killed twenty-eight people, she had been so surprised. She'd demanded to know how I knew that. I had thought nothing of it at the time, but she must have known the exact number. It must have been scrawled on her memory like bloody graffiti, a scarlet number twenty-eight across her chest, branding her the child of monsters.

So far, I've only considered a limited number of reasons someone would want to hurt Annabelle. I've been imagining it's a sexually motivated kidnapping, or perhaps motivated by some hometown grudge or thwarted crush. But now I understand that there might be any number of people with a motive for hurting Annabelle, any number of people with a grudge against her, any number of people who might want to kill the only living relative of the woman responsible for dozens of deaths all across the state of Texas.

"Holy shit," I whisper again.

"Bitch," she says as though in agreement and takes a sip of her beer.

Protectiveness flares up inside me. "You can't blame Annabelle for not wanting people to know that. How do you think it felt for her to be related to…holy shit. I was there when she scattered the ashes. I helped scatter Deadly Annie's ashes. That's wild!"

"I'm glad that woman is dead. I hope she burns in hell."

"Did people here in Lone Herman treat Annabelle badly because of her grandmother?"

She considers. "She was only a little girl. How can you blame her? But they didn't like her, either. She could be spooky. Too smart. Too goody-goody." I remember what my impression had been of the high school and how I'd known Annabelle hadn't fit in here.

Her eyes drift sideways. I follow her gaze through a tiny dining room whose off-texture walls shine orange in lamplight shining from a ceiling fan's single remaining bulb. Beyond, a tiny living room sports only enough room for a love seat and a coffee table. The wall behind the sofa is filled with framed pictures, from the back of the sofa to the ceiling. A crocheted blanket has been arranged on the couch, and its worn tassels make me feel sort of sad. It's a reminder that this girl plays house here in this run-down trailer surrounded by junk, that she tries to make it comfortable and homey.

I follow her eyes, expecting to see something, but nothing's changed in the quiet room. She sees my curiosity and pushes herself off the counter. "C'mere." She leads me across the squashed, dirty-looking carpet.

She stops in front of the love seat and indicates the wall of photos. "That's Rob," she says, pointing with her beer can. I lean in. It's a crappy snapshot of a group of high school kids standing in front of a new-looking car from the late seventies. "That's me, that's Rob," she points. "That's Annabelle, that's Preston."

"Preston? The kid who died in the car crash?"

She nods, her eyes never leaving the framed photo. "He was my first love."

I lean gingerly over the back of the flowered couch. In the photo, Annabelle stands between Stacey and one of the guys, the older one, his age made evident by the broadness of his shoulders and the thickness of the mustache that flowers over his top lip like a fat caterpillar. All of them are smiling, Annabelle included. Her bangs are hair-sprayed into a small-town fashion, her clothes cheap-looking. Stacey looks pretty in the photo, her hair a more natural shade of blond, her face more animated. Preston looks like a jock, slimmer than Rob but not anywhere near as wiry as me.

She's still looking at the photos. None of them are any more recent than the one I've been examining. I recognize Preston's face and tousled blond hair in almost all of them.

Gently, I ask, "Have you dated anyone since Preston?"

She's surprised. "I dated Rob. We went out until he moved to Austin." She looks at the wall again. "But…it wasn't the same. It's never been the same. Rob's such a good guy. He, like, saved me. I think he felt bad for me more than anything else, and he…we…we always liked each other when I was with Preston. But then we hooked up and it felt…empty. And he had to get out of here. I don't blame him. He had more to get over than I did, what with Deadly Annie and everything; it was just too much." She swallows. "It was too much for all of us. Still is. I should have left, too. I wish I had. I don't know why I didn't. I don't know what—" She looks around, as though just now taking in the squalor of her surroundings.

Her mouth quivers and she wipes at it with the back of a hand. Grief turns her aura the color of old, soggy denim, so thick it's almost opaque. I want to reach out and touch it. I watch it fade into sad whorls around her, my stomach sick with the stench of her loss.

This is going to be me. I'm never going to get over losing Annabelle. I'll never move on, never leave Austin, never stop going to Four Corners. I'll retrace my steps every day, always hoping she'll somehow be back there at the fountain, waiting for me with her map of the park and her geometric backpack. What irony, that Annabelle should be related to such a monster and that a monster should fall in love with her.

In a hushed voice, I ask Stacey, "What was Deadly Annie like? Did you ever meet her?"

"She lived outside of town in a big house with her son, Annabelle's father. They kept to themselves, seemed like nice enough people, just, you know, more interested in their own business than anybody else's. It wasn't until Annabelle's father killed himself that Deadly Annie went a little more crazy, set some fires around the area, wasn't as careful to keep her murders away from home. They caught her that same year."

"How old were you guys?"

"That would have been the year we were in seventh grade?

Eighth? Took them forever to execute her. Annabelle never talked about her, never went to visit her, seemed like she wanted to put the whole thing behind her. Wanted to pretend it never happened."

"And did the other kids let her pretend it never happened?"

"Some people had family or friends who had died in one of the fires. That made it harder. A lot harder." Her gaze returns to the pictures.

I feel pity for Annabelle, feel so sorry for her that it hurts as I imagine a life lived in shame and humiliation for something that had nothing to do with her.

"Can you think of anyone who had—"

A banging on the front door interrupts us. She frowns. I watch her in profile as she hurries to open the flimsy door. "Oh," she says, surprised, to whoever's out there.

"You all right?" asks a gruff voice.

"All right?"

The door pushes forward, nudging her back a little, and Officer MacFarlane appears in the small hallway. He spots me right away. His face is dark and angry.

"What'd I tell you?" he growls.

"I'm sorry, sir. I just remembered, Miss Burns had mentioned that Stacey might—"

He's on me in two seconds and spins me in a smooth movement, catching my hands behind my back.

"What's wrong?" Stacey asks.

"You don't want to be hanging out with him, young lady," says Officer MacFarlane. He snaps handcuffs on me and pushes me toward the front door. I protest but he silences me with a slap to the head. He shoves me down the two front steps of the trailer and through the dry grass toward his cruiser, which shines like Christmas with its flashers reflecting off the grass all around. As we pass the main house, he waves at the front door, behind which a shadowy figure waves back.

He shoves me into the back seat of the cruiser. My heart is going to pound its way out of my chest. I don't like the handcuffs. I don't like them at all. My heart pounds harder. My breath is short and shallow, and I *don't...like...the handcuffs*.

I have to breathe. I'm not in the institution. That's far away. It's over. Officer MacFarlane slams the door behind me and gets in the front seat. He turns the flashers off and hits the gas. The cruiser bumps its way onto the two-lane road and roars into gear.

"I'm sorry, officer," I say.

He ignores me.

"Will you be driving me back to the Chevron? Or are you arresting me?"

He doesn't answer, but I watch the darkening landscape fly by. We are not going to the Chevron. We are going the opposite way, away from the main highway, away from civilization, down a long, empty country road.

CHAPTER FIFTEEN

After an hour, he pulls the cruiser onto the gravel shoulder. He turns around in the bench seat to face me through the grate. His Old Spice deodorant sickens me, and I'm grateful I didn't finish the bag of Cheetos. My wrists ache from straining against the metal cuffs.

At least I don't have the photos on me. That's one small thing to be grateful for.

"I called Austin," he says just as I'm about to break the silence. "Got a little bit of interesting information on you, Sean *Suh*. You a gook?"

"Excuse me?"

"Are—you—a—gook?"

"You mean, am I from Vietnam? No, I'm Korean."

"That's a gook."

"Oh. But… I was born in America. I don't even speak Korean." *Shut up*, I command myself.

There is a pause as he examines me through the wire mesh. "The detectives in Austin have your juvenile record from California, Sean. They got it in the mail today. Said it got some real interesting stuff in it. They thought it was real interesting that you were here, asking around after Annabelle."

"They have my juvenile record?"

"Yes."

"Fuck," I whisper, which makes him laugh.

"Yeah. Fuck is right." He keeps studying me. "You a psycho? Some kind of sicko?"

"No, sir," I say firmly. I try the door handle in vain with my cuffed hands. Locked. I'm trapped. My heart pounds out a frantic beat.

"NO?" His voice roars out at me so loud it hurts. "Then what in the *hell* are you doing at Stacey Burton's trailer?"

I can't quite breathe. "Annabelle has been missing. I was trying to—"

"Austin PD thinks you kidnapped her. *Kidnapped* her. You didn't mention that she was kidnapped. Abducted."

"I didn't want to scare her mom. I didn't think it was my place. The police didn't tell her."

He gets out of the car and opens the back door. I flinch away from him. He reaches for me and I'm certain he's going to hit me, maybe beat me to death, but instead he displays a black bandanna. He wraps it around my eyes and ties it behind my head, then adjusts it, widening it until there's no way I can see anything at all. He shuts the door. I hear him get behind the wheel. He guns the engine and we're driving again.

We drive for a long time. I don't know exactly how much time passes, but it has to be a couple of hours. Maybe it's less; my sense of time is messed up from the adrenaline pounding through my veins. We drive fast; we must still be on highways, but we stop occasionally, like we're hitting stop signs or streetlights.

Austin has my file. The knowledge hits me a thousand times. Austin has my file. They know. They know. They *know*.

My mom is right. They'll never believe I didn't kidnap Annabelle myself. If I don't figure out what really happened to her, institutionalization is the least of my worries.

They can't convict me without a body. Can they? The thought pops into my head and is followed by a tsunami of remorse and guilt. How can I think of such a thing? If Annabelle is dead, how can I even care what happens to me?

The road beneath the cruiser changes, gets bumpy.

What if she is dead, and what if they find her body? What if it's buried out in the desert somewhere with no evidence pointing to anyone at all? Would they still be able to convict me?

By the time the cruiser belches to a stop, I've almost forgotten Officer MacFarlane in my frantic worrying about the Austin police. When he opens the door and shoves me to the ground, I realize I had been wrong to forget.

A hard kick lands in my left ribs and I can't think about anything but the red-hot pain. Another kick, this one to the stomach as I curl in on myself, and now I can't breathe, either. While I'm sucking wisps of air into the vacuum of my rib cage, he pulls the blindfold off me, and the moonlight shines brighter than day against my dilated pupils.

He kicks me again and shoves me onto my stomach. His boot smells like gasoline. The boot is replaced with a knee. I can't breathe. I'm going to pass out. He messes with my handcuffs and I feel them come unlocked. The knee is removed, allowing air to partially fill my lungs, and I suck it in gratefully. My stomach rolls over and I'm filled with seasickness and relief that the handcuffs are gone.

He kicks me so that I roll onto my back. I stare up at the blurry stars, trying to breathe, my arms wrapped around my stomach. "Get up," he pants, getting to his feet above me. "Come fight me like a man. Come and get it."

"I'm not going to fight with a cop, man, are you crazy?"

He gets his gun out and points it at my face. The hole in the barrel is dark on dark. "You piece of shit," he hisses. "Cock-sucking psycho."

The words send me spiraling backward into a pit of memory. Alfonso on top of me, pinning me down from behind, my prison scrubs torn, wrists shackled, psych meds syrupy in my veins, thicker than blood.

My stomach is shuddering—it's going to come up—I roll to the side and vomit into the dirt and grass beside my head. I heave until my stomach cramps and I gasp for air. When I'm done, I wipe my mouth with my forearm. Should I get up and run? Can MacFarlane aim at me if I'm running away in the dark? Would it anger him more if I ran away or if I stayed and was docile? With Alfonso, it never seemed to matter. He came after me when I was asleep or awake, whether I raged or stayed limp.

MacFarlane lowers the gun to his side. "Can't kill you today. Austin knows you're here." He holsters the gun. "But come back to Lone Herman, come bothering our girls again, and I won't call it in. I'll bury you out here. No one will ever find you. You hear me?"

I can't talk. I clutch my knees, pulling them into my chest, and try to breathe. The grass and dirt are bumpy beneath me. He walks back toward the cruiser. He slams the back door shut and calls back to me, "Try to follow me and I might accidentally run you over. That'd be a shame." He gets in, shuts the front door and the car drives away, down the dirt-packed hill, and out of earshot.

I'm left alone, hollow, sweating through my shirt.

I feel like Alfonso is here with me, laughing at me in his dispassionate orderly's voice. "C'mon, get up," he'd say when he was done with me, like it was my own personal shortcomings that kept me on the ground, like the blood that leaked from me was an illustration of my inability to contain my weakness, and it disgusted him.

Part of me wants to just stay here on the dirt and rocks, far away from Austin and the detectives who know me, and my mother, above all, my mother.

I wonder if I could walk away from my life. Could I disappear from one day to the next? Would people think *I'd* been kidnapped?

The memory of the gun twists through me, and I find myself crying into my forearm. One of my worst fears is that what happened with Alfonso has somehow branded me, that other men can tell, that it left some sort of stench on me, that I'll always be weak now, the pathetic, hapless victim.

It takes time to stop crying and pull myself together. Sobbing into the dirt like a baby isn't going to make me feel any tougher. I need to get up. *Get up. Get up!*

I couldn't protect myself from Alfonso. I was just a kid, I was high on a thousand antipsychotics, I was thirty pounds underweight, I was handcuffed. It wasn't my fault. I tell myself this over and over again, and at last I sit up and wrap my arms around my knees. I couldn't protect myself from Alfonso. I couldn't stop Annabelle from being kidnapped, and I couldn't protect Elise or Betty from my own self, but I can keep looking for Annabelle. That is the one thing I can do to redeem all the things I've done and that have been done to me. I can keep going. I can get up.

I get unsteadily to my feet, brush myself off, check my pocket for my wallet and stretch a little, which hurts. I don't think my ribs are broken, but I feel bruised and sore. I survey the oak trees in the distance, the hills and cedars around me, and find no sign of civilization.

The cruiser had disappeared around a bend to the left, through a break in the trees, so I decide to walk that way. No matter which way I go, I suppose eventually I'll find a road. Does it matter if it takes me a day or two to get back? Does it matter if something happens to me? Does anything matter? Annabelle is gone and I'm no closer to figuring out who might have taken her. The news about Deadly Annie has hit me hard. I suppose I should get a list of all her victims and go through it one by one, but how would that help? If a vengeful spouse or family member is taking his or her anger out on Annabelle, I'd have no way of knowing who that person is by looking at a list of people who died in the fires Deadly Annie set.

I'm a terrible detective, I decide. A heavy, dense apathy settles over me like a lead blanket as I turn my footsteps toward the horizon and try to care if I ever find my way out of this endless Texas wilderness.

As it turns out, I only have to walk for an hour until I come to a little country road, and it's only half an hour more until I find a rather normal-looking house surrounded by pastures and horse fencing. A giant Texas star adorns the garage. I can't imagine a guy like me will be very welcome at two in the morning, and I haven't spent all this time walking just to run into the wrong end of a shotgun. I decide to spend the rest of the night tucked into a grove of oak trees on the shoulder of the road.

I lie down under cover of high grass and trees, my head cradled on my forearms, gazing up at the pieces of sky laced through with leaves. It's sort of comfortable, actually, on the soft grassy earth, and I feel like I'm camping, which is something I've never done but I decide I might enjoy. I'm painfully thirsty and my ribs ache and burn where Officer Hick kicked me with his cop boots. I find myself shivering and pull my arms into my chest, but that doesn't help at all. I wonder if I have a fever. This feels a little bit like that.

I keep remembering his words. *Psycho.* Tears fall down my cheeks and I rub them away angrily. The detectives have my file. I don't want to go home and face my mother. Where else is there for me to go, though?

I don't know what to do about the backpack with the photos and drugs in it. It's hidden from view, nowhere near where anyone would see it unless they were digging through the bushes, and why would they? Regardless, it seems dumb to leave the photos and pills there, but it seems even dumber to carry them on me. Officer McFarlane's threat didn't seem empty; if I go back to Stacey's house to move them, not only will I risk being caught with the photos in my possession, but I'm pretty sure he might actually kill me.

So that's it, then. I have to leave them.

But they have my fingerprints on them.

It's going to rain soon. It always rains in the summer here. That will destroy the prints, the photos. Right?

I don't know what else to do. I decide to leave the photos for now.

I knock on the house's front door a little after dawn, which is punctuated by the nearby crowing of roosters, something I've never heard in person before. A man answers, looking exactly as I would imagine: short-sleeved button-down a little tight over a hard belly tucked into a pair of crisply ironed, belted jeans. He glares at me suspiciously as I stammer out an excuse about friends from UT ditching me in the woods as a

fraternity prank. Despite all I've heard about Texan hospital-
ity, he makes me wait outside for an hour before he lets me
ride in the back of his red pickup truck to the nearest town,
where I ask to be dropped off at a gas station. I make a meal
out of bad coffee and packaged pastries, and the gas station
owner fixes me up with a ride to Greenville with a trucker
who comes in around noon. The ride is boring and uncomfortable; the trucker smokes like a chimney, doesn't talk and
has no less than five missing front teeth. In Greenville, I walk
a few miles to a bus stop. By eight o'clock at night, I'm on
my way back to Austin by way of Dallas, and the twenty-
four hours of travel hang on my shoulders like a tired, smelly
blanket. In the darkness of the bus, tall billboards and endless miles of cow pastures flying by me, exhaustion catches
up with me and I sink deeper into a lake of sadness where
every stroke of my tired arms brings me closer to the knowledge that Annabelle is dead. The bus eventually lets me off
at the Austin Greyhound station. I walk the few miles home
through warm, steamy darkness.

My mom's car is in the driveway but the house is dark. It's
long past midnight. In my room, which is beautifully clean
and gloriously familiar and quiet, I cram my meds down my
throat, fall into bed fully clothed and pass out.

CHAPTER SIXTEEN

Sleep shrugs off me like a mudslide, leaving me with another hangover and a roiling stomach. I stay in bed, hiding under the pillow for a long time. I remember waking up a number of times in the night, and I try to remember the last time I had a good night's sleep. Through my headache I know I should call Dr. Shandra; there has to be something wrong with my meds. I don't want to, though. I don't want to go back on the old meds, hangovers or no. I don't want to feel so underwater and apathetic. I finally feel like myself again.

I throw on a pair of jeans and limp downstairs with a hand over my eyes. I fumble in the cabinet for some aspirin. I gulp it down with a glass of stinky tap water, missing Northern California's, which always tasted cold and crisp. I start the coffeemaker and stop with a hand on the fridge handle, confronted with a note in my mom's uneven doctor's scrawl.

You missed an appointment yesterday. You need to call Dr. Beck to reschedule. —Mom

It's weird when she signs notes "Mom." It would feel more natural if she signed them "Dr. Suh."

Whatever. I can't care right now. I crumple the note and dig some eggs, cheese and bread out of the fridge. I wince whenever I move in such a way that my ribs pinch and groan. I heat up a pan and reach for the knife block to cut the cheese. My hand freezes on the hilt of a small paring knife. I'm not going to do anything with this except cut the cheese, one half of my brain snarls at the other half. No one's even home. What am I afraid of?

In response, vivid pictures of me stashing the knife in my pocket and using it in a number of future violent acts flash through my brain like a demented slide show. I snap my hand open and shake it out. The palm is itching. I rub it on the counter.

The pan is burning. "Shit," I mutter. I turn off the stove.

I get out a butter knife and cut some chunks of cheese that are mildly slice-like. When it's done, I take my fried egg sandwich and coffee to the kitchen counter. I take a bite and wince. The bread and egg feel rough and greasy in my mouth. I force myself to chew the bite and swallow it; I should be starving. I've hardly been eating since Annabelle went missing. I set the sandwich down and rub a hand across my bare stomach. The muscles feel tender from Officer MacFarlane's boot. I glance down at my torso and notice that my hipbones are poking out above the waistband of my jeans. I need to eat, but the idea of putting another bite of the sandwich into my mouth is repugnant.

The doorbell rings. It echoes tinnily up and around the high ceilings.

I frown. Who could it be? I brush the crumbs off my hands and approach the door with caution. Through the glass pane next to the front door, I see that it is the two Austin PD detectives. Their silhouettes are distorted into palefaced reapers through the leaded glass.

"Shit," I whisper. Are they here to arrest me? As much as I want to turn and run upstairs, I pull the door open and face them. "Hello," I say, wishing I had put a shirt on.

They look me over, Benton with the mustached solemnity of a grieving Tom Selleck. Ridgeway like a middle school PE teacher whose class is misbehaving. Behind them, two squad cars pull up to the curb.

Benton says, "We're executing a search warrant, Sean." He pulls a folded paper out of a manila folder he holds by his side and hands it to me. I don't even know what I'm supposed to be looking for on the xeroxed sheet, but I try to make sense of it anyway. The hangover isn't helping.

"Can I call my mom?" I ask.

"You can call whoever you want once we're done, but we're going to execute our warrant." He takes the paper back and gestures that I should step aside.

"Can I go get a shirt from my room?" I ask.

"Just stay right here."

I hover anxiously by the wall while Ridgeway lets a group of uniformed officers into the house. "Don't mess up my mom's stuff; she'll get really mad," is all I can think to say. After I say it, I kick myself inwardly for doing so. I sound like some psycho who lives in his mom's basement and buries women who look like his mom in the backyard, but not before taking souvenirs from their dead bodies and displaying them in his mother's china cabinet.

Ridgeway takes two officers upstairs. Benton pulls me into the dining room. I'm still clutching my mug of cold coffee. I set it aside on the table and then wonder if he might want some. I almost offer it to him but then worry that this would seem very suspicious. In the end, I hover in awkward silence while Benton stares at me over his YMCA mustache. More uniformed cops spread out into the living room, the garage, up the stairs. A few guys get down on the kitchen floor and start going through the drawers. They have kits, cameras and equipment with them and look like they plan to be here for a while.

Suddenly I remember the photos, still in Lone Herman. Thank God I left them. I actually sigh with relief. I always thought that was just a figure of speech.

Benton clears his throat. He rocks back onto his heels, almost bored with the proceedings. "So, here's some news. We have your juvenile records from California." He taps the folder he's holding.

Ridgeway trots down the stairs and joins us. "What do you think about that, Sean?" she asks.

"I dunno."

"You don't know?"

Her aura is distracting me. It's pulsating with red-hot anger. Officer Benton isn't so angry. He's more curious, purple mixing with her red to make a magenta fog between them.

"Do you want to explain any of this to us?" Benton taps the file again.

"Probably not without a lawyer."

A long silence vibrates around us. Ridgeway's red-hot tentacles of fury poke at me from the periphery of my vision. She can't keep quiet. "This is horrible, Sean. This is shocking. This is…this is…"

I know how bad it is. I don't need her to tell me. I stare at the floor.

"You're having fun here? Playing some kind of sick game with us?"

"No."

"That's what it seems like. It seems like you're enjoying playing the concerned boyfriend, keeping yourself in the loop, waiting for us to find her body. A lot of killers do that, try to stay near the investigation. They can't stay away; they like it too much. Is that what you're doing?"

"No." My protest sounds wrong, too loud, too weak, too forced, too young.

She steps closer. "Did you kill Annabelle?"

My voice won't work. Eyes huge, I shake my head.

"You don't like me, do you? I'm not afraid enough. Not young enough, not helpless enough, right? Not like Elise."

I wish her words would stop coming. I wish I could hide from her hate-filled blue eyes. I close my eyes and catch the scent of her deodorant. "It's not like that," I manage to whisper. The corners of my mouth pull down hard. My throat stings.

"What is it like, then, Sean?"

I cover my face with my hands. My fingers smell like sweat. I remember the knife block, my fear of using the knives. Could I hurt someone with them? Would I?

"Tell me," she hisses. "Tell me what it was like with Elise, then."

"I loved her," I whisper. My voice is choked. I'm filled with longing, but this time it's not for Annabelle. It's for Elise, with her stupid teenage giggling and her incessant phone calls and the way she'd played with my earrings. She had always been ready to laugh, always ready to make a game out of any little thing. If we were waiting in line, she'd make me do Thumb War with her a thousand times. If we were stuck in class, she'd make some little project out of paper and drag reluctant chuckles out of me with the funny things she'd write inside them. She was always smiling, teasing, poking at me, pinching my cheeks, pressing her forehead into my chest. She was the first person to ever truly touch me.

Detective Ridgeway steps back. "We're going to look into anyone else who's gone missing after visiting Four Corners, any other missing girls who might have spent some time there over the last few years. Does that worry you?"

"No," I say into my hands. I take a breath, pull myself together and remove my hands from my face. "I haven't done anything. It doesn't worry me."

It actually does worry me. What if they turn up some random girl who happened to go to Four Corners on a vacation and get murdered a few months later? I've been going there for years. Statistically, there could absolutely have been some girl who went missing after a visit to the park. Could I get blamed for someone else's crime?

Benton clears his throat. "What were you doing out in Lone Herman? Officer MacFarlane was very disturbed by your going out there, stalking the girls, going to Annabelle's old high school. It was creepy. Weird."

I'd never noticed, but the grout between the tiles is a little too dark. It makes the floor look dirty. They should have used white grout.

Benton leans a hand onto the wall next to me, trapping me. "Why'd you go there? Trying to make yourself look real concerned? Like a nice guy trying to help? Or maybe you were just getting off on seeing where she grew up, this girl you killed."

I can't help but stare at his mustache. It's so bushy.

I look into his gray eyes. "I was just asking around to see

if anyone might know where Annabelle could be. I'm worried about her. I didn't…do anything to her. I don't know anything more than I've already told you."

Ridgeway's red-orange fury slaps me on the side of my head. "I didn't," I snap in response. "You should be out there looking for her instead of wasting your time with my juvenile record and…and…" I clench my jaw. I need to shut the fuck up. My hangover is an annoying, low-grade throbbing on the side of my head.

Benton says, "This file is *very* concerning." I'm pretty sure *concerning* is not a word. "We've opened a missing persons file."

"Good. Finally." After an awkward silence during which five different emotions battle for my attention, I appeal to Benton. "Look, I get that you're suspicious of me. Fine. I can't blame you, not if you have that." I gesture toward the folder. "But at least look into other options, other people. You're the professionals. At least consider that I'm telling you the truth. I understand that you have to look into me, but at least *try* to find out who else might have taken her. Please? Isn't that your job? To consider all angles?" My words come out so rushed and pathetic that I can hardly bear the sound of them. My left shoulder starts tingling and prickling, and I struggle to restrain myself from rubbing it.

Ridgeway can barely even function through her fury. She wants to hit me. I stare at the floor again, ashamed and small, hating myself, hating them, full of guilt and shame and self-loathing. I've underestimated these detectives. I've been considering them hick cops because this is Texas and everything here feels garish and half-assed to me, but I've been wrong. Officer MacFarlane is a hick cop. Austin is the state capital; these are real, intelligent detectives, and I haven't paid any attention to the complexities of their personalities. Officer

Ridgeway is hard and tough, but she's also full of empathy and horror for the victims of violent crime. Her eyes, so full of taut, soured sadness examine me from head to toe, and I feel like no part of me can be hidden from them, like in her desperation to save Annabelle, she will mine me for every last piece of information until I've given her every part of myself that could possibly be used to incriminate me. Officer Benton, too, is much more incisive than I'd given him credit for. I feel the ebb and flow that goes between them, the unspoken communication that allows them to know which of them should play which role when talking to a suspect or victim.

These are good detectives. They're on the right side, and the right side is not my side because I am not the good guy.

"Here's a question," Benton says, as though he's been mulling something over. "You were sentenced to twelve years, yet you served only three. Why?"

I look down at the tile.

"I mean, look, criminals get off all the time," Benton continued. "I wasn't so much wondering about the reduced sentence until I came here and got a look at your house. Top-of-the-line personal computer, nice stereo system...your mom drives an Audi?"

I shrug.

"Must've had some pretty good lawyers, huh?" His voice is full of loathing.

I feel young, spoiled and pathetically small, but I force myself to say, "I was sick. I got treatment."

"Sick," he scoffs. "You told that to the appeals court? They ate it up, I bet. California bleeding-heart judges. I'm sure Annabelle's family will be glad to know you're all better now when we find her body."

One of the uniformed officers comes downstairs holding

four of my sketchbooks. He calls Ridgeway over and pages through them with her.

"What are you doing with those?" I demand. "Those are private. Those aren't evidence."

Ridgeway glances through one. "You're a real artist."

I shrug.

"Who's she?" she asks casually, her tone carrying more weight than the question warrants. I look at the sketch she's indicating, the one the officer came to show her, and my stomach drops down to the floor.

It's Rebecca, one hand resting on the steam wand of the espresso machine, other hand gripping a silver pitcher of milk. She's smiling down at the milk as she steams it with practiced ease, hair pulled into a high puff of a ponytail. Hers was a youthful, perky beauty, all freckles and russet skin and golden-streaked, spring-curled hair. I went to that coffee shop every day for months, watching her, ordering cups of coffee I got too absorbed in my drawings to finish. Her aura was almost always a soft, aqua turquoise, making me think of islands and dolphins, everything pure and sunny and clean.

Ridgeway murmurs, "They say they found hundreds of drawings of this girl in your sketchbooks. Hundreds. Books full."

I back away from the book. I can't go far; there's a wall behind me. "I didn't do anything wrong," I manage.

"What's her name?" Ridgeway demands, teeth sharpening under her angry, tightened lips.

"She stopped working there. I never saw her again. One day she just wasn't there."

"What is her name, Sean?"

I sigh. "Rebecca. I never found out her last name. I never even spoke with her. She just...she always had a name tag on."

She holds the book up. "This is stalking. Do you under-stand that? What coffee shop was this?"

"It was called Hopped Up, just a mile or a mile and a half from Four Corners. You can check, find out about her. I swear to you, I didn't hurt her. I never even spoke to her! She never knew I was there."

My voice cuts off, leaving a hollow silence in its wake. I hope my words ring with truthfulness. Ridgeway looks at me like she wants to spit on me. "Those notes you found were interesting, Sean, the ones you say were given to you by the kidnapper. Do you know what kind of paper they were on?"

Taken aback by the change in subject, it takes me a min-ute, but then I shake my head. "No. It just looked plain white to me."

"They're on 50 pound matte white. It's pretty common. You know what it's used for?"

I shake my head again.

"Sketchbooks. Like the ones you use."

My head reels. She has to be wrong. "This paper has to be used for other things, too," I stammer.

She levels her stare at me and keeps her mouth pinched an-noyingly shut.

I toss my hands up in exasperation. "You're just trying to find things to use against me. You want this to be my fault, but it isn't. This isn't even real evidence. Why would I have given the notes to you if I had written them? It makes no sense!"

To the officer, who is still waiting for instructions, Ridge-way says, "Make sure you take pictures of every drawing in every sketchbook. And look for pages that have been torn or cut. Let me know what you find."

He gives her a look of protest; clearly this is a task that will take him a million hours. Her expression makes him think twice about arguing and he retreats up the stairs.

I can't watch this. I'm going to hit her. I'm going to scream. I turn around and walk to the kitchen. Benton is outside with one of the officers and some equipment, probably digging up the yard. The cop from the kitchen keeps a close eye on me.

I pick up the kitchen phone receiver and bring it shakily to my ear. I tangle the curly cord around itself by accident and have to swing the receiver in circles to untangle it. It feels like a weapon and makes me want to use it like a bludgeon. I page my mom, fingers almost unable to hit the right buttons, and set the receiver back into its cradle. I press my face into my hands for a moment, afraid I'm going to cry. They're reading my journals *right now*. They're reading all the ones from high school. They're reading all the ones from when I was first released from the asylum. They're reading all the ones from Four Corners, and they're reading all the stuff I've written about Annabelle this week, all the pictures I've drawn of her from memory, all the words I've written about loving her and about wishing we could be together, about her sweet copper innocence and her pulsing, darkly beautiful melancholy. They're reading about the auras, my confusion about my diagnosis, my private pain. Did I write anything about Alfonso? God, I hope not. All those private images and words are right now being defiled by some fat-bellied pig of a cop and I can't do anything about it. Sobs come out along with tears and I'm shocked by the intensity of the emotion. Usually I feel so dim and away from everything, remote and apathetic. Now the feelings are up close and personal. They're right here, and they're crushing me—Annabelle's absence, my dream, my guilt, the knowledge that if it weren't for me and my past, the cops would actually be *looking for Annabelle* right now instead of wasting their time reading all of my diaries. It's my fault, the whole thing, and I hate myself so much for it in this moment that images of stabbing myself with one of the kitchen knives overwhelm me and I have to sit on my hands to reassure myself that I won't actually do it.

There's no way around it. I'm completely and totally screwed. I am going to jail for this unless I figure out who actually kidnapped Annabelle, and it's not looking very good on that front.

My mom is going to be so pleased. She's finally getting her wish.

CHAPTER SEVENTEEN

The cops leave the house trashed. My mom never returned my page. By four o'clock, the house is empty and I'm left alone in my room until I can't stay here any longer. I shower, change and set off on my bike with no destination in mind.

As I ride, I wonder if I'm being followed by the police. Is that something they would do? I look behind me a bunch of times but don't see any cars that seem to be tailing me, and at last I decide that I really don't care. Let them follow me.

My bike takes me on a familiar route, and before I know it, I'm pulling into the Four Corners parking lot. It's a crowded day, a pretty, sunny afternoon, and I get in line with the tourists. I show the girl at the turnstile my season pass and then I'm inside.

My heart kind of soars. It's so familiar here, so comforting. I stand in the entry square for a few minutes, soaking up the crowds of happy tourists and the big empty Texas sky. The smells of concession food and cigarette smoke blend into each other; nearby, a family poses for a picture against a fountain and one of the kids throws a nickel into the water with her eyes squinted shut, wishing hard.

I follow my familiar route to the tree house and climb up into the branches of the big oak. I hide up there and look down at the creek where I'd seen Annabelle's copper hair as she searched for a spot to dump her grandma's ashes. It seems so long ago. I can almost pretend the last two weeks have been nothing but a bad dream.

Staring down at that spot, I can't help but think that, if I had left Annabelle alone like I should have, she'd still be alive right now. I can't help but think that I somehow brought this on her. I can never allow myself to get close to anyone again. I have to leave people alone.

I climb down the tree and wander through the paths, running my eyes over the tourists, trying to ignore the rainbow of auras all around me. Around six o'clock, I duck into a little restaurant near the High Tower that serves good hamburgers. I order one at the counter and sit at a table near the register to wait. I kill some time lighting matches from the custom restaurant matchbook and dropping them one by one into the ashtray.

The cashier is a pretty blonde, maybe nineteen years old. Behind her, a man in his midtwenties with an already receding hairline and bad acne is packing up the food that gets handed to him by the cooks on the line. He stuffs burgers, fries and ketchup into bags and hurries to the counter to call out a number, then returns to his place on the line. When he trots by the cashier, he brushes against her ass as though by accident. It's completely intentional. She has no clue; she just steps forward, out of the way, and smiles more broadly at the woman whose order she's taking.

Creep, I think. His name tag tells me that he is Greg and that he is the assistant manager. He resumes his duties, staring at her ass with a little smirk on his face.

Something about the incident eats at me. I examine the feeling and wonder why.

The match I'm holding burns my fingers and I snap them apart, dropping it into the pile of ashes and cigarette butts.

"Order 43," the cashier calls, and I take my bag from her, searching her face for answers and finding none.

I wander through the park with my burger, forcing myself to chew without tasting, hating the feel of the food in my mouth, turning everything over in my mind. I end up at the Black House with a stomach full of something darker than butterflies. I enter slowly and approach the wax sculpture of Deadly Annie, who graces the passersby with her motionless, benevolent smile. I study her face, searching for Annabelle in it, and read the statistics on her plaque even though I have the whole thing memorized. I remember Annabelle's face when I'd recounted Deadly Annie's body count. It must have horrified her, tortured her. I understand now with complete clarity that killing a person is not a final act. It continues to reverberate and echo back in unforeseen ways. All the people around the victim are affected, as are all the people around the killer. It's like dropping two rocks in a lake; all the ripples around the rocks spread out and cross paths with each other, messing each other up, muddying the clean surface of the water, and they send ripples out all the way to the edges. Annabelle is one of those ripples. Her killer is another.

Her killer. There. I've thought the words.

She is dead and someone killed her. That's the truth, and I have to accept it.

There's one small moment of peace where I know the truth and I believe the truth, and then the truth is hot and sickening, and I push it away and go back to thinking about the ripples.

Out there somewhere is a person who was affected by one

of Deadly Annie's killings. That person thought killing Annabelle was a fair form of revenge. Little did they know they were just dropping two more rocks in the lake.

Annabelle never told anyone in Austin that she was related to Deadly Annie. Whoever that person is, he or she must have known Annabelle in Lone Herman. So I'm looking for someone athletic enough to drag Annabelle away screaming, motivated by a personal connection to one of Deadly Annie's victims and connected to Annabelle through Lone Herman.

Greg pops into my head, leering at the cashier's ass. The restaurant manager. Something about the restaurant manager. For a moment I don't know why this is resonating with me, and then suddenly I *do* know. The thought hits me in the stomach so brutally that I gasp for breath. My burger falls to the ground. The air spins around me.

The restaurant manager.

Where's a phone? I need a goddamned phone.

I run out of the Black House and straight for the exit. I push through pedestrians and burst through the gate onto the pavilion, which is crowded with tourists and people selling toys and refreshments out of pushcarts. I scan the pavilion. There's a gate, there's another gate, there's a million fucking tourists… There! There's a bank of pay phones.

I run unsteadily, digging change out of my pocket. I drop a dime as I'm trying to insert it into the slot. My hands are shaking so violently, I can't even pick it up. It's like I'm wearing oven mitts. I fumble a different one into the slot and dial the number for Information and then again as I dial the number for Duke's.

It rings twice and then connects. The hollow restaurant sound of voices and laughter fills my ear and a high-pitched female voice says, "Thank you for calling Duke's, this is Lisa, how may I help you?"

"Hello. I have a question for you." I clear my throat; my voice is all off. "I think I may have hit your manager's car in the parking lot. What kind of car does he drive?"

A pause. "What kind of *car*?"

"Yes, yes, what kind of car?"

"Rob? He drives an Explorer."

My heart is not beating. "What color is it?"

"What *color*?"

"Yes, what fucking color is it?!"

"It's white!"

"Is it dented?"

"What?"

"Like, does it have damage to the rear end of the truck, near the bumper?"

"Oh, I get it. Yeah. Why? You hit it with your car? You want me to put him on the phone?"

Holy shit.

I set the receiver down.

And now my blood can start flowing again. When it starts flowing and my heart starts beating, it beats the color red. Red fills the air around me. Red seeps out of my pores. Red clouds my vision. Red, red, red.

I grab my wallet from my back pocket and open it up. Inside is the folded slip of paper on which I'd written Stacey's address and phone number. I shove change into the slots until it lets me dial the long distance area code.

When she answers, I say, "Stacey, it's Sean, Annabelle's friend. Don't hang up."

A pause, and then, "Oh, Sean, you all right? What was up with MacFarlane?"

"Just a misunderstanding. Speeding ticket in Austin. Look—"

She laughs. "He's always been such a tool." Her voice is rubbery with alcohol.

"I have a question for you. Remember when you told me that it wasn't respectful for Annabelle to...to...not tell people about her grandmother? You said it when we were talking about Rob. You said you didn't understand how he could pretend along with her. Do you remember that?"

"Kind of."

"What did you mean about that? Does Rob have some sort of connection to any of Deadly Annie's victims?"

"Does he have a connection? You serious? His baby cousin was in one of the houses she burned down, along with her mama, who was Rob's uncle's ex-girlfriend. His whole family was just...messed up by it."

"That's why you were so mad she contacted Rob about a job."

"Bitch," she confirms.

"Was *he* mad?"

She's quiet for a moment. "He was nice about it, but he never liked her. He always called her devil spawn, stuff like that. You can't really blame him, can you?"

I hang up the phone.

I stare at it.

Woodenly, I retrieve the receiver and dial Information. When the lady picks up, I ask for the address of Rob Shiner, hoping against hope that it's listed.

It is.

★ ★ ★

I didn't care much about being followed before, but I do now.

I ride away from Four Corners, trying to look like I'm not in the biggest hurry of my life. I glance over my shoulder a number of times on my way home but can't tell if any of the sets of headlights on the streets around me are the same ones I've just seen.

At home, I fumble through the darkness, tripping over things the cops have scattered about, and turn on the light in the den. I scour a bookshelf until I come across the atlas of Austin city maps. I fumble for the index, searching for the street name I'd been given by the operator. It's Oak Pass Street. Texans are obsessed with their damn oak trees. I don't know why. You don't see California cities stippled with ten thousand Palm Tree Drives.

Oak Pass is across the freeway, in a neighborhood on the southwest side of town. I tear the page out of the book, write turn-by-turn directions on it and stuff it into my pocket.

Now I have to be a little bit careful.

I go upstairs and turn the light on in my bedroom. The whole place is trashed. I can't imagine my mom's reaction when she comes home tonight. I start the shower and turn the water up to the hottest setting. I open the little window in the shower stall so that steam will rise out of it if it is viewed from the outside.

Downstairs again, I keep low to the ground in case anyone is looking in the windows. In the kitchen, I crouch down by the cabinets, reach up and seize a steak knife out of the knife block. I slide it into my belt. On second thought, I open a drawer without standing and fish around for a flashlight. I test it against a cupped hand and then squeeze it into my front pocket.

I crab-crawl to the garage door and open it slowly. The garage is dark, hot and smells like engine grease. I close the door behind me and am in the oily dark. I feel my way to the nearby door that leads into the backyard. I crack the door and poke my head out. I listen.

Nothing.

I don't trust the silence. I sit there for a long time and nothing happens. I have to imagine they can't station an officer on private property. Anyone who's watching me is watching the front of the house.

I crawl out the door and shut it quietly behind me. I crouch next to it in the outside air that feels cool and smells fragrant in comparison to the stuffy garage. I keep low, glad for my black clothes, trying not to stab myself in the leg with the steak knife, and make my way to the back fence that borders the neighbors' yard. I want to go through the neighbors' directly to our rear and thus emerge onto the next block, but that house has a little yapping dog who is sometimes in the yard.

I make sure the coast is clear and hop the six-foot wooden fence that separates us from the old couple next door. Quietly I make my way across their yard to the one back to back with theirs. I keep low and close to the fence line, picking my way along the fence and through flower beds, until I come to their side gate. I fumble for the latch and let myself out as quietly as possible onto the driveway. I hold my breath and look around. Nothing.

I creep through their front yard and onto the street, and then I hurry as fast as my legs will take me to the left and west. This will let me out onto a different busy street than the one I take home from Four Corners every day. I plan to keep to side streets as much as possible, so I'll cross the busy street and make my way through the neighborhoods. Some of them don't connect with other streets and some do. I have my map marked and my directions listed.

Rob. Rob. Rob. His name bleeps through my head and I'm honing in on him, tracking him like a missile.

Rob. Rob. Rob.

I wonder if he can feel an impending sense of doom as the grim reaper's sickle swings in his direction.

The apathy is gone, and all my rage is loaded, the safety disengaged. For the first time, I really might kill a man tonight.

I wonder what it will feel like.

CHAPTER EIGHTEEN

Rob lives in a shitty little house on a shitty street south of downtown. His windows are dark and there is no car in his shitty driveway. It looks like the lawn has never been watered, not once, and in the sickly yellow streetlight, the windows seem coated with an oily sheen. Weeds creep around the worn gray siding and up to the front windows.

I pass quietly through the chain-link fence into the backyard. Back here, the grass is as dead as that in the front. I find the back door, a decrepit glass slider, and try it. It's locked. I move from one window to the next. All locked.

I reinvestigate the windows. They slide upward; I just need to get the screens off and hope that one is unlocked. I try first one, then another, until one lifts with a great echoing of screeching. I hoist myself inside.

Inside, I slide the window shut behind me. The room is stale and hot. I'm in a bedroom that's been turned into a game room of sorts with an old pool table and a kegerator in the corner. In the gray light trickling in from the window, posters of women look at me over mounds of exposed breasts from the walls. They all seem to be posed on various beaches and cars that are being washed, wetting their bodies and thin T-shirts and bikinis. I turn and bump into a furry head. My heart stops beating and I jump back two steps.

It stares at me with glass eyes, an antlered buck's head with a curved neck and slightly parted lips, mounted on a plaque and attached to the wall. Near the plaque, a framed eight-by-ten photograph shows Rob in camouflage clothes, holding a rifle, one hand lifting the deer's head by the antlers, the animal's body prone beside him. In the background of the picture, a white Ford Explorer nuzzles against a bank of oak trees.

I pull my flashlight out of my pocket and flick it on. It's too bright; it'll be visible through the windows. I put it under my black T-shirt and shine a little bit of dark yellow light around.

I move into a tight hallway. One dirty bathroom on my right and a master bedroom straight ahead make up this side of the house. I move into a living room and kitchen, both carpeted rust-orange like the bedrooms. This house feels gross, unclean. I can imagine Rob lounging around here after work with greasy food and buckets of cheap beer.

I search the house for Annabelle, tapping back walls of closets and pulling the attic ladder down from the hallway ceiling. I find nothing in the attic but boxes, rat droppings, insulation and cockroaches.

Back downstairs, I go through all the rooms again, starting with the master bedroom, which is papered with posters of Cindy Crawford and Elle MacPherson. I search under the bed, in the closet, pushing all the clothes around and shining my flashlight on the ceiling and walls, searching every crevice for signs of Annabelle.

I find nothing.

The game room yields even less. I spend some time on

a tall, locked cabinet about the size of a high school locker tucked inside the closet, but it's padlocked and not quite large enough to hold a person. I find a giant box of pornographic videotapes and magazines as well as a hanging camouflage outfit that I recognize from the hunting photo.

I stare at the outfit for a minute, then look back at that locked wooden cabinet.

I frown, the gears turning.

I hurry back into the master bedroom and open the top drawer of the nightstand. The bed doesn't even have a frame on it; it's just a janky mattress and box spring sitting on the dirty carpet. The nightstand is full of candy wrappers, empty condom wrappers and, at the bottom, an assortment of change and keys. I take the ring of keys into my hands, marveling that someone this disgusting manages to get himself laid at all. I've heard the jokes about women preferring assholes and have to concur that the empty condom wrappers provide some evidence to support this theory.

Keys in hand, I return to the game room cabinet. I fiddle with the padlock until a small silver key clicks it open.

Anyone from Texas would have recognized this cabinet right away for what it is: a gun safe. Being from San Francisco, where no one except hardened criminals believes in owning guns, I had never encountered a gun safe.

I swing open the door and sit back onto my heels. Inside, on specialty racks with barrels pointing down, are two hunting rifles and three different handguns. On the bottom of the safe is a stack of cardboard boxes that I have to assume are ammunition.

None of these things help me. None of them point to Annabelle.

I stare at the handguns in the dark. Next to them, the rifles glimmer dully.

I pick up one of the handguns. It feels cool and heavy. I don't know if this is a revolver or a pistol or what. I practice pointing it at one of the half-naked girls. I like the heavy feeling in my hand. I wonder if that's because I'm a bad guy or because I'm a man. Perhaps it's a testosterone thing. I can't imagine shooting a woman with this. There would be no satisfaction in that, no intimacy.

I can, however, picture myself shooting Rob with this.

I keep the gun. I drop the keys onto the closet floor and slide the door shut.

Annabelle isn't here. Just to be safe, I creep out into the backyard, gun in hand, and search every inch for any sign of a trap door, basement or storm cellar. Nothing. She can't be buried here, either. All the grass is hard and brown beneath my feet. Nothing has been recently disturbed.

Back in the house, the green numerals of his nightstand clock tell me that it is eleven o'clock. I make sure my knife is easy to withdraw from my pocket and settle down to wait.

I change spots a few times, but I end up standing beside the front door, where I'll be hidden when he swings the door open. He won't see me until he's inside the house.

I stand there with the gun pointed at the ceiling like I'm in some cheesy cop movie.

What the hell do I think I'm doing, exactly? I don't even know if this thing is loaded. Arnold Schwarzenegger over here, skinny arms pointing a potentially unloaded gun at the ceiling, planning to, what? Wave it at the bad guy and scare him?

I practice holding the gun so that that my finger is not on the trigger but rests on the little metal piece in front. I cover that hand with the other hand, supporting the weight like they do in cop movies, and point it fiercely at various things. That ought to at least make him think I know how to hold the thing.

I'm put out of my suspenseful misery when the flash of headlights brightens the room and the sound of a motor being shut off interrupts my reverie. I get into cop stance and take a deep breath. I am ready.

Car doors. Footsteps. The front door rattles as a key unlocks the deadbolt.

It occurs to me that, covered in jelly bracelets and half-long hair, I look more like one of David Bowie's backup singers than any sort of law enforcement officer.

The door opens and a male shape steps into the shadows of the living room. I wait a breath until he is all the way in and then step between him and the door. I bring the gun up in his face and yell, "Don't move!"

He jumps back like he's already been shot and lets out a high shriek of surprise.

"Don't fucking move!" I yell. My voice sounds fierce and manly.

"What—" he screams.

"Down on your knees!" I'm not sure if that's a good thing to tell him to do, but I want to give him some instructions so he doesn't go running for the safe and get a gun of his own.

That reminds me. I really should have locked the gun safe. I'm an idiot.

"Shit," he murmurs.

"Down!" I yell.

He drops down.

Behind me, the door bumps into my ass and I almost squeeze the trigger.

"Get out of here!" he yells, which makes no sense until I

realize that someone else is coming into the house. He's not alone.

A female voice behind me says, "What?"

I yell, "Get out of here!"

"Get out of here!" Rob echoes. It's like we've made up a little song and we're singing it in rounds.

"Why?" cries the female voice.

I'm desperate. "I'll shoot her," I tell Rob, and I mean it, I really do, my heart is exploding and I think maybe the best thing is to just kill everyone.

"Get out of here! I'm being robbed!" he yells, and there is a silence followed by a screaming gasp and running footsteps.

Now my time is limited. How long will it take her to call the police? Can I be gone before they can get here?

I can barely see him. He's black on gray. The tip of the gun is only two feet from his head. I can smell his sweat, or is that mine?

"You need to hold still," I say in a voice that is full of resolve. "You need to tell me right now what you did with her."

A pause.

"Put your hands on your head," I say, realizing that I should have told him that at the beginning. "What did you do with her?"

He puts his hands on his head. "With who?" Waves of emotion are rolling off him, confusing me, turning the air a weird shade of brown.

"Annabelle," I say.

A turquoise swirl mists into the brown. "Annabelle? From Duke's?"

"Where is she?"

"Where is *Annabelle*?"

"*Yes*, you *fuck*, where is she?"

"I don't know." He swallows. "Fuck. I think she's on vacation. Why? What do you mean?"

"I mean where is she? I know you have her! I know you know her from Lone Herman!"

He chokes out an incredulous laugh. "Yeah. I mean, I know her. But I don't know where she is. She's just...on vacation. Why? Who are you? Why are you asking me?"

I keep the gun trained on him. My arms are weakening. No one ever mentions how heavy guns are. The thought, clear and calm, weaves its way through the brown and teal confusion.

"Do you have her?" I ask, examining his aura. "Tell me the truth. I'll know if you don't."

He makes a scoffing noise. "You came here to ask about one of my fucking *waitresses*? Of course I don't have Annabelle. She's on vacation. What the fuck is your damage?"

His color doesn't change. He's not lying.

I don't know what to say. I don't know how to breathe. "But your cousin. Deadly Annie. You don't hate Annabelle?"

Teal swirls around him, no change in the aura visible to my eye. "Dude, I mess with her, yeah, I give her a hard time, but I don't really give a shit. My cousin was just a kid, and it was ten years ago. What the hell?"

His color doesn't change. He feels nothing for this relative of his. I think I'd like him more if he *had* taken revenge on behalf of his small, innocent cousin, but he didn't. He's not the guy.

I open my mouth to reply but he launches off the ground. With one meaty hand he wrenches the gun out of my hand; with the other, he explodes a punch onto my cheekbone. Lightning-hot pain soars through my head. My vision blurs and I'm on the ground with him on top, punching me in the stomach, the kidneys, the head. Through it, I hear him say, "Is this my gun? You took my fucking gun and broke into my house?" Punch, punch, punch. It all blurs together.

I go into a haze and come a little bit out of it when the lights get turned on. A set of cops in black uniforms is standing over me, and then a set of paramedics is standing over me, and then I'm floating off into an ambulance. I was wrong. It wasn't Rob. I don't know where Annabelle is, and now I probably never will.

CHAPTER NINETEEN

Being arrested, booked and charged with a crime is slightly different in Texas. Well, also, I'm injured, so there's less annoyance on the front end. They handle most of the paperwork while I'm being patched up at the hospital. It takes them a few hours to determine that I am pretty much fine, just bruised. None of the nurses seem to give a shit that there's a cop waiting for me to be treated. It's just a breaking-and-entering case, and it's noticeable how differently I'm treated by the cops compared to the last time I was arrested. They seem to think it's kind of funny, a weird-looking Asian kid breaking into a good old Texas boy's house and getting a proper ass-whupping.

As I sit on the examination table, hands handcuffed behind me, I stare at the little glass-and-mesh window in the puke-green door and remember the door in the asylum. I remember the drugged apathy that had made time stop passing and, for the first time, I miss it with every cell in my body. I miss it so much that it literally hurts. I search my body for some comforting feeling of medicine, but I can't find it. I'm completely alone.

Eventually I'm shipped to the police station. I'm brought in through a side entrance and my vitals are recorded by bored-looking desk cops. I'm measured and fingerprinted and given something to hold while my photograph is taken. The cops who brought me in tell the other cops why I'm here and they all have a good laugh. I say nothing. When they ask me questions, I tell them I want my lawyer. I know the drill. Phones ring around us, shrill and loud against the ever-present clickety-clack of typewriters.

I don't like to look at the cops when I'm being handled and questioned. It makes me remember those two cops in the cruiser, that first night I was arrested at the scene of the crime.

When they're done with my identification, have taken my clothes and my wallet, and have searched all of my orifices for whatever I could be smuggling in, I'm allowed to make a call from a designated phone that allows me to call any number in the area. I'm warned that I only get one call from this phone; after this, I'm going to have to use the pay phone in the holding cell to make collect calls. I stand there in my baggy scrubs, staring at the beige phone in front of me. The cop stands with his hand on the receiver, ready to dial whatever number I give him.

I could page my mom, but it will take hours for her to call back.

I have no one else.

Is this really my life? I stand there staring at the phone with no one to call, not a single person. I did have a few friends growing up, other artsy, nerdy kids. I guess I always figured that things would get better when I got older. I'd get better at keeping friends. I'd grow out of whatever was wrong with me.

Yet here I am.

The cop clears his throat. "You gonna give me a number?"

Finally I have him dial Dr. Shandra's office line. I leave a number with her emergency answering service. I ask them to have Dr. Shandra page my mom since I'm not able to get an incoming call here. I tell them where I am and the lady taking the message exhibits no surprise.

I follow the cop into the cell where I am supposed to wait. It's much better than the crowded holding area. It looks like I'll be sharing with only a couple of people, both of them old and homeless-looking, both of them cozily asleep on the benches. I find a spot on the concrete floor against the wall and settle down to wait. I lean my head back and stare up at the fluorescent lights.

The homeless guy nearest me snorts and jolts himself awake, rising to a sitting position that seems to shock him. He looks wildly around the cell. His eyes land on me, on the floor. He's a gray-haired white man with red-rimmed eyes and crinkly, sunbaked skin. I make eye contact with him but am unable to smile. My arms are locked around my knees, hands wound together.

He rubs his hands over his forehead. "They serve dinner yet?" he asks in a thick Southern accent.

I shake my head.

"Good." He clears his throat, which triggers a coughing fit from deep inside his lungs. He covers his mouth with a wobbly, ashen hand.

"You should get that cough looked at," I say.

He waves a hand at me in a gesture of mirth and coughs into his other fist. "I'll get right on it," he laughs as his cough-ing fit subsides.

We sit in silence. He gets comfortable on the bench again, head cradled in his arms. He stares at the ceiling like an out-doorsman admiring the stars. I lean my head back and look up at the ceiling with him. I follow the pattern of cracks and shadows from one end to the other, allowing myself to be soothed by the simple act of observing. He doesn't smell great, but I suppose I probably don't, either.

"What you in for?" he asks after a little while. "You get into a fight?"

I nod my head, rubbing it on the rough wall behind me. "It's not just that. They think I killed someone. A girl."

After a pause, he says, "Your old lady?"

"Kind of."

He doesn't respond. I don't blame him.

"I'm not guilty," I say, a shade too loud. "I'm not some crazy psycho."

He looks doubtful. Do I sound defensive? I didn't do anything to Annabelle—of course not. I loved her. Love her. I would never. I remember the cops in the interrogation room that first night, when they'd grilled me about the evening, looking for a way to make it my fault, looking for a hole in my story that would prove I'd been the one to abduct her.

That memory makes my stomach uneasy. It's one little detail, something I've been avoiding and that I wish wasn't popping into my mind right now.

I lost time between when Annabelle was taken and when I called the cops. What happened to that missing forty-five minutes? I don't remember calling the police at all. I remember being confused. Maybe I was confused about more things than I'd been willing to admit. Maybe I'm crazier than I want to believe.

No. I'm fucked up in the head, but I'm not capable of killing someone and forgetting about it altogether.

In this moment, everything comes into focus: Elise's dead face, wide brown eyes staring, horror welling up inside my chest; the fancy San Francisco lawyer's suggestion of schizo-phrenia and his search for the perfect psychiatrist to diagnose me; my mom watching all this happen, eyes shrouded; and finally my release into the world and the knowledge that it was wrong, that I'd successfully manipulated the system and that I did not deserve my freedom. I picture myself at Four Corners, in my self-imposed institutionalization, waiting out the sentence I knew I'd earned.

Annabelle is dead. I know it. They'll eventually find her, and I'll be convicted of the crime. Perhaps I am finally going to get exactly what I deserve. I can't deny the justice. Maybe this is God correcting a mistake or fate finally making good.

Jail is like a waterslide. I don't have to do anything once I've done the work of getting on. The ground drops out from underneath me and all that's left is for me to fold my arms across my chest and wait to hit the ground.

This waterslide ride consists of half sleep, a couple of sand-wiches served at weird hours, peeing in a public toilet, smell-ing the homeless guys' shits when they use the toilet, and eventually facing my stone-faced mother, her lawyer, Steve Ross, an aging redheaded man who wears cowboy boots with his suit, and a judge who releases me on bail.

The ride takes me in front of Detectives Benton and Ridge-way, who meet us at the police station so the lawyer can sign paperwork. In the interrogation room where we're crowded around a table full of forms, Ridgeway looks at me and says, "Thanks for getting yourself in here to be fingerprinted. You saved me the trouble of bringing you down."

I stare at her stupidly.

"We have prints collected from your home, but of course we need the official set for comparison," she explains.

My lawyer looks up and scans her face.

She continues. "We found some interesting prints in An-nabelle's apartment. Anything you might know about, Sean?"

I look back and forth between her and my lawyer. To him, I say, "I don't understand. They already knew I went to An-nabelle's apartment. I wanted to talk to Jenny, her roommate. I spoke to Ridgeway on the phone from there."

He looks at the detectives. "What—" he begins, but Ridge-way interrupts him.

"We found unidentified prints on unexpected surfaces," she explains. "We wonder if they might be your client's."

He raises his eyebrows. "Such as…?"

"Such as the knives in the kitchen."

I try to keep my face still while inside my guts are tum-bling down onto the linoleum.

Ridgeway leans forward onto the scratched table, her wrists stretching the buttoned sleeves of her blue shirt. She folds her hands together in front of her and asks, "Are you a serial killer, Sean? Are there more bodies that no one's ever found? Are things about to get really, really interesting?"

"No," I whisper.

"We're looking into everyone who's gone missing since you moved to Austin, looking into which ones might have visited Four Corners, your little hunting ground."

Mute, I shake my head at her in wordless horror.

"So, I've been researching serial killers," Ridgeway con-tinues, almost cheerfully. "You know, the last ten or fifteen years have been very active years for serial killers. I was sur-prised by how many different stories I found. Weren't you?" she asks Benton lightly, who nods in the affirmative, eyes twinkling. "The seventies in particular," she goes on. "There was the Freeway Phantom in the DC area. Killed six young women. There's the Connecticut River Valley killer—he's still at large. You know where there have been some very interesting serial killers, Sean? California."

I look to the lawyer for help. He's watching her with a frown but doesn't protest.

"The Doodler. You've heard of him, haven't you, Sean? He was active in San Francisco in '74 and '75. You'd have been, what, thirteen? A formative time in your life. Do you know what he did? He sketched his victims before he killed them."

I've heard of The Doodler. Everyone in San Francisco has; he's famous for killing gay guys in the Castro. I don't know what this has to do with me until she says, "Doesn't that remind you of yourself a little bit? You and your sketches of all the folks who come through Four Corners? It makes me wonder if most of those sketches are just decoys to keep us from looking at the real ones, the ones of your victims. Like the coffee shop girl. Rebecca."

"I never did anything to Rebecca," I protest.

"We know. We got in touch with her. She quit her job and works at a restaurant across town now. Do you know why?"

"No, I never spoke with her, like I told you."

"Because of you. You stalked her, followed her, sat through her entire shift, drawing picture after picture of her while she worked. Her manager asked you to stop, but then you stood at the window outside and drew her picture from there."

I don't know what to say. I look down at my hands, ashamed. "I didn't mean to creep her out," I whisper. "I didn't realize she even knew I was there."

The lawyer's hand comes up in a sharp motion for me to be quiet. "This is all very interesting," he says calmly. "But can you come to the point? My client is tired and would like to go home, and so far I'm not hearing anything that should keep us here."

She goes on as though he hadn't interrupted. "There was the Zodiac Killer a little earlier. Much more famous; everyone in the country knew about him. You remember him, don't you, Mr. Ross? He was active in Northern California as well. You know what I find interesting about the Zodiac Killer?" She reaches under the stack of papers on the table and extracts a large, flat Ziploc bag. It contains the note I'd received from the kidnapper, the one that reads, THIS IS WHAT HAPPENS WHEN YOU LEAVE THE FISH IN THE CARE OF THE CAT. As I stare at the writing through the Austin PD imprint on the bag, Ridgeway's voice drops lower. "The Zodiac Killer sent letters to the police. He liked to send little puzzles. Cryptograms. He was egotistical. He liked to play games. Does that sound familiar at all?"

I shake my head.

"There's something unique about this expression, the fish in the care of the cat. That's strange. I haven't ever heard that before. I've heard an expression about a fox guarding a hen-house, but not a cat with a fish. That was interesting to me, and it occurred to me that it might be a similar analogy in another language. Does that make sense?"

Steve Ross stares at me like I have some explaining to do. "I really have no idea what she's talking about," I say.

"I bet your mother knows," Ridgeway says. "I bet she's known the whole time."

"Known what?" I plead.

She says it to me, but she's looking at my mom. "It's a Korean proverb." She flips the bag over. A line of Korean characters and a corresponding English translation are printed neatly on an index card taped to the reverse side of the plastic bag.

고양이에게 생선을 맡기다
Leave the fish in the care of the cat

"It's like leaving the fish in the care of the cat. Same idea as leaving the fox to guard the henhouse."

"I don't know any Korean proverbs," I protest. "I don't speak Korean. I couldn't read that if I tried." I jab a finger toward the Korean letters.

"You knew," Ridgeway says to my mom, ignoring me.

My mom shakes her head. Her lips are tight.

Ridgeway stares at my mother for a long moment. A muscle in my mother's jaw twitches visibly through the porcelain skin. At last, Ridgeway says, "You have to stop protecting him. Do you want to be responsible for this?" She indicates the file in front of her, as though Annabelle's death is contained neatly within.

My arms explode into prickling, like someone's electrocuting me with a thousand tiny needles. I shudder and rub at them furiously, and then the nausea hits me in a wave. I clap a hand to my mouth and leap to my feet. I cast a panicked glance around and race to a trash can in the corner, where I vomit explosively, almost missing the can in my hurry. I pant and gasp, spitting bile, trying to keep my hair out of the way.

"What's wrong with him?" Ridgeway asks behind me. My mom hurries to my side, where she leans forward to study me with a diagnostic frown. She touches my neck lightly, pulls away a fingerful of sweat.

"He's experiencing withdrawals from his antipsychotics," she says at last, straightening to a standing position. "We'll get him back on his medication schedule at home."

"We're done here anyway," the lawyer says. "Until you charge my client with a crime, your speculations about serial killers from ten years ago and a possible Korean reference to a cat are just that: speculations."

The ride is sliding me away from here, out of this horrible room where. I'm an insect under a magnifying glass and back out into the hot, stagnant Texas air.

The ride takes me into my mom's air-conditioned Audi, where I sit smelling the leather seats and my own body odor. I look out the window at the freeway speeding by, my bruised cheek and ribs aching and burning. I am too ashamed to break my mom's horrified silence. Ridgeway's words seem to echo between us. *"Are you a serial killer, Sean?"*

My mom breaks the silence for me. She asks, "Have you been taking your meds?"

I look at her, surprised. "In jail? How could I?"

"No, at home. Before you were arrested."

"Of course."

"You wouldn't be having these symptoms after only a day and a half off your meds," she says.

I blink at her. "You think I'm lying? You think I've been, what, flushing my meds? Why would I do that? I've always taken my meds."

She keeps her eyes on the windshield. I can feel her disbelief.

"I have no reason to lie. I'm a grown man. I can take them or not if I want."

Nothing.

I heave a frustrated sigh and look out the windshield. The day is muggy. It looks like rain. "I've been feeling like shit all week, for the record," I tell her. "Not that it matters. I think I have a stomach bug or something."

Silence.

The ride takes me back home to a house that has been professionally reorganized. It slides me up to my room, which has been cleaned, as well. It deposits me onto my bed, on the exact spot where Annabelle sat, and that's where I'm left to crumple into a heap, my face pressed into my arms, my hands clutching the back of my sweaty T-shirt. The thing that eventually gets me up is my stench. In the hot shower, my skin starts prickling again, and I press my hands to my face, letting the hot water run down them into my eyes like tears. I want to cry, but the tears won't come. I'm hollowed out and numb, like I've been emptied by the emptiness around me.

When I go back downstairs, my mom is on the phone, leaning against the kitchen wall and wrapping the cord around her fingers. She's talking in quiet, urgent Korean. When she spots me, her eyes sharpen and she says a few last things, then hang up. She moves to the dining table, where she sits behind a mountain of paperwork and settles her reading glasses on her nose. I search the fridge and come up with a carton of milk. I pour myself a glass and sip it cautiously.

From the table, my mom says, "Drink that quickly. We're going to Dr. Beck's."

"Fine." I glance at the kitchen clock. It's noon on Saturday. I sit near her at the table. She ignores me and flips through patient files, taking notes on a legal pad in her illegible, tiny scrawl. "Who were you talking to?" I ask.

She doesn't look at me. "Your grandmother."

"Did you tell her?"

"No." Maybe I'm imagining it, but I think her mouth pinches shut a little tighter. Her gaze flickers across my black T-shirt and old black jeans. "Where did those clothes come from?"

"They were in the hamper."

She returns her eyes to her work.

I set my glass down. "Mom. Don't you think it's stupid for us to fight about clothes when—"

"Finish your milk." She won't say another word to me.

I stare at the clock and trace time backward. I haven't been keeping track of it, but I haven't lost it either. I don't think I've lost a single minute since Annabelle's been gone.

Why?

CHAPTER TWENTY

Dr. Shandra's ice-cold office feels different because it's the weekend. She's waiting for us in her usual chair. My mom and I take possession of the couch, sitting on opposite ends.

My mom sees no need for formalities. "Our lawyer thinks that our best option is to get in front of the correlation between these new charges and the case they're building against Sean around this missing girl."

Dr. Shandra taps her pen on her pad of paper. "What's he recommending? Sean, how are you, by the way?" She awards me a warm, sympathetic smile.

"Doin' super, Dr. Shandra."

My mom says to me, "You've committed a felony. Breaking and entering, aggravated assault with a deadly weapon. It's a felony, Sean. Armed robbery? A *felony*."

"I wasn't robbing him. I was interrogating him."

She is unmoved. "Once the prosecutor feels that Detectives Ridgeway and Benton have a strong enough case against you on this missing girl, you're looking at another felony. You heard Ridgeway. Are they going to find your fingerprints on the knives?"

"Yes."

It's silent for a minute.

"I touched a lot of things in that house. The knife thing is bullshit. I just touched them, fidgeting around. I didn't use them for anything. Jenny was on the phone, I was in the kitchen, and I was just, I don't know. Fidgeting." The words sound hollow and useless, like I'm telling a lie.

They exchange a look.

"Mom. Look at me. I didn't do anything with them. They know I was in her apartment. I spoke to them myself from her kitchen! Right where the knives are!"

"You could have called them for that express purpose, so there would be a plausible explanation for the fingerprints you knew would be found in her apartment."

"God, you're as bad as they are. There's no body. How can everybody be so sure I killed someone when no one knows she's dead? There's *no body!*" It sounds like I'm screaming *There's nobody!*

"Yet," she hisses.

"I did not kill her."

"You could be looking at the death penalty. You're not a minor anymore. With your record, no jury will find you sympathetic."

"Well, that works out perfectly for you, then, doesn't it?"

Dr. Shandra says, "Sean, I want you to feel heard. Would you like to—"

My mom cuts her off. "Steve Ross says our best bet is to commit Sean to an inpatient facility, or rather, for Sean to commit himself voluntarily. He says this will strengthen another plea of insanity. It's our best strategy, our only strategy."

I look down at my hands. I forgot to ask the cops to return my jelly bracelets. My hands look naked.

I hate my mother at this moment, hate how perfectly this is all working out for her, like God himself has come down to screw me over on her behalf.

Dr. Shandra clears her throat. "Sean? What are your thoughts about inpatient?"

"What you're talking about—it's permanent placement, isn't it? We're not talking about a couple of years."

My mother says, "Yes."

Just like that. No mercy.

Flashbacks to the asylum splash over me: Alfonso, wrinkling his nose at a puddle of my blood on the bathroom floor; Betty's face turning blue under my hands; drugs like lead flowing slower and slower through my veins as the weeks blurred into months...

Dr. Shandra is looking super worried. "I want you to know that I feel we've made significant progress. I think you can be proud of the work we've done, and I hope you continue to make these types of gains in the future. Inpatient doesn't have to be an end. It could potentially be a beginning for you. You could focus on your art and finish your education through correspondence. And who knows what the future holds? Down the road, perhaps you'll be rehabilitated to the point that you can revisit the idea of outpatient therapy."

I don't know what to say. I can't breathe at all. Dr. Shandra starts to say something, but I cut her off by getting to my feet. "I'm not going back," I tell them.

"Yes, you are," my mom says, her voice made of steel.

"No, I'm not!" My voice cracks. "I'm not," I say, and then I roar, "I'm NOT GOING BACK! I won't. I'm not your puppet."

Before I walk out of the office, I take one more look at my mom's face. It's cold and placid. This is it. This is our big goodbye, and I'm no closer to understanding her than I ever have been. I push though the door and I'm out of her life for good.

The air-conditioned lobby spits me out onto the sweaty, asphalt-and-exhaust-scented street. Cars and trucks roar past me. I walk west along the sidewalk. The way I figure it, I have two choices. I can run or I can kill myself.

The sun burns my eyes. I wish I had sunglasses. I'm walking in the direction of UT, like Annabelle's presence is drawing me there.

Maybe I could go down to Mexico. I could get some money out of my mom's bank account. I know where she keeps her checkbook. I try to form plans, try to figure out how long it would take me to learn Spanish. The thoughts are stupid and fizzle out. I can't keep any of them straight. Ridgeway's words haunt me. Am I a serial killer? If I had killed Betty, that's exactly what I would be. The only thing separating me from that title are the orderlies who interrupted me.

The thought sends spiders up my spine, and I shudder from head to toe. Am I like those guys you hear about who keep pieces of their victims' corpses around their houses? I can't be. Am I? The idea makes me want to throw up and crawl out of my skin. Is this what all serial killers feel like? Are they horrified to be themselves?

The afternoon takes me in circles, each with a memory of Annabelle at the epicenter. I wander the UT campus, trying to imagine Annabelle wandering under these trees, sitting on a bench, studying for a test. I walk the five miles to pace the outskirts of Four Corners. As the sun sets, I stare at the place in the fence where the hole has been patched and am flooded with memories of the dented white truck speeding away, Annabelle's scream ringing in my ears. I stay there for a while, just standing on the side of the road, staring at the fence. This is the spot where all this began, ground zero for what will ultimately prove to be my undoing, and I can't help but wish with all my might, and against the painful love for Annabelle that eats me alive, that I had never met her. After a long time, I begin walking around again, enjoying the darkness as it sets in. I sit cross-legged on the dirty gravel for a long time, until my butt falls asleep and my legs stiffen up. It's only when I can't stand to sit still with myself any longer that I get up and resume my wandering.

My circling eventually takes me downtown. The air is warm and humid. College kids and tourists clog the sidewalks, celebrating the weekend with booze and fried food. Clubs leak electric guitar solos onto the street; oversized bouncers stand at doors with hands outstretched for IDs. For just a moment, I feel like I'm back at Four Corners, lost in the crowds of tourists, and it makes me feel safe and alone.

I pause outside the club where the bartender had recognized Annabelle. On a whim, I walk through the door. The bar area is packed and the dance floor is half empty. It's still relatively early for a nightclub; people aren't quite drunk enough to let loose. I squeeze between people and am relieved to see that the fifties greaser bartender is working again.

When he makes his way to me, he does a double take. "Hey!" he cries. "You found your friend yet?"

"Not yet." The music changes from loud to soft. The lights dim so that everything glows blue.

"You drinking?"

"I guess I'll have a beer?"

He retrieves a bottle and waves my wallet away, which is

nice of him. I lay down a dollar for a tip and sip my beer. If only I had been able to figure out who had taken Annabelle. I could have redeemed myself. It's driving me crazy, the not knowing. It just doesn't make sense. It should be Rob, but it's not. I know he was telling the truth. I'm as sure as I've ever been in my life. I'm never wrong about these things—but he has the white dented truck. It's *the* truck, it's the one I searched for all over Texas. How else…it just doesn't make sense. Could someone else have used Rob's truck to kidnap Annabelle? Why would they do that?

I suppose there could be any number of reasons. First, they could just have needed a truck. If they're someone who drives a particularly recognizable kind of car, they might have looked through Annabelle's acquaintances for someone with a larger vehicle, one that would be easier to load a struggling girl into.

But Rob fits the profile. It makes sense. He has a motive. Deadly Annie killed his cousin. Could someone be framing Rob for Annabelle's kidnapping? That doesn't make sense. If someone's getting framed here, it's me.

But why would someone be framing *me*? No one here knows anything about me. I've made no friends. I don't talk to people. Before Annabelle, I don't think I've even told anyone in Texas my name.

My beer is empty. The bartender—Johnny, I remember—approaches me from his spot behind the bar. "Hey again! Another?" he asks.

I nod and pass him a five-dollar bill. He gives me a beer and again waves the bill away. I slide it toward him anyway as a tip.

Johnny pockets the five dollars and gives me a toothy grin. "You from around here? You look like you're not."

"San Francisco."

"I knew it! I totally called it!" He leans even closer. "Let's hang out after work. I get off at two thirty. You'll be up. You look like someone who stays up late."

"Sorry. I can't." I try to smile, which probably looks like gloomy pity. It's all I can muster.

See? I think as he walks away to help another customer. *I still haven't told him my name.* Until Annabelle, no one in the entire state of Texas has known my name except my mom and my psychiatrist. I'm completely antisocial. No one knows me. No one except Dr. Shandra, and what motivation could my doctor have to frame me? It's not like *she* needs me out of her hair, locked up neatly in jail or an institution where I can never contaminate her world with my messiness again.

A group of people next to me laughs loudly in unison. They're doing shots; the other bartender is lining them up in colorful rows. I frown down at my beer, not in the mood for festivities. One of them jostles me and I move my body sideways, putting my shoulder between us. I chug the rest of my beer, ready to get out of here. Johnny rematerializes as I set my empty bottle down on the bar. "Another?" he asks.

"I'm good. Thanks." I pat my pockets, looking for a last tip for him.

"You getting phone numbers?" he asks.

I look up at him, confused. He points to a folded white paper at my elbow. "Getting numbers?" he repeats, teasing me.

"It's not mine," I say.

"It wasn't there a minute ago."

I tap the guy next to me, a young Latino with a long, jet-black ponytail. "You dropped something," I tell him, indicating the paper.

He glances at it. "Nope. Not mine." He returns to his friends, who are now daring each other to do tequila shots.

I take the paper, exchange a confused look with Johnny and unfold it. Immediately, I realize it's another note, written in the now-familiar block handwriting on plain white paper cut into a neat square. "Oh, shit," I gasp, unable to focus on the writing. I grab the shoulder of the ponytailed guy. "Did you see who left this here?"

"Naw, man. People have been coming through, buying drinks, I don't know. I'm not keeping track."

"Did you see what any of them looked like?" I'm desperate, reaching.

He frowns. "How many times I got to tell you? No."

I let out an exasperated groan and return my attention to the note. Johnny leans forward to read it, obviously interested in my reaction. "Is it a phone number?" he asks.

"No." I feel my face go white as I read the printing.

"A love note?"

I look at him blankly. "No," I say at last.

"You all right?"

"I'm fine." I push myself back and away from the bar. "I have to go," I mumble. I fold the note up, shove it in the back pocket of my jeans and stumble for the exit. All indecision has deserted me, leaving me cold in my fingers and chest. I know where I'm going, but I don't know what I'm going to find there.

The note feels heavy and hot in my pocket, like the words are burning through the paper and denim, working their way off the page and worming into my bloodstream like a parasite. They're burnt into my retinas. I don't know who wrote it, but I know exactly what I'm supposed to do next.

THIS GAME ENDS WHERE IT BEGAN.

COME ALONE. I'M WATCHING YOU.

SHE'S STILL ALIVE. FOR NOW.

I hadn't thought of this as a game before, but it's clear to me now. This is definitely a game, and I am not some lover-turned-detective. I can't win the game; I was never even playing it. I'm *being* played—I'm just a chess piece—and the knowledge fills me with hopelessness.

With or without hope, I'll push forward. I don't know what else to do.

CHAPTER TWENTY-ONE

It takes me almost an hour to get to Four Corners. I catch a ride down the highway for a few miles with some college guys, and those ten minutes in the back seat of their car, surrounded by their laughter with Duran Duran pounding an insistent beat, mark a surreal contrast to the darkness inside me. The word *why* keeps echoing around my head, singing a useless refrain. Why me? Why Annabelle? Why bring me here? Why kidnap her at all? I understand violence, but why draw out this complicated game? What do I have to do with anything? It feels so random, so pointless. I harbor no illusions that I'm being brought here for any reason except for someone to kill me, but why? Why not just shoot me in my bed? Why bother leaving these notes? Why drag me down here on a fruitless rescue mission? For all I know, Annabelle is already dead and I'm a lamb to the slaughter.

Here I am, though, on my way. This guy knows me well enough to know I'll risk my life to save Annabelle, which in itself is strange. I haven't known her long. How does he know

I'll react this way? What's to stop me from bringing the note to the detectives and washing my hands of the whole thing?

Yet here I am.

The guys let me off at the junction of the two-lane country road that borders the park.

I have no plan. I'm no hero.

I suppose every villain is the hero of his own story.

I jog through the Four Corners parking lot. It's midnight; the park has been closed for hours. The lot is empty except for some of the Four Corners golf carts lined up at the front end. I run around the corner, following the two-lane highway that runs alongside the back of the park, searching for the place Annabelle had been dragged through the fence.

Rob's white Explorer is pulled up alongside the chain-link fence. It hadn't been there earlier, and the sight turns my stomach in a nervous somersault. The car is dark. I walk around to the front and put a hand on the hood.

Still warm. I'm not far behind.

I move around the Explorer. Next to the passenger's side door, the chain-link fence has been cut into a door-sized opening. I inspect it. Sure enough, this is the same part of the fence that had been cut before; I can see the joints in the surrounding chain-link where it's been patched onto the posts.

Something shiny catches my eye on the dirt near the passenger's side front tire. I approach it.

It's a little card. It looks like something laminated.

I pick it up. It's sticky with blood.

It's my Four Corners season pass, my old one from last year. I keep it in my desk at home. I hold it pinched between two fingers. I don't like the fact that it's bloody. I don't like it at all. The blood is tacky but still wet. I don't know how long blood takes to dry; this blood could be an hour or a day old for all I know.

I stare at it for a long moment. This is no accident, the fact that this is my season pass. *Am* I being framed? Is that possible? But why? I tuck it into my pocket with the folded note, blood and all, unwilling to leave it here for anyone to find.

When I'd been about to get released from the institution, my mom had sent me a letter. It was the one time she'd written to me. It read, *The night is nearly over; the day is almost here. So let us put aside the deeds of darkness and put on the armor of light. Sean, I've secured a position at a hospital in Austin, Texas. You'll be joining me upon your release. —Mom*

It had taken me a few minutes; the language was so poetic and pretty and unlike her. Was she finally going to really love me? Was she saying she forgave me?

Then I realized it was a Bible verse, which had hurt my feelings so much. She hadn't even bothered to come up with her own words. I wonder how she will feel when my body is found. Will she cry for me? Will she be relieved?

The image of my mother being given the news of my death makes this whole thing too real, and I find myself unable to take even one step forward. I don't want to die. It doesn't matter if I deserve death. I don't want it, and I'm filled with such cowardice that my stomach twists with nauseous shame. Annabelle is surely in there, dead or alive, and I have to go in and try to find her, whatever the outcome.

A little voice in my head reminds me that I'm a bad guy. This guy doesn't know me. He doesn't know what I'm capable of. I can do this.

I talk myself up like this for a moment, take a deep breath, square my shoulders and face the fence. This is it, the moment I've imagined in a hundred male fantasies: fighting to the death for some damsel in distress. As a child, I read stories about knights slaying dragons to save princesses. Would I be a brave knight one day, I wondered?

Well, will I?

Poor Annabelle, assigned me for a champion. I'm the shittiest knight ever. She deserves better.

Well, then, I'll have to become the knight she deserves.

I duck through the hole in the chain-link. I'm passing through the curtain, moving into the realm between life and death.

I creep through the forest in the direction of the theme park. I get back onto the main walking path near the High Tower, searching everywhere for signs of life. I remember all the times I've sneaked in here after closing to wander the darkened pathways. Once I almost got caught by the late-night cleaning crew and had a great adventure sneaking back out. That seems like a thousand years ago.

My reverie is interrupted by a loud clanging sound somewhere to the south, toward the center of the park. I walk in the direction of the sound, keeping to the shadows that line the walkways. I reach the central intersection of the park, near the fountain.

Now what?

The clanging sound comes again, in the direction of Jungle Land. I slink deeper into the shadows and move.

I'm being summoned.

As I move through the pressing, close-scented dark, it occurs to me that I might be dreaming this whole thing, like Alice trailing the white rabbit. I actually stop walking and pinch my forearm. It hurts. That doesn't prove anything.

I push my feet forward into the dark, past battened-down food shacks and dark-windowed restaurants. The jungle-themed greenery swishes gently in the night breeze. Goose bumps stand up on my arms.

Ahead, a narrow shaft of gold cuts through the gray night. A door hangs open, spilling yellow light onto the asphalt walkway.

And now I know where I'm going.

"Shit," I whisper, dizzy with fear.

I reach the door. I know this entrance well. This is one of the entrances into the secret passageways used by employees to move around the park. The lights are not usually on at this time of night.

I enter the concrete-floored, white-walled corridor. My eyes sting from the sudden onslaught of light. I stay as quiet as possible. It's not quiet enough. I can hear my own footsteps and the rustling of my clothing every step of the way.

The passage curves left. To my right, a closed door appears. This door leads into a loading dock for ambulances. When people get injured or sick at Four Corners, they're taken through these corridors and into these loading areas, where they get picked up by ambulances and expedited out of the park the back way, behind the restaurants and rides.

I stand flat alongside the door and try the handle. Locked.

Okay, then. Onward toward death.

Any last thoughts? I ask myself, in case my head suddenly explodes or someone appears from behind to slash my throat.

I glance behind me. No one's there.

I keep walking, slowly and in my weird half crouch.

Ahead, the path widens. Fluorescents flicker overhead. I'm nearing the big theater, where productions are held throughout the day. The path opens up here, turning into a backstage area large enough for twenty people to wait for their cues. To my left, double doors lead to the stage and are visibly bolted.

To my right, doors lead into male and female dressing rooms. This isn't a swanky enough joint to boast individual changing rooms; they just have large open-air mirrored rooms with benches and attached multiple-stall restrooms.

The door to the men's changing area is partly open. Light shines brightly inside.

Shit.

I look around me.

No one.

Shit. Shit, shit, shit.

Okay. Fine. Okay.

I leap across the open space, expecting the sound of shots, and peek into the changing room.

No movement. Nothing on the white walls. A large huddled lump on the white-tiled floor.

I'm being watched. I feel it.

My heart is pounding a psychotic beat and has somehow moved into my head. I'm paralyzed, head rotating on the axis of my spine like a disoriented owl.

It's too late to turn back now.

Finally I urge myself forward with the single whispered phrase: "Fuck it."

I push my way into the changing room.

I expect the kidnapper to leap out from behind the door or for the adjoining door to the bathrooms to open, but nothing happens, nothing at all. The lump on the floor is still and silent. It's an oblong shape, flatter than I'd realized. As I near it, it resolves into the shape of a young man in his late twenties, dressed in baggy jeans and Texas Longhorns T-shirt, arms by his sides, in what seems like a deep sleep.

Rob?

I stand over him.

It is Rob. He's got a purple aura, faint but there. As I watch, his chest rises and falls faintly.

"The fuck?" I whisper shakily.

I'm suddenly aware of the flavor of another person, the metallic glimmer of personality.

A bang—Rob's head shatters open, blood and brains splashing out. His skull bounces back into the tile. Two more shots bang out; one opens a hole in his chest, red splattering up onto my pants, and another opens another hole in his temple. It's so fast, *bang-bang-bang,* over before I can turn to face the shooter.

She's wearing all black. Her skin is pale in the fluorescent light, her cheeks pink against her freckles, eyes bright with excitement.

"Annabelle," I breathe.

Her copper-and-shadows halo unfurls gloriously around her like chiffon; she's as beautiful as I remember. No, scratch that. She's more beautiful than I remember. For a moment I think I've died, that the kidnapper has shot me or I'm crazy after all. Maybe Annabelle was always a hallucination. Maybe she's a shade, my personal grim reaper sent to lure me into the dark rivers of the afterlife.

Annabelle crooks an eyebrow and shoots her gun four more times, into Rob's lifeless body and the tiles around him. The sharp roars make my ears ring.

I find my voice. "What are you doing?" I ask.

"I've got to miss a few times. You're not a very good shot, I'd imagine, growing up in California. Probably never touched a gun in your life." She's wearing gloves. They're *my* gloves, black-and-white-striped, left over from last winter. I stare at them stupidly. Where did she get them? From my room, obviously, but how? Why?

She lifts the gun, aims it at my forehead. "I'm glad to see

you. I knew you wouldn't bring the detectives. I feel like I've gotten to know you so well, Sean." One side of her mouth creases into a playful smile.

I'm stunned into silence. Despite the gun pointed at my face and the immediate proximity of a newly dead body, despite the blood splatter on my jeans and hands, her smile gives me butterflies. Her hand holds the gun steady, index finger firmly on the trigger. This is the third time this week I'm staring down the barrel of a gun, but it's the first time I've felt the true proximity of the afterlife. It brushes across my skin like cobwebs. Through heart-skipping fear, I can't help but be filled with an intense, overwhelming rush of relief that her body is not decaying somewhere in the Texas wilderness, that she glows with life and strength, gloriously vital and alive.

I try to gather my thoughts. "So you weren't kidnapped? There's no other guy—it was *you*? The notes, everything?"

Annabelle chuckles. "You know you're the worst detective, right?"

"I—" My throat is dry.

"I mean, I kidnapped myself in Rob's truck right in front of you. I guess I should have drawn you a map." She reaches into her pocket with her free hand. She digs out a set of keys. "Catch," she says. She tosses them to me.

I catch them and turn them over in my hands. "What is this?"

"Rob's keys. Fingerprints. It'll look more natural if you handle them while you're still alive."

I drop them immediately, instinctively, and she laughs. "I'll just put them in your hand after you're dead. It's not that big a difference."

"Annabelle." My voice cracks. "You're framing me for... for Rob's murder? *Why?* Do you know how hard I've been looking for you? I've been...you've..." I hate that I'm going to cry. I hate that I can't make the words come out to describe my love and longing for her, my pain and horror and the waking nightmare of thinking she was dead.

She's watching me as though fascinated, the gun pointed unwaveringly at my chest. "Why what? Why you, or why Rob?"

"Why any of this?"

"This is what I do. I'm a hunter of hunters. A predator of predators. It's my..." Her eyes turn thoughtful. "Not job. It's my life's work, I guess you could say. My calling."

I glance down at Rob's caved-in skull. "Is Rob...some kind of predator? Like a pedophile or something?"

She steps forward and taps me on the side of the head with the gun. "You're the predator. You're my target. He's just annoying."

I meet her eyes, speechless.

"I know about Elise," she says. She's so smug, so self-possessed. It would make me angry if I weren't full of so much hurt.

"How?" I manage to whisper.

"I was premed at USF, one mile from UCSF. Your mother, like, owned the neurology department on that campus. She's a legend, the only female neurosurgeon west of the Mississippi. Didn't it occur to you that I would have heard of her? Of course I know Dr. Suh. Everyone knows Dr. Suh. You know what everyone's favorite thing about your mother was?"

I shake my head in mute shock.

"Her son. Can you imagine? Dr. Suh, the great ballbuster, shattering the glass ceiling, and all the while, her serial killer son is murdering girls in her basement."

This hurts my feelings. "We didn't have a basement."

She ignores this. "Everyone in my class knew about you. It was the best story any of them had ever heard. They all wondered if your mother is really some sort of evil scientist, performing experiments on your brain at home, ridiculous stuff. I never believed any of the hype. I studied you. I know everything about your case. I drove down to the institution and interviewed your doctors for a pretend research paper. I've saved every newspaper article about you and your mother. I broke into her house in San Francisco and read your records while you were incarcerated. You are the biggest, best game I've ever hunted. Today is an important day for me." Her eyes flash. "This is the culmination of everything I've been working toward, everything I've been preparing for. You. All these idiot rapists I've been tracking all these years—they're all just practice, just a warm up, just preparation for this moment." She runs out of air and sucks in a draft of air. "You are number twenty-eight."

The number hovers between us, waiting to be inhaled and understood. "Like your grandma," I realize aloud. "Twenty-eight. Jesus, Annabelle. You've killed twenty-eight people?"

"Yes, like my grandmother. But this isn't my last kill. It's the end of something and the beginning of something new. I can feel it. It's special. You're special. You don't know how long I've been waiting for this."

Her childhood, dark and dusty, rears up in my memory. I picture the high school, the photos of Annabelle in cheap seventies blouses, the somber look on her twelve-year-old face and the pity I'd seen on the faces of her mother, her teacher, even Officer MacFarlane. How wrong they'd been to pity her. How condescending the pity was, I realize now. How humiliating it must have been for her.

"Was your father the first person you killed?" I guess. "Because of the custody thing?"

"He deserved it."

"And Preston?"

She snorts. "Now that's a story. I walked in on Preston raping a freshman girl in Stacey's bedroom. Stacey was passed out downstairs; it was her birthday party. This girl's face was covered in blood from him punching her while he... It was..." She frowns, her aura swirling around her. "My father was easy. Too much blood pressure medication, too many drinks. I was twelve. Anyone could have done it. But Preston was a work of art. To get him just the right amount of intoxicated, just the right combination of drugs, and yet coherent enough to get behind the wheel—to control his route, to suggest he take the highway instead of streets—I followed him, made him swerve off the road into a wall—can you imagine? Without getting even a scratch on my car? I'm an artist. A vigilante. You know?" Her aura flashes, searing the air around us. I can almost smell the ozone where it scorches the atmosphere, crackling like lightning. She's a force of nature, a human thunderstorm.

"You're beautiful," I murmur, the words out of my mouth without my permission.

Her face goes cold. She taps my temple with the gun, harder this time. "Come on. Let's have you put some fingerprints in the room where you've been holding me hostage."

She makes me walk in front of her so she can keep her gun on the back of my head. She leads me out the door, across the hall and into a janitor's closet. "Push that door open," she says. It takes me a minute to find the door she means; it's dark in here and my heart is beating like a drum.

"I never knew this room existed," I say as I turn the handle and push. Inside, it's black as night.

"Reach forward and to the left. There's a string attached to a bulb on the ceiling."

I do as she says. When I pull the string, a flickering bulb illuminates a room full of cloth mountains. It takes me a minute, but I register that this is some sort of storage unit; the mountains are piles of stuff covered in tarps. "What is this place?" I ask.

"It's where they store the Christmas decorations. Now go on. Forward march." The gun digs into the back of my scalp. I take slow steps, looking around me for an opportunity to flee from her. I could just run, I guess. Could she make it look like a suicide if she shoots me in the back? Would she need to? She could probably concoct a believable story about a fight over the gun. She's obviously a good actress. Had she been faking it with me the whole time, pretending to like me, kissing me because she had to, not because she wanted to? The idea stings more than it should given the circumstances. I feel like I've been slapped.

"To the left," she instructs. I turn and, sure enough, I find an alcove created by shelves of what look like rolled-up strings of lights. On the floor is a pile of folded blankets. "Now I want you to turn around slowly and start touching the shelves," she says. "Just get your fingerprints on whatever surfaces you can."

I turn to face her. She presses the point of the gun into my forehead. I reach out and touch the wooden shelves on either side of me. "Is this where you'll say I was keeping you?"

"Yes. I'll be discovered by the cleaning crew. I'll be very traumatized. Now, reach up and touch those higher shelves. There you go." She smiles as I obey. The unsteady golden light does otherworldly things to her hair and aura. It's glittery, like it's made of individual particles of light. I want to lose myself in it, to study it, to paint it. "Hey, how are you feeling?" she asks almost conversationally.

"Excuse me?"

"I took you off your meds. Replaced them with placebos."

I stare at her in shock for a full five seconds. My mom—she'd accused me of being in withdrawal. *Holy shit, she was right.* Finally, I say, "Mentally, I feel clear. But I've been getting these hangovers. And my body feels like shit. I'm throwing up and stuff. My skin's all prickly. And I feel like I can't sleep, but then I crash out like I've been hit with a baseball bat."

Annabelle gives me a guilty smile. "That's to be expected. And I've been giving you sleeping pills in your evening meds, so that'll make your withdrawals worse, I bet. I just needed you not to wake up while I was, um…searching through your house. Anyway. You should be feeling better soon. Or, well, you would have felt better soon."

"But wait." I try to think, praying she'll give me another minute so I can ask her one of the thousand questions exploding in my head. "I'm still seeing auras. If you took me off my antipsychotics…wouldn't that affect the hallucinations?"

"You're not hallucinating. You have synesthesia."

I stare at her stupidly. "I have what?"

"Synesthesia. Your brain is translating one type of input into visual experiences. It's a new term; it's no wonder you haven't heard of it. You have no idea how many researchers would want to study you."

"So I'm not hallucinating? I'm not… I'm not schizophrenic?"

"Of course you're not schizophrenic."

"Are you sure?"

"Not even close."

Hearing her say this in her matter-of-fact, scientific voice fills me with so much relief that my head swims. "I'm not crazy," I say, just to hear it out loud and know it's true.

"Most predators aren't."

I stare at her for a long, blank moment, trying to make sense of the feelings inside my chest. At last, I say, "I knew it. I was right."

"It really doesn't matter now."

Anger flushes through me, and for the first time, I want to hurt her. "Do you always do this when you kill someone?" I ask bitterly. "Do you always set them up so thoroughly, fuck them so royally?"

"Fingerprints," she reminds me. I run my fingers down to a lower shelf and press them to the surface. "No. Not at all. This is a special case. I've been preparing for this for years. You're special. I took a lot of time with you. The notes were—well, I felt like they were my best work yet." She adopts a pleased expression that is almost bashful.

"Thanks. I'm super flattered," I say bitterly.

She laughs. "I usually use a system. I send each case through a complex rubric to make sure there are enough degrees of sep- aration between him and me. I get most of my referrals from the crisis line. Sometimes I have a connection with a victim or predator that I hadn't anticipated. Also, of course I have to make sure he's truly a predator, make sure the victim isn't ex- aggerating, et cetera. I lure the predator into a club and help him overdose in a quiet corner. It's very humane."

Her gun hand shakes a little and then recovers. I remem- ber holding the gun at Rob's house. They get heavy after a while. Maybe I could rush her, get the gun away from her. I bet I could.

My heart hammers inside me, pumping adrenaline into my veins. I feel my hands growing stronger.

Don't take the gun, I command myself, but I feel the beast rising inside me, growing, like a balloon inflating.

I say, "If you're going to target anyone, it should be your professor, Spike. He's sick. He's a rapist."

"You *know*?"

"I found a bunch of photos at his house."

"*Dammit.* I wish I had found those. I could have done a lot with those. You still have them?"

"I left them in Lone Herman."

We stare at each other for a second. My hands itch. The beast inside me rustles.

Her aim wavers, just a little.

"Wait," I say, realizing something. "You said you've been giving me sleeping pills so you could go through stuff in my house. Did you...were you... I have this memory that I thought was a dream—"

"Was I in your bed?" she finishes for me.

I nod slowly, my eyes locked with hers. A mischievous sparkle plays with the corners of her mouth. I remember the hot skin of her breasts against my chest, and with desire comes the need to touch her, to feel her against me, to make her my own. "Let me kiss you," I whisper.

Her eyes darken. They're beautiful against the rosy skin of her cheeks.

Don't think, just act. I raise my hands in a gesture of surrender, lean down and brush my lips against hers. Her breath catches, which sends a tornado of sensation through my body. *She likes it.* I press into her, moving my lips slowly, tasting her skin and a faint trace of fruity lip gloss. Hunger and need sweep through me. A moan escapes my lips, and her teeth graze my bottom lip. The gun snaps coolly to my temple. My heart speeds up, skipping double-time. She kisses me harder, pressing the gun into my skull. Her tongue is hot and soft against mine. Fear and arousal tangle painfully inside me. I want her. I *need her.*

Don't—

The monster rears up inside me like a tsunami. I duck down and push her gun hand out of the way. The gun goes off—my ears ring—but I get her hand under mine and pin her arms against her, the gun pointing to her own stomach. I slam her into the shelves. They rattle under our weight. Strings of light fall and crackle to the floor. One hand pinning her gun hand to her side, I move the other hand to her throat. My fingers close around the skin and I moan. The veins pump hard and hot against my palm and I squeeze.

Mine.

Her face is red, furious, blue, and she is *mine*. After all the searching, *mine*. This moment, *mine*.

She pounds her head into mine and her gun arm comes up. The gun presses into my chest. I wait for the gunshot to rip through me, but it doesn't come. I knock her gun hand aside and trap it behind her back. She slips out from beneath me like a snake and comes up outside the circle of my arms. She lifts the gun to my temple. Her eyes are wild, her lips parted, her breath coming in short, hard pants.

I push her to the side and get hold of the wrist that holds the gun again. I'm feral now, all thoughts clear. She fights me but I hold that wrist. I grab her in a bear hug, lower my face to her neck and bite it, hard.

Delicious. Hot. Juicy. *Mine.* My blood pounds red hot inside my chest.

She screams, writhes and kicks, landing a good one on my

shin. She whips her gun hand free and clubs me on the neck with it, which sends a flash of pain through my vision like lightning. She hits me with it again in the stomach and backs me into the shelves. She tumbles to the floor, rolls into a neighboring shelf and pulls herself to her feet. Gun still in hand, she points it at me and shoots wildly into the ceiling. I lunge for her and she slips away, back through the cloth mountains. I run after her, slip on the slick concrete, catapult into a pile of something soft, push off and lurch toward the door. I explode into the janitor's closet and pass through into the hallway. She's in the doorway of the changing room, a hand on the door handle; she's going to slam it shut on me and lock me out.

I bash into the changing room door just as she's closing it and send her rocketing backward. She slips on a finger of Rob's blood and falls back hard on her ass. She raises her gun hand but I'm coming too fast. I grab her by the neck and wrist, heave her up like she weighs nothing and slam her against the tile wall. Her eyes are wild, terrified.

"Stop fighting," I say. I let my hand ease up on her throat. She pulls left, right, trying to twist away. "Stop," I repeat. I kiss her cheek, her throat. Copper flames flash and burn around us. I let my lips rest on hers, and she freezes. Her lips move against mine, parting, her tongue slick against mine. For one soft, timeless moment, we kiss, bodies pressed together, death forgotten.

The beast rears up inside me and, even as I try to grab the reins and my heart screams *don't*, it's too late.

She's not expecting it. I grip her gun hand and move it away from me. She gasps and tries to scream, but my hand is tight on her throat again. The glove is slippery inside my grip. I press my lips to her throat and pin her other hand behind her. The monster inside me screams with excitement.

She's squirming, struggling. Carefully, I press her finger with mine and the gun goes off again, kicking back against the wall. White splinters fly off a tile on the floor. I press again four times until the gun is empty. Tiles splinter. I press my thumb into the palm of her gloved hand, hard, and she hisses. The gun clatters to the floor next to us.

"Better," I murmur, and I press her harder into the wall. *Finally.*

She shrieks, grunts, tries to twist and squirm away from me. She half succeeds, gets her right hand free, reaches into her back pocket. I press her harder into the wall with my body and kiss her neck. "Mine," I whisper.

"No." She writhes, probably as hard as she can, and produces a knife from behind her. She snaps it open in a fluid gesture and digs it against my throat.

I pause for a beat. Our breaths come fast between us. I like the feeling of the sharp point against my flesh.

I wait for her to press a little harder, just hard enough to draw blood, and then I whip my hand up, quick as a snake, and knock the knife out of her hand.

She curses, hurt. I ignore her free hand and get my palm up under her chin. It presses her head back into the white-tiled wall. She hits me, punching at me with hands that don't hurt at all. I lean down to press my lips to hers. She tries to bite me. I like the pinch of her teeth on my lips.

I choke her harder. She makes small, wet gagging noises. Her face contorts, her eyes squinting shut. It's all panting and copper glitter and bloodlust around and inside me. My heart is going to explode out of my chest. Everything inside me screams *yes*.

The knife is on the floor near my foot. It's a shiny thing, black and oily-looking.

No, I beg myself, but I'm not listening.

I give her one last squeeze. Her face is purple. I let go and she gasps a breath in. Her knees are weak and try to crumple. I squat down for a second, bringing her with me by a fistful of bronze hair, and I grab the knife. I pull her back up and press her into the wall. I lean forward to kiss her cheek.

I don't want to do this. I don't want to do this. *Stop*, I beg.

"I can't," I whisper. I lift the knife. It's warm and heavy in my hand.

I have to know. I've always wondered what it would feel like.

She's woozy, struggling only half as much as before. I run the knife up inside her sweatshirt—*my* sweatshirt—and press the point into her back between her shoulder blades. She's not wearing a bra. Arousal mixes with bloodlust, and I dig the point into her skin, cutting through.

She stiffens. We stare into each other's eyes.

"Don't," she croaks.

"I don't want to." I press the blade into the skin and she screams. It sinks in, the skin juicy and soft, and I groan. It's just what I'd imagined. I keep it light, not wanting to pierce through the ribs just yet. A trickle of blood runs down the hilt of the knife and along my knuckles.

"I'm sorry," I whisper. I drag the knife down, slicing the skin open as I go.

She screams hard, loud, rough, shrill. My heart pounds. My body sings. "I'm so sorry," I murmur. I run my free hand up, cup her neck and squeeze. I drag the knife down further, slicing the skin open to the small of her back.

She twists out of my arms. She's fast and my hand, wet with her blood, slips. The knife clatters onto the tile, speckling it with blood.

She spins and runs. Blood splashes behind her in a speckled trail. I'm right behind her but she's got a head start. She hurtles out the door and down the concrete hall. I turn the corner and see her flying toward the exit. I push my legs harder.

I fly outside and skid to a stop. I look left and right, into the dark passageways between buildings. I see nothing, hear nothing.

I slide along the side of the concrete wall to the right, inching, holding my breath.

Lights flood the pathway to my left. A car explodes out from behind a building, its headlights blinding me. It hurtles by me, bumping over the curb that borders a planter. I catch a glimpse of her bronze hair behind the wheel. It skids and screeches around the corner. It's plenty small enough to fit on these paths, which can fit the pickup trucks the maintenance guys use. It sails around the corner and disappears in the direction I'd come, toward the back of the park where she'd vanished the first time.

I look down at my hands. They're quaking. I'm crying. Tears drip onto my palms.

I have to get out of here.

But Rob. His body. Blood everywhere. I can't just leave it like this. They'll find it, find *me*.

My heart pounds explosions inside my body.

I wipe my eyes with the backs of my hands.

After all this searching, all this hoping and praying for Annabelle's safe return, how have I done this?

Underneath, I think I always knew it would be better for her if I didn't find her.

Suddenly I'm back in Elise's bedroom. My hands are locked around her dead throat. Her empty brown eyes are staring at some point I can't see. Her face, disfigured and purple, horrifies me, accuses me, judges me. I try to drop her. My hands won't come loose. I scream, terror and horror filling me like the plague. No one's home. We had come here because her family was out. We had wanted a chance to have sex.

I wrench my hands off her throat. They won't straighten out. They look like claws. If I had a knife, I would probably try to saw them off. I scream and scream, and eventually someone comes. When they arrive, they scream, too.

Stop, I command myself. I have no time for this right now. I can't go back—I can't be locked up—I can't let them catch me.

I go back into the hallway and pull the exterior door closed behind me.

Inside the changing room, I lean against the wall where I'd held Annabelle. I look at the blood on the floor: hers, Rob's. I look at the gun, the car keys. I have to get rid of all this evidence. Then I can run. How much time do I have until Annabelle sends the cops here? Half an hour? I have to run. I have to get away.

I press my hands to my face and try to breathe.

"I love you, Annabelle," I whisper into my hands. They're sticky with her blood.

CHAPTER TWENTY-TWO

The changing room is cold. I hadn't noticed before, but now I shiver so hard my teeth chatter.

I push the mountain of guilt and self-loathing aside and try being logical. Rob is dead. This room is full of forensic evidence that implicates me in every possible way. How much time do I have?

I grab hold of Rob's ankles and pull. I immediately reconsider every cop show I've seen in which people stash dead bodies in the trunks of their cars. It would take two or three people to lift this guy; he's not just heavy but impossibly floppy. I grunt and heave, pushing my muscles to their limit, welcoming the pain of exertion. His head leaves a dark trail of blood in its wake as it scrapes across the tiles. I have to assume that Annabelle is en route to the hospital, where she will call the police, who will come here as soon as they hear her story. The nearest hospital is ten minutes away. Once she gets there, it will probably take them at least ten minutes to get her into a treatment room and make sense of her story. I imagine another five minutes to contact the police, five or

ten minutes for them to get to Four Corners and then another
five or ten minutes for them to find this place. So I have about
thirty minutes before they show up.

Panting and heaving, I drag him down the moonlit asphalt
paths, stopping occasionally to wipe sweat from my brow and
catch my breath. I'm aiming for a seldom-used storage shed
I've hidden in many times. When I get there, I shove the door
open with a shoulder. A few minutes of pulling and grunting
and I get Rob over the threshold. I shove him next to a pile
of brown cardboard boxes.

Back in the hallway, I head for the janitor's closet Annabelle had shown me. I fill the yellow mop bucket with water
from the floor sink, grab hold of the mop and push it out of
the closet toward the changing room. Water sloshes everywhere, on my jeans, on the floor. A hysterical laugh escapes
my throat at the ridiculousness of me, psycho killer, unable
to get a mop bucket down a hallway.

Blood cleaned up, I shove the pile of sludgy, blood-soaked
mop heads into a plastic trash bag. I stuff the gun in there with
them, but I fold the knife up and tuck it into my pocket with
Rob's car keys. I glance around quickly, looking for any last
things. In the corner of the room, half-hidden by a wooden
changing bench, a black tote bag is crumpled on the floor.

I crouch down and open it gingerly. Inside are a tangle of
rope, a set of house keys on a cheap key ring, the kind they
give you when you get keys made at the hardware store, and
a girl's delicate cardigan. I pull a sleeve of the cardigan out of
the bag and smell it. Annabelle's scent floods my brain.

At the bottom of the bag, hidden underneath everything,
a small black book is almost invisible against the black cloth.
Worried about fingerprints, I use the sleeve of the cardigan to
pull the book out. It's a leather journal with a tiny pen clipped

onto the binding. I use the cardigan to clumsily page through it. It's full of notes in shorthand, but I catch my name on a page and peer closer. I can't read shorthand, but I see my address, some kind of combination—to a safe, maybe—as well as some notes about Dr. Suh. A few pages further along, I notice Rob's address along with some dates and scribbles that look like his work schedule.

I laugh with relief and elation, the sound incongruous and stupid. I don't know if it's enough to convince the police of my innocence, but I bet Annabelle's fingerprints are on this coil of rope, and I bet these are keys to things she isn't supposed to have keys for. Rob's house, maybe?

"Dammit," I whisper. If I had known this was here, I would have just left everything as it was. Now I've made myself look suspicious by cleaning up. "Fuck, fuck, fuck, fuck," I hiss.

Fingers pinched through the soft knitted cotton, not wanting to smear any of Annabelle's fingerprints, I pull the pen off the journal's binding and tear out a page. I let the journal fall back into the bag and jot a note down onto the torn page, using my knee as a desk.

Benton and Ridgeway: It's not me. It's Annabelle. She killed Rob. She's framing me. She killed her father, a guy named Preston from Lone Herman, and a bunch of guys here in Austin. Check her out.

I run out of room, sign the paper and drop it into the tote bag. I'll leave this with Rob's body in the shed. By the time they find it, I hope to be in Mexico.

I turn off all the lights and close the door behind me. I stash my trash bag and the black tote bag in the shed with Rob and pull the door tightly shut. I sprint away unencumbered, black-on-black against the backdrop of night, needing no light to guide me along paths more familiar to me than home.

I'm going to have to stop by my house. I need to get into my mom's purse, get her checkbook so I can get real money out of her account. I know where she keeps a stash of emergency cash, too. I'll hitchhike to Mexico. From there, I'll keep an eye on the news. Hopefully the cops will figure out that it was Annabelle who killed Rob. If they do, I'll come back. If not, I'll just... I guess I'll live in Mexico for the rest of my life. I've always wondered if I could make a living with my portraits. Maybe I could find a touristy area and do those caricature drawings you see people buying. A couple of those artists work in Four Corners occasionally. They charge a lot, like twenty bucks a pop. I bet I could live off that in Mexico. As I climb through the hole in the fence, I wonder if there is a chance the police will be at my house and decide it's unlikely. Annabelle will tell them I'm here, so they'll come to Four Corners first.

I'm behind the wheel of Rob's car, engine running, when I remember I don't really know how to drive. I was halfway through driver's ed when I was arrested in San Francisco. Since moving to Texas, getting behind the wheel has been the last thing on my mind. It takes me a minute to figure out what I'm doing. The gearshift is up by the steering wheel, not down by my knee. I keep my foot on the brake pedal, figure out how to shift into Drive and then ease my foot up. I inch forward along the shoulder of the dark road. Cautiously, I edge the truck onto the county road and take a breath. I push the gas harder and shoot like *The Dukes of Hazzard* onto the asphalt. I cry out and slam on the brake, coming to a horrible, screeching stop halfway though an intersection.

"Fuck's sake," I whisper and try the gas again, more carefully this time. I inch forward, try to straighten the car out, overshoot and almost crash into a tree. With more cursing and heart-pounding and checking of the mirrors, I manage to get the truck into the appropriate lane and make my way south. The streets are dark and empty; it's almost two o'clock in the morning. My heart pounds in my ears. I'm more vulnerable now, during this five-minute drive, than I was at Four Corners, dragging a dead body around. If I get pulled over by a traffic cop looking for drunk drivers, I'm done. I grip the steering wheel to control the shaking of my hands. "No cops, no cops, no cops," I whisper like the rosary as I pull off the main drag and into the quiet suburbs near my house.

I park jerkily around the corner from my house. I sit in the driver's seat for a minute, trying to breathe, willing myself to stop sweating. My stomach quivers and churns. I remember Annabelle's lips against mine and the silky way her skin had opened up under the knife. I'm hyperventilating; I think I might pass out. *Get it together,* I command myself. Once I've done what needs to be done, I can sink into a lifetime of self-flagellation.

I creep through my back neighbor's yard and do a silent pull-up on their back fence. I get a view of the rear of my house and, from the side, the street in front. Everything looks dark and quiet. No cars are parked in front of the house, police or otherwise. I pull myself all the way over the fence and drop silently onto the grass on the other side. As I sidle along the side of the house, light glows from the kitchen windows, spilling onto the lawn. My mom is awake.

I flatten myself against the wall and try to catch my breath. It's coming in short, fast pants. *Shit. Shit shit shit.* This is bad. I'd been counting on my mom being asleep. How am I going to get the stuff I need? I can't think of a single other way to get money. Why is she awake—or maybe she just left the kitchen light on?

I slink along to the kitchen window and grip the narrow frame. I pull myself up with my fingertips, toes on the wall, until I can just peek over the window pane.

Inside, I see my mother. She's kneeling on the kitchen floor, by the refrigerator. The white tiles are speckled liberally with blood. She's bent over something—a person—a bloody, sliced-up woman lying facedown on the kitchen floor. Annabelle. The back of her T-shirt has been slit open to reveal the wound I've inflicted. The skin from her shoulder blades to tailbone is washed in an ugly orange. Iodine? My mom is stitching up the wound, wielding a needle and thread with rapid, surgical precision. A stainless steel tray sits on the floor at her elbow. It overflows with used syringes, scissors and discarded paper wrappings. A wad of gauze stained bright red rests on the edge of the tray, and as I watch, my mom reaches a latex-gloved hand for it and uses it to blot a trickle of blood that seeps from the edge of Annabelle's wound.

My fingertips give out and I tumble backward onto the grass. I lie there stunned, stars and trees lacing together above me.

Why aren't there cops everywhere? Why didn't she just call an ambulance? Why is my mom helping her? Is my mom… involved in this somehow? No. She wouldn't. How could she? I'm sure Annabelle just showed up here and my mom didn't know what else to do. She probably feels partly responsible for this. The weight of what I've done, to Elise and now to Annabelle, piles on top of me like bricks. Shame floods me. I want to tear my own skin off. My mom is stitching up the wound *I* created in my moment of lust and weakness. Bile rises up in my throat. I choke it down. I feel filthy, like I've been caught masturbating.

I drag myself back from the brink. *Stop thinking about yourself. Annabelle is dangerous.* Whatever her plan is here, her reasoning for involving my mother, it can't be good. Protective rage takes over where the shame leaves off, and I push myself up in one smooth motion.

I jog around the house to the downstairs bathroom window. Standing in a flowerbed, I pull the screen off, toss it aside and raise the window slowly with a faint scraping sound. I pull myself up and into the bathroom, snaking through the narrow window and almost landing on my head as I push myself hurriedly into the darkened powder room. I tumble forward onto the peach bath mat and catch myself in a low pushup. I freeze like that, breath held, listening for any indication they'd heard me. All is silent. Adrenaline sharpens my senses. I can smell hand soap and the detergent that clings to the fluffy bath towels.

I hop to my feet and poke my head out, wrapping myself around the doorjamb like Wile E. Coyote. Murmuring voices filter along the hallway. I set one foot delicately onto the soft white carpet, then one more. My hair falls down into my eyes, a sweaty mess.

I make my way carefully along the hallway, sticking to the wall, straining my ears. When I near the corner that lets out into the living room, I begin to make out words from the kitchen. It sounds like my mom and Annabelle are arguing. I catch the word *hospital*.

At the end of the hallway, I take a deep breath, press my back into the plaster wall and peer around the corner. From here, I can see the living room and, reflected in the mirrored wall, the kitchen, where Annabelle's supine lower half is vis-

ible around the breakfast bar. I catch glimpses of my mother
as she kneels beside her, bending and straightening in time
with her stitching. She's wearing her unisex cotton pajamas.
Above the latex gloves, her forearms are streaked with blood.
Her face is hidden behind her hair, which falls forward delicately, exposing her thin, girlish neck.

"...morphine," I hear my mother say.

"No," Annabelle replies in a voice tight with pain. "Just
give me another lidocaine injection at the incision site."

My mom heaves an exasperated sigh that I recognize well.
"We're almost at maximum dosage. I'm not going to risk lidocaine toxicity."

"Just hurry," Annabelle whimpers.

"You're almost done," my mother says. "We'll get you
comfortable, get through the shock, and then talk about how
we're going to handle the police."

"What do you think we should do?" Annabelle asks in a
high, frightened voice. "If we call them, they'll go looking
for him. This is Texas; they'll shoot him for sure. Trust me,
I know. I grew up with a lot of cops."

It takes me a moment to process this. First, it's strange that
Annabelle is deferring to my mom's judgment. I don't picture
her ever being willing to relinquish control. Second, what
does she care if the cops kill me? She was about to shoot me
herself. Third, she didn't grow up with a lot of cops. Not one
that I ever met.

My mom says, "Well, Sean's had some time to get away.
That's good and bad. He'll be on the run without his meds.
He'll be dangerous."

I expect Annabelle to snap at her and point out the obvious,
that I'm already dangerous with or without the meds, even
tell her about Betty, but instead, she cries quietly, helplessly,

into the kitchen tiles. "I'm so scared," she whimpers. "What if the police catch him and then let him go or something? What if he realizes I told the police about him? He'll kill me. He'll be so angry. You don't understand how scary it's been."

She's playing my mom, I realize. She's manipulating her, trying to keep her from calling the police, pretending I've been holding her hostage all this time. Why?

Air floods my lungs: she *can't* call the police. Not yet. She can't let them find that black bag. She thinks it's still sitting there at the crime scene. She needs to get back there before the cleaning crew starts work so she can finish setting up her tableau.

I actually smile—she doesn't know about the note I left. And she'll never find her bag. That shed I hid it in with Rob's body is way off the beaten path.

"What time is it?" Annabelle asks my mother.

"Why do you keep—"

"Just tell me!" She pauses. "Please. Please tell me."

My mom cranes around the breakfast bar to look at the dining room clock. I throw myself back into the hallway. "Two forty," she answers. My mom returns to work on Annabelle's back. I wonder how many stitches it's taking to fix what I did, the thought bringing stinging embarrassment along with it. When my mother speaks again, her voice is broken, low and rough. "I'm sorry," she says. "I knew he was... He's not well. I'm so sorry. I never wanted this to happen again. He's mentally ill. He doesn't know what he's doing."

"Do you really think he's schizophrenic?" Annabelle asks innocently. "I'd considered synesthesia to explain the visual hallucinations."

My mom makes a scoffing sound. "That's pop psychology."

"It's a documented phenomenon."

"What two senses are his brain connecting, then? His impressions aren't linked to graphemes or anything concrete."

"Just because you haven't seen a case like his doesn't mean it doesn't exist."

There is a pause and a rustling of supplies on the tray. "It's irrelevant," my mom murmurs. "The antipsychotic acts as a chemical restraint. That's the priority. Safety."

"Do you think it's working?"

A snuffling noise makes me crane my head around the corner. My mother has set the needle and scissors on the tray and is kneeling on the tiles, crying into the crook of her forearm so the tears don't contaminate her latex gloves. "I knew it was him," she chokes out with broken breath. "I knew it when I saw the notes. I knew."

Annabelle pushes herself into a half-sitting position, her stitches complete. "It's not your fault," she tells my mom, reaching out to pat her shoulder. Her face is taught, tense and I know why: she only has an hour and twenty minutes until the janitorial crew arrives. As I watch, her hand steals surreptitiously to the medical tray, where it hovers over a scalpel. Her indecision is palpable, and I can't believe my mom has no idea she's in any danger. As I watch, Annabelle's hand moves to clasp the handle of the scalpel.

Unable to control myself, I cry out and leap forward, around the corner. Annabelle jumps, taken by surprise, jolts backward from the tray and spins to face me. They're frozen in place, two pairs of owl eyes set into two pale faces. My mom, kneeling on the tiles, stares up at me with panic in her red-rimmed eyes.

"Sean," my mother begins, a hand reaching out as though to stay my progress.

To Annabelle, I say, "Your bag is with Rob. I hid him.

It'll be a fun game for you to try and find him before the park opens."

Her face goes white with horror and fury. "You fucking asshole," she manages.

I brush my bangs out of my face. "I know," I confess sadly.

My mom asks, "What do you mean, you hid something with Rob?" She looks at Annabelle, an expression of mistrust and confusion crossing her face.

Annabelle's eyes flit back and forth as though she's reading. When they focus again, her face is calm. "You're going to show me where you hid it."

"I'm not showing you shit," I tell her.

My mom asks, "Is this the same Rob whose house you broke into? Sean, what did you do? What did you do to Rob?" Her voice is high, hysterical.

I forget about Annabelle and turn on my mom. "I didn't do anything to Rob. Just like I didn't kidnap Annabelle, and I didn't hurt the coffee shop girl. You don't know me." My voice breaks and I swallow hard. "You've never known me. You've never bothered. Annabelle killed Rob. Annabelle is a murderer. She's the real deal."

Annabelle hisses, "I'm no murderer. That's you, Sean. I'm a vigilante."

"Tell that to the twenty-seven dead bodies you've left strewn around God knows where." My mom makes a choking noise and regards Annabelle with horror. I say, "I've never lied to you, Mom." For one poignant moment, my mom and I lock eyes, and I realize how much I look like her, how much I love her and how much I have always longed for her to truly *see* me.

"I believe you," she says.

Annabelle makes a grand, sweeping hand gesture, speaking

to an imaginary audience. "And thus, female Dr. Franken-stein reconciles herself to having created a monster, one of the great American family dramas, now in theaters." She gets to her feet, brushing her torn shirt off, straightening it as much as she can. It seems to make her dizzy; she reaches a hand out and steadies herself on the kitchen counter. She smooths her tangled hair, drawing it into a high ponytail and fastening it with a scrunchie that has somehow managed to stay on her wrist through all this.

Taking her cue from Annabelle, my mother pushes herself forward, getting ready to stand. "Don't get up." Annabelle tells her, reaching for the surgical tray.

"What are you—" my mom begins.

Abruptly, I understand what is happening and let out a wordless cry of warning, launch myself forward, hands out-stretched. It's too late. Annabelle has a scalpel in hand and flits to a position behind my mother, pressing the scalpel to my mother's neck. My mom cries out, arms flailing out in panic. I come to a screeching halt, frozen in a reaching, lunging arc.

"Annabelle, no," I croak.

Her eyes are cold, but a smile plays at the corners of her mouth. "You're going to show me where the bag is."

I put my hands up. "All right. Please don't hurt her. Please." The last "please" lingers between us pathetically. My mom's eyes are wide with panic, her breath coming in gasps. The scalpel, surgically sharp, digs into the soft skin under her left ear. Annabelle's hand shakes and a drop of blood trails down my mother's neck, running along her collarbone and stain-ing her shirt.

"Annabelle," my mom manages to whisper without mov-ing her jaw. "Annabelle, what are you doing?"

To Annabelle, I say, "You're right. I'm going to show you.

Let my mom go and I'll take you to the exact spot." My stomach lurches. I picture my mom's throat opening up, picture her blood spraying the kitchen floor.

Annabelle says, "Tell me where it is."

"It's in a shed. I can't really describe it."

"Try." She makes a show of digging the knife into my mom's skin just a little more. Another trickle of blood joins the first.

"I'll take you there right n—" Annabelle's hand slips, cutting the skin again, leaving a trail of cuts. My mom whimpers and looks like she's going to faint. "Keep it together, Mom," I say. My voice cracks. I can't watch her die. I beg reality to shift, praying against reason for God himself to come down and snatch my mother up from this room full of blood and death.

Annabelle studies my face. "I can kill your mom. It's no problem. I can think of four different stories I can tell the police. They'll never suspect me."

Desperate, I plead with her. "I know. You've bested me. Okay? You win."

Annabelle cocks her head, her face running through a few different expressions before it lands on anger. "You think I don't know that? Of course I've bested you. Fuck you, Sean."

She shoves my mother forward, pulling her knife hand around and slashing my mom's back as she falls face-first down onto the tiles. My mom screams out a sharp cry of pain. Red blood blossoms from a six-inch cut down her back, staining the lavender cotton of her pajamas. Annabelle flattens a palm against my mother's cheek, pressing her face down into the tile and digs a knee into her back like a huntress about to skin a lion. "Does it hurt?" Annabelle asks her.

My mom nods, sobbing, her head barely able to move.

"Tell Sean how much it hurts."

"It hurts," my mother screams. It kills me to hear her like this, so weak.

My heart is breaking. "Annabelle, please—"

"Let's hurt Sean a little now," Annabelle says to my mom. "Let's tell him how you've been feeding him extra drugs, chemically castrating him. Should we tell him about that, Nancy?"

My mom squeezes her eyes shut, tears pouring out of the corners. "What do you mean?" I whisper.

Annabelle reaches back and slashes again, opening a wound on my mom's upper arm. My mom screams shrilly and dissolves into sobs. I look around, frantic for anything I can launch at Annabelle's head, but she returns the knife to my mom's throat, straddling her from behind. I'm helpless, my arms and legs leaden, heart in my throat, ready to plummet to the floor.

"Come near me and I open up her jugular." Annabelle grins up at me, back in her element. The wound on my mom's arm drips blood onto the tiles. It's deep; I can see fat under the top layer of skin, red and greasy. "Anyway, she knows you aren't schizophrenic," Annabelle continues, nicking at my mom's neck as though for fun. Little red flecks drip onto the blood-streaked tiles. "She's been adding extra antipsychotics, upping your dosages, since you've been home from prison. She's tired of your shit. She wants to make sure you can't murder anybody else. Right, Nancy?" She directs that last line to my mom, who sobs incoherently into the tiles. "Anyway, I don't know if you know this, but that's illegal. She could lose her medical license, go to jail. She's not supposed to be prescribing you anything, much less performing psychiatric experiments on your brain chemistry off the books." Using the scalpel like a razor, Annabelle rakes it up the side of my mom's neck, teasing her, torturing her. My mom starts screaming, a horrible, futile, grisly wail. It reverberates around the kitchen, loud enough to make my ears ring. "Oh, Jesus Christ," Annabelle hisses. Quick as a snake, she reaches for one of the syringes on the surgical tray with her free hand and stabs it into my mother's neck, depressing the plunger with a practiced hand. My mom slumps forward onto the floor, silent.

"No," I shriek, the word too small to convey the burning *no* that screams inside my every frozen nerve ending.

"Oh, stop. She's going to take a little nap now. Let's see how much she likes drugs, right? She could go to jail. Did you know that? Prescription fraud, I think. I forget what the charge would be. Something like that." Her breath comes fast now, excited, but her neck is tight with tension, like she's holding back some deeper emotion. She adjusts her position so that she's pressing the knife onto my mother's exposed neck from above. My mom's blood leaks onto the floor from her arm and back, her aura a barely visible, faint, sickly green. Annabelle is going to kill her, without a doubt. She can pin it on me. She's like a cat now, playing with her prey before she eats it.

"Don't kill her," I manage, my voice breaking. "I thought you killed rapists, bad guys, guys like me. Come kill *me*. I'm the one you really want. Besides, think of the mess, all the extra lies you'd have to tell. Is she worth all that hassle?"

She hesitates, the knife pulling an inch from my mother's skin, her eyes scanning, considering.

I take the opening and bound forward, smashing her backward into the tile. The knife flies out of her hand and clatters against the fridge. Her eyes go wild and she squirms and thrashes, fists useless against my ribs and shoulders. I use my body weight to pin her down, hands tight on her throat, cutting off her air supply. She's weaker now that she's wounded. The smell of blood excites me, sending adrenaline coursing through my fingertips. I shudder, quaking with visceral excitement. She wrestles her way to the side, freeing her throat for a moment, gasping in a breath of air.

"Stop fighting," I whisper.

We lock eyes, our faces inches apart, her eyes filling with tears, throat fragile under my hands. "I hesitated," she whimpers through quivering lips. "Back at Four Corners, I could have shot you twice. And again now. How could I fuck up like this? I don't understand." She squeezes her eyes shut, face slumping sideways.

My hands go soft. I collapse forward onto her chest, cheek pressed to her breastbone. Her heart beats fast inside her ribs. I wind my hands under her shoulders, pulling her closer to me, careful with her stitches. I inhale the scent of her shirt, the sweat and blood, the warmth and salt of my own tears, the sweet aroma of her deodorant. I don't want her to be a corpse decaying in some Texas graveyard. I want her alive, wild and free and smelling like this forever. From the corner of my eye, my mother's chest rises and falls softly. All her frown lines have been swept away. She looks young, peaceful, beautiful. I'm not angry with her. I love her. I love both of them, with their savage, reckless intelligence that threatens to consume them.

I push myself up onto an elbow and run a hand over Annabelle's forehead. Her ponytail has gone lopsided. I pull the scrunchie out and run my hands through the bronze strands, smoothing it out around her face. She watches me, amber eyes striated like gemstones in the fluorescent light. My heart pounds against hers, almost syncing rhythms. "I don't want to do this anymore," I murmur. I lean down and kiss her lips gently. She returns the kiss, a hand lifting to tangle itself in my hair. She moans quietly, a soft, sensual sound, and my body tingles from head to toe. I kiss her harder, deeper, hands cupping her cheeks, relishing their silky warmth. There has to be a way for us to walk away from this together. Can't we come up with a way out?

I pull back, an idea playing itself inside my head. "Hey. Spike."

Her brow furrows. "Spike?"

"Remember? The photos. And we have time. The park doesn't open for hours."

She pulls me down and kisses me again. Into my lips, she murmurs, "You're not boring, Sean. I have to give you that."

CHAPTER TWENTY-THREE

One year later

I'm sitting on the couch, drawing on my arm and watching an after-school special on TV, when the front door opens, admitting Annabelle and her glorious copper glitter-fog. She kicks the door shut and throws a pile of mail down on the kitchen table.

"Why aren't you on campus?" she asks. "I figured you'd still be in the studio prepping for your show next week."

"I'm procrastinating. For a change."

"Slacker." She drops her backpack onto the floor and pours herself a glass of sweet tea from the fridge.

"How was today?" I ask. Sometimes she wants to talk about work and sometimes she doesn't. She's on a pediatric rotation right now that she detests.

"Whatever." She drains the glass, leaves it on the counter and approaches the couch. She snuggles on my lap in such a way that I cannot see the TV.

"You're such a cat." I trail my fingertips through her copper aura and then through the tips of her silky hair. She kisses me. Her lips are soft and stir up all my lust and love at the same time. I murmur, "You nervous about court tomorrow?"

"Nope." She smiles her angelic smile. "It will be a piece of cake."

"Don't oversell it."

She raises an eyebrow, insulted. "Please." She takes my hands, guides them behind my back. I'm a goner. I press my lips to hers and the animal in me takes over. I lose myself in the softness of her lips, her tongue, and then something yanks me out of my trance.

I pull away. "You smell weird."

"Oh yeah?" She sniffs the sleeve of her cardigan. "Like what?"

"Cigarettes."

"Oh. Yeah, lots of the doctors smoke. Such hypocrites." She hops off my lap. "I'll take a shower. I'm sure I smell like kid puke, too."

I follow her into the bathroom. "You had a kid throw up on you? Gross."

She cranks the water on and sheds her sweater and dress. "Yeah. They're cute, but not when they have the stomach flu. I can't believe I have to do this peds rotation." She says it like "peeds."

I hold the shower curtain open for her in a gentlemanly way and take a nice long look at her naked body as she steps into the stall. She notices and pats me on the cheek. As she turns her back to me and tilts her face up to meet the warm water, my eyes fixate onto the long, straight scar that stretches all the way down her spine. My stomach turns over and I'm filled with shame even as my blood boils with pleasure at the memory of slicing through her skin. I shove it aside. I can't let myself think about it. It's forbidden. I try to remember what we're talking about. Pediatrics. Kids. Her job.

"We should have kids someday," I joke. "Imagine the demon children we'd create."

She laughs. "We could make an evil army."

I hate myself so much for the pleasure the memory of hurting her brings. It's more shameful than any other memory I have, worse even than Elise somehow because of how much I love Annabelle and how hard I've worked to be safe for her.

I pull the curtain shut. "I love you," I say. Steam and the hissing of water fill the small room. She pulls the curtain aside and kisses me. Her hair and skin drip warm water onto my shirt. I run my hands down her silky-wet arms and up to her cheeks. Before I can get to the good parts, she pushes me away and pulls the curtain shut again.

It bugs me how she always dumps her clothes in a pile on the floor. She's so sloppy. It's like living with a teenager. I grumble to myself as I pick her dress up and fold it. I lay it aside on the fluffy toilet lid cover, then pick up her cardigan. My hands freeze over one of the sleeves.

A small, damp crust of rust-brown lines the cuff. I bring it to my nose and sniff it. I already know what it's going to smell like.

Blood.

My heart beats three times.

I drop the sweater onto the floor. I swipe her dress off the toilet, on top of the sweater where she'd left it.

I say, "I'm going to make something to eat. You want anything?"

"I'm washing my hair! Can't hear you!"

I raise my voice. "Want some food?"

"Yes! I'm starved. Hey, are you working tomorrow night? You going to be downtown?"

I can't take my eyes off the clothes on the floor. My brain races around. "Why?"

"I'm going out."

"Out? Like...*out?*" This means she's on a case.

"Yeah."

"I'll be downtown, yeah."

"Maybe I'll come see you."

"Okay."

In the kitchen, I open the fridge and stare inside it, not seeing the food. She doesn't wear her street clothes at the hospital. She changes into scrubs and leaves her clothes in a locker. There's no reason she should get blood on her sweater. She always, always wears one of two sweatshirts when she gets cold on rotations. They're white hoodies, and she bought them specifically because she can bleach the crap out of them. The cardigan with the blood on it is soft, fragile. She would never wear it at work.

So she wasn't at work. She's lying. She was on a case.

Her cases don't involve blood, though. There's no blood when someone overdoses. I can imagine puke, spit, all sorts of other bodily fluids, but not blood. And she's taking another case tomorrow? So soon? She usually goes a few months between cases. They're never back-to-back like this.

Unless she's been lying to me.

I'm still staring when she sneaks up behind me. She wraps her arms around my waist and presses her wet, naked body against my back. "What's wrong?" she murmurs into my shoulder blades.

I look down at her hands, clasped together on my stomach. Faint copper tendrils furl out from between her fingers.

"I'm worried about you," I whisper. It's the truth.

"Why?"

"I'm worried about tomorrow."

"About my testimony? Sean, come on. It's not a big deal."

"No, about your— About the case you're taking."

She stiffens. "What about it?" I'm not really supposed to ask about her cases.

"The cops could be watching you. They could be following you."

She kisses my back. "I'll make sure they aren't."

I turn inside the circle of her arms. It says something about my love for her that I'm able to keep my eyes off her breasts and on her face. "I'm worried you're not thinking clearly. You're usually such a scientist, logical about this stuff. With your rubrics and everything. This seems…risky. Wouldn't it be better to wait a few months, let everything settle down? Once Spike's in jail, the whole thing will be yesterday's news and we can go back to normal." I try to read the truth in her eyes, try to figure out what she'd really done, what she's planning.

Nothing but clearheaded innocence meets my gaze. "Everything is fine. Court will be a piece of cake. They have all the forensic evidence in the world. My testimony is a formality, it's overkill. No one suspects me of anything."

"You're not the only smart person in the world, Annabelle. They know how to smell bullshit. I know those detectives. They're really—"

"I know. It's not a problem. Trust me. I'm a victim to them. If anything, they worry about me because of you, because of what I experienced with Spike." She gives me her best baby-kitten face. "I'm so fragile. Can you imagine me hurting a soul?" She lays her Texas accent on thick and I have to laugh a little.

Fuck it. She's a killer. That's who she is. I give in and kiss the side of her neck. Automatically, I put my hands behind my back. That's our routine. If both hands ever come into her view, she's off me in a hot second. Glad I'm done lecturing, she wraps her arms around me, and the blood on her sweater is the last thing on my mind.

She loves this game. She loves that I'm her beast on a leash. I suppose I love it, too.

Downtown Austin is always packed full of college kids and tourists. Today is no different. I park my beat-up Toyota on a side street and carry my gear to my usual corner in front of a Mexican restaurant, juggling the giant portfolio and folding stools with practiced ease. From the portfolio, I remove my three-sided board that displays some samples of my work and pricing. I set my easel in front of my stool and unfold a second stool for customers. Onto the easel, I load a big pad of expensive drawing paper. I'm not even done opening up and arranging my toolbox when a middle-aged woman plants her ass on the folding stool facing me and her husband starts dictating what kind of portrait he wants.

I listen to his instructions, nod mutely, pull my Walkman out of my backpack, settle the headphones over my ears, rewind my favorite mixtape, and dig some graphite pencils out of my toolbox. I take about fifteen minutes per portrait and have developed a style that combines graphite, colored pencil and ink. I usually do shoulders-up portraits, but I do fullbody or couples portraits for a higher price if that's what they want. I turn the volume high, cranking up the first track on the new Cure album until my eardrums protest.

The middle-aged man stands over my shoulder and watches me work. I feel his hot breath on my neck and know he's talking to me, but I'm not really in the mood to hear all about how hard it must be to "draw this good" and how warm a night it is. It's always warm. It's July in South Texas, for Christ's sake. Of course it's warm. Even the mosquitos are hot.

A flash of frustration burns through me. Why did Annabelle pick tonight for one of her cases? I know she's not worried about court tomorrow, but I am. I want it to go perfectly. I want to put all this behind us.

Spike's defense has been built on his reputation and the ludicrousness of the charges against him, but it's been pretty much buried under the prosecution's avalanche of evidence. They've had an easy job, linking Spike not only to Rob's murder—the body was found buried in a vacant lot near the stack of photographs and medication I'd taken from his house—but Annabelle's testimony that he had kidnapped her and held her captive in his home was completely damning. She had been rescued by a neighbor while Spike was at work, having escaped her bindings and run semiclothed and half-starved into the front yard, where she'd collapsed into traumatized sobbing. As the case unfolded, a number of girls from the photographs came forward to testify against him. Annabelle is right. I need to stop worrying. Still, I think she should be more careful.

The middle-aged blonde is exchanged for a pair of kids who squirm a lot and make drawing them quite difficult. It's a good challenge. After that comes an older lady, which is interesting, and after her a beautiful Hispanic teenager with a protective boyfriend who eyes me suspiciously the whole time I'm drawing. I hit a lull around ten o'clock and bend down to pull a water bottle out of my backpack. When I turn around, a young brunette is sitting on the folding stool, smiling at me with no recognition on her face whatsoever.

I sigh, exasperated. She loves to play these little games. I push the headphones down onto my neck and hit the Stop button on my Walkman. "How can I help you?" I ask.

She looks up at the tall college guy who stands behind her with thumbs crooked into his belt loops. On his feet he wears cowboy boots and a UT T-shirt stretches across his massive chest.

The guy tells me, "The lady wants her picture drawn."

"Just the standard portrait? Shoulders, neck and head? In color?"

"Yes, thank you," she says, stretching her accent to the max. I almost roll my eyes. I brush the drawing pad off and begin sketching. I don't need to look at her, but I do.

"You draw here every day?" she asks conversationally.

"Pretty much." I make a show of examining her nose and eyes.

"You're an art student? At UT?"

"How'd you guess?"

She laughs. "Maybe the outfit."

"Fair enough."

I didn't finish my high school diploma or do anything really to qualify for college, but when I showed them a portfolio of my work and explained that I'd been institutionalized through most of high school, they accepted me immediately.

"Do you have a girlfriend?" she asks, still in a light conversational tone. Her date makes a doubtful laughing-snorting sound.

"Actually, yes," I say. I begin drawing her hair, which I really do have to look at. I don't like the wig, not at all.

"You must draw her all the time," she says.

"I do indeed."

"She must like that. It must make her feel special."

"Nah, I think she's used to it by now."

"I'm sure it does make her feel special. She's probably just too proud to tell you so."

I meet her eyes; they twinkle in the streetlight, and the moment is so sweet, I almost break her cover and kiss her.

Her date steps forward to look over my shoulder. "Shit, man. That looks just like her!"

"What a coincidence," I grumble, returning to my work. Annabelle's soft expression hardens, and I know I'm on the edge of pissing her off. "So how did you lovebirds meet?" I ask in a falsely interested voice.

She giggles in a high-pitched tone I've never heard from her. "Just now. At a bar. He asked me out. How could I say no?"

Right. I'm so sure it was that simple. I'm sure Annabelle didn't plan it just so, engineer it so she was near him, give him just the look she knew would draw him over, say the right things to flatter him...

When the portrait is done, I hand it to the guy. "Twenty bucks," I say, and he shoves it into my hand with thick, manly fingers. She gives me a wink and they twine arms.

"Hungry?" she asks him. "I know a great spot..." She begins a string of chatter that sounds so foreign I can't help but stare at their receding backs.

He reaches back, wrapping a muscular arm around her waist, and pats her on the ass. It's a territorial gesture, way too forward for a first date, and I do not like it. Rage and possessiveness boil inside my gut. This furious helplessness, feeling so small here while they walk away, tints my vision red. When did I become the harmless, hapless boyfriend—when did I stop being one of the predators? It's irrational and darkly male, and I know it makes no sense, but I don't care. I shove my pencils into my backpack and fold my easel up. I flip the "Back in 10 minutes" sign over the top of the easel, which I created for bathroom breaks, and sling my backpack onto my shoulders. Staying to the edge of the sidewalk, I follow them down Sixth Street. They turn in to a Japanese restaurant. I watch from across the street as the hostess finds them a table. Once they're seated, I make a run for my car.

I park on a side street about half a block from the restaurant and wait, fingers drumming on the peeling dashboard. I don't know why she's eating with this guy. She supposedly only takes them to nightclubs.

It's an hour before they emerge laughing onto the sidewalk. I wonder if I should have left my car where it was; they head down Sixth Street and I assume they're going to hit a nearby club after all. They're almost out of eyesight when they approach a large black pickup parked at the curb. He opens the passenger door for her, helping her up into the raised cab. I start my car.

I follow them at a distance, a little surprised that, instead of heading further into the city, they head away from it on I-35. *What the hell, Annabelle?* I keep a couple of cars between us on the freeway. The glow of dusk clings to the low-lying hills. They exit the freeway fifteen minutes later and head due west, toward Lake Travis.

Is Annabelle…could she be actually cheating on me with this guy? No. He's a case. He has to be. Jealousy floods me and I almost can't see the truck through the haze. She does like her games. But this guy? He's the beer-fueled date rape type, exactly the kind of guy who would send a girl crying to the crisis line. He has to be a case. So what are they doing out here?

I trail a few cars behind them on the wide, winding road

up through the dry hill country. It gets prettier as you get outside the city. Now that I'm off my meds and have a car, it's been nice getting to know the area. Austin is surrounded by beautiful nature I'd never seen.

My old life feels like a dream. I can't believe I wasted so many years doped up on psych meds. This last year has felt like waking up in every possible way. Once I moved out, my mom took her old job back in San Francisco. With her gone, I'm finally at rest. With me gone, she's probably at rest, too.

I'm not angry with her anymore. I feel sad more than anything, sad that I burdened her so much and for so long. I should have never moved back in with her when I was released. I should have found a way to be independent. I was lazy, immature, irresponsible, and it was too much to expect her to have enough objectivity to navigate all of that. What she did was wrong, but I was wrong, too.

Having Annabelle has freed me, too. Finally, someone *knows* me. It's a feeling like no other. I try to give her that same feeling. I don't judge her. I don't control her. All I want is to be near her and to love her. Sometimes, though, I wish I could control her, just a little. Like tonight.

Forty-five minutes later, we're on a two-lane county road in the brushy, woodsy hills that surround Lake Travis. I'm giving them at least seven car lengths, so I almost miss it when the truck turns left down a narrow dirt lane.

Shit. It's too sparse out here. They're going to see me if I follow.

I pass their turnoff and get around a few bends before executing a haphazard three-point-turn (I still suck at driving) and creeping back along the deserted county road. I scout out a fairly discreet shoulder, pull as close to the bushes as possible and kill my headlights.

It's completely dark now. Down below, moonlight glints white on the oily black surface of Lake Travis.

She's always told me definitively that no, she doesn't sleep with the guys she kills, but now I wonder. Maybe this is a part of her routine she's never told me about.

Regardless, this guy is a sexual predator. What does she think he's going to do to her alone out here in the woods? I picture her slender legs parted for him, his broad shoulders tensed as he pulls her into his lap.

No. Fuck this. No. She's mine.

I switch off the dome light and open my car door. I ease out into the cedar-flavored night, instantly awash with the rustling of brush and the chirping of crickets. I move down the gravel lane, my Converse crunching lightly. To my left and right, trees form a tunnel. It's like a gateway.

About six months ago, Annabelle and I were walking through the UT campus, hand in hand, and she stopped me. "Look," she pointed. Above, two squirrels chased each other from branch to branch, back and forth between oak trees whose limbs had grown intertwined.

"What about 'em?" I asked.

She smiled a little secret smile. Copper played around her shoulders. "Just cute, I guess." That's how Annabelle is: she always seems to be holding something back. Her skin was so pretty, her eyes so bright, that I kissed her, cupping the back of her head with my hands itching like mad.

I stop walking. Do I really want to know? If sleeping with them is part of her ritual, is that for me to judge? We don't live by normal relationship rules. Maybe this doesn't count as cheating. Maybe this is something else.

No. There's a line, and this is where I draw it. I move onto the side of the lane so the gravel won't crunch under my feet.

WENDY HEARD

Black-on-black, blending into the night, I step forward into the rich aromas of loam and evergreens. I walk at least half a mile, wondering the whole way if I've got the wrong road, if I only imagined seeing the truck turn here, when I scrape against something metallic tucked into the trees.

I scuttle back a few feet, surprised, and then investigate. It's the tail of the truck, which has been parked in a space between two trees off the road. The truck is off. All is silent.

My heart explodes into pounding. I bite my jaw shut tight and crouch down. I feel my way around the truck. I get to the driver's side and slowly raise myself up into a standing position, peek into the window. From what I can see, the truck is dark and empty.

No no no. This isn't good.

Should I call out? If he's attacking her, raping her or worse out in the woods, would that make him stop or would it create panic, make him speed up whatever he's doing? My breath is coming in sharp pants.

I step forward, feel the hood. The engine is almost cool, just a little warmer than the night air. Around me are trees and bushes, dry leaves and darkness. The lake should be off to my left, I think, but the road is curvy and I might be turned around. I don't want to get lost in the woods like an idiot.

Well, standing here isn't going to do any good. I take a step and crunch some leaves underfoot.

Shit. I can't stomp through this forest, crunching leaves all the way like Godzilla. What am I going to do?

Sometimes when I stand still for too long in front of one of my paintings, Annabelle sneaks up on me and smacks me in the back of the head. She always laughs when I jump. She thinks it's funny that I can get so absorbed in my thoughts, I forget about the world around me.

To my left, dim yellow light flickers through the trees deep inside the woods. I hear a faint cry, unmistakably feminine.

Hot rage empties into my intestines. I don't care about being heard. I charge the flickering light like a bull. I open my mouth to scream her name, but then I explode into a clearing and the breath gets sucked back into my chest.

A kerosene lantern sits on a pile of dirt. A shovel hangs out of a messy hole.

Movement to my right, near the trees.

I spin around. I catch the image of tangled legs, a flurry of human movement. It's Annabelle, struggling with the cowboy, their bodies a blur of motion in the eerie half light. Annabelle grunt-cries again, tumbles forward and straddles the guy. She lifts the knife up and slices sideways, a swift backhand motion that misses his neck by half an inch. He's injured, blood trailing down over one eye and staining his T-shirt. Annabelle's dress is ripped down the front, exposing her torn bra and half of a breast. Her face is wild but calm, thirsty eyes stretched wide. As I stand frozen he regains the advantage, locking his legs around Annabelle and flipping her onto her back. She bares her teeth and slashes sideways with her knife, missing him again.

I search around, eyes landing on the shovel.

I hesitate. She's no helpless maiden; she's a killer with a decade of experience.

I can hear the deep intake of the cowboy's breath as he looms over Annabelle. His blood drips down onto her cheek as he pins her knife hand, her small fist disappearing into his meaty palm. She squirms and thrashes. He wipes his forehead with the back of his free hand, looks at the blood. "Bitch," he pants. He grips Annabelle by the hair and pins her head back.

With his other hand, he pries the knife out of her hand, tosses it aside and reaches down to hike up her dress.

Thought evaporates into action. I run forward, grab the shovel by its handle, swing it back and unleash a World Series blow on the back of his skull. Metal whacks bone with a satisfying clang and he topples sideways. Rage and bloodlust roar inside me. I want to kill this guy; I want to see his blood soak the forest floor. I heave the shovel backward and launch it forward into his temple, knocking him sideways and splitting his skull open. My heart soars with pleasure. I reach back and hit him again, in the forehead this time, sending blood splattering off into the forest. He rolls back to look at the stars, the lower half of his body convulsing jerkily. Blood and drool bubble out of his mouth as he half opens it as though to speak.

Annabelle makes a brutal roaring sound, wriggles out from underneath him, snatches her hunting knife off the ground and plunges it deep into his chest. It quivers there, hilt wet and glinting in the kerosene lamplight. She wriggles it out and slices it across his neck from ear to ear. Blood spurts weakly out of the wound; he's already dead. His face is frozen into a bewildered expression as though he's been greeted by something stranger than dead relatives on the other side of the curtain.

Annabelle pushes herself up and stands to face me. We regard each other warily. Her arms, chest and legs are splashed red with blood. Pine needles and dirt cling to her blood-streaked calves. Her strappy sandals and wig are missing, leaving her barefoot with waves of auburn hair tumbling into the mysterious folds of her glinting aura. She's glorious, terrifying, a goddess to whom you'd gladly make sacrifices.

I break the silence. "What the fuck was that?" I manage shakily.

"He was harder than I expected." Already she's regaining her composure, breath slowing. She tries to draw her bra together between her breasts. It's a lost cause, and she shakes her head at the torn clasp as though the destruction of her favorite undergarment is the real crime here. She turns her eyes back onto me, focusing on the shovel I hold clenched in my hand, veins bulging under the skin of my forearm. I'm concerned she finds my posture threatening, but then a new worry occurs to me: I've intruded on her tableau. I eye the knife, still clutched tight by her side.

"Are you mad?" I ask cautiously.

She considers this. Her eyes travel down to the dead man.

"He was going to rape you," I point out.

The amber eyes turn on me, their depths inscrutable. "So what are you, my bodyguard?" She grips the knife tighter. It's a true hunting blade, its curved edge threateningly serrated. It had sliced through the cowboy's neck like butter.

Does she think she's in danger? Is that why she's still holding the knife?

Is she in danger? I perform my automatic scan, searching my body for hints of impending violence.

In a flash, I realize I have no urge to hurt her. The bloodlust seems to have passed out of me into the corpse on the ground, purged from me with the ferocity of the blow I dealt him. I'm not subduing any gory images; the memory of slicing her down the back doesn't taunt me. It holds no interest—it's just a memory like any other. I force myself to picture my hands on her neck, which is the most forbidden of all thoughts, but again the idea does nothing to me. It's just an image, nothing more. "I don't want to hurt you," I tell her. The words burn my chest coming out; it means too much. This is everything, this moment. I run back through the images again, this time forcing myself to see my hands on her throat, really imagine what it would feel like.

Nothing.

Her aura sparkles bronze in the half light, mysterious and shadowed against the backdrop of night. She narrows her eyes, tracks my facial expressions clinically.

"It's gone," I say, my voice rough.

"Gone? You think you're, what? Cured?"

"No, I mean…" I motion toward the corpse with the shovel, the gesture comical given the gravity of the situation. "It's, like, spent? Used up. At least for now."

She raises her eyebrows. "Completely?"

"I think so."

"I would have predicted that violence would…exacerbate your condition."

"I know. Me, too."

"Put the shovel down," she commands. With some trepidation I obey, tossing it onto the loose earth near the dead guy's cowboy boots.

She steps forward. With her free hand, she reaches up and runs a hand through the back of my hair. Her fingernails trail lightly down the nape of my neck. A chill sweeps through me. She grips my hair by the roots and pulls my face down to hers, kissing me deeply.

It shocks me. I'm unprepared. Her hot, silky lips unravel me. I hear myself moan, feel my hands close in on her waist. She doesn't stop me. I run them up her sides—both hands, recklessly, eagerly—over her chest and the sides of her neck.

In a flash, the knife digs into the skin at the hollow of my throat. I pull back, hands flying into the air in a gesture of surrender.

She regards me suspiciously.

"It's not like that," I say. My heart leaps because it's true. I'm in control. I bring my hands back to her waist. "Keep your knife," I warn her. I lean down to kiss her, the serrated blade sharp against my throat. It stirs my blood up and my heart pounds a hard beat inside my ribs. "Let me do this," I breathe, willing her to understand. I run my hands over her neck, pulling back to look at my skin against hers. The blade spurs the skin of my throat. I run my thumbs across her throat, waiting for the urge to squeeze to overcome me, bracing myself for the moment when the monster rears up inside me.

It doesn't happen.

"I don't want to," I say, my voice cracking with emotion. "It's not there. For now. I think… I think I used that energy up on him."

She looks down at the fallen cowboy. "Let's try it again," she says.

I look at the corpse skeptically. "He's already dead. I don't think—"

"No, not on him. On someone else. Once you're back to normal."

"You want to test the hypothesis. Fuck, Annabelle."

She shrugs. "I'm a scientist. I want to duplicate the results."

"You can't just keep killing people like this. You're being reckless. You're going to get caught. Look at this." I indicate the crime scene with a sweeping gesture to include the hole, the shovel, the dead body, the kerosene lantern, her torn, blood-soaked dress. "What if he'd gotten away? You were lucky I followed you. You can't just lure guys out into the woods and slaughter them. Some of them will escape; some will overpower you. You need to go back to your old way of killing them. Or stop."

She hesitates. "I know. But…"

"You need to do it," I finish for her.

"Yes." She lifts a hand to examine the darkening blood-stains. "And the old way isn't…it's not enough anymore. I need…more."

The admission is huge, and with it I can feel the weight of her grandmother and her dark, haunted childhood. She is a killer as surely as I am; she can hide behind science and vigilantism all she wants, but the truth is, she kills because she likes killing.

I swallow and meet her eyes. "I need it, too," I whisper.

I step toward her, and she lets the knife tumble to the ground. She looks up at me with eyes that are more vulnerable than I've ever seen them. I clasp her blood-smeared hands gently in mine.

"Okay," I say. "We can try it again."

A smile breaks across her face, dimpling her left cheek like a schoolgirl. "We can find someone in Dallas—or we could go out of state. That's even safer."

"All right," I agree, and I know what I'm doing. I'm making a deal with the devil: her life for many, many others.

I don't care.

★ ★ ★ ★ ★

Author's Note

The research process for every book is different. For *Hunting Annabelle*, I needed to research in four distinct areas. First, the eighties—I was a small child in 1986, so I had to research this time period deeply, especially in the setting of Texas. Second, I had to research psychiatry in the eighties as it related to Sean's diagnosis of schizophrenia. Third, I did research around Sean and Dr. Suh's Korean heritage, connecting with interviewees and readers in my quest for positive and accurate representation. Fourth, I researched police work in the eighties, checking my knowledge of investigative procedures against those in practice in 1986. Creative license was taken with the University of Texas at Austin, which did not have a medical school in 1986 but which now boasts state-of-the-art facilities. All this said, I hope readers forgive any inaccuracies. Like any artist, I am learning and growing, and I hope to improve with every undertaking. If you have comments about my treatment of this material or suggestions for future endeavors, I would love to hear from you via my website or on social media. Thank you for your readership. I hope you'll enjoy Sean and his strange, twisted love story as much as I enjoyed writing it.

Acknowledgments

As with all works of fiction, *Hunting Annabelle* was a collaboration. My agent, Lauren Spieller, was my most influential collaborator, and her expertise drove crucial revisions that proved integral to the book's success. I also want to thank Michelle Meade, my editor and the deliverer of feedback that both nourishes and challenges me beyond measure. Without these two women who manage to be both blunt and kind, both coach and cheerleader, both partner and friend, there would be no *Hunting Annabelle*. I cannot thank them enough for taking a chance on me, and on Sean. This book was similarly influenced by the masterful input of Mary Widdicks and Tracie Martin, my co-conspirators, critique partners, therapists and sometimes hostage negotiators. Other invaluable readers and interviewees included Laura Park, E.J. Zain, Christopher Hanson, Meghan O'Flynn, Ethel Lung and Dr. Treasa Davis.

One must acknowledge that behind every novelist lies a family who patiently tolerates bouts of muteness, ecstatic highs and despair-soaked lows. I'm blessed beyond measure to do life with fellow artists who understand and support the creative process, and I can't thank them enough for their contributions to my work. My mother and daughter are my intergenerational adventure companions and best friends, and I'd have dedicated this book to them if it weren't such a very creepy book that cannot really be dedicated to anyone without raising serious concerns. My partner/live-in musician is always there to provide creative support and reminders that I am not alone in this journey. My father, provider of counter-inspirational anecdotes; my close friend, who printed and bound my very first book fifteen years ago; my cherished family and lifelong friends—these people have shared my sacrifices and given me the chutzpah to persevere.

HUNTING
ANNABELLE

WENDY HEARD

Reader's Guide

Hunting Annabelle is an enthralling psychological thriller that digs into themes of identity, desire, violence and redemption. What was the inspiration for this story?

This story was built around an idea I'd been mulling over, that all of us have this potential within us to do Bad Things. Ever been on a bridge and wanted to jump off? Ever wanted to yank the steering wheel and drive off a cliff? Ever wanted to stab yourself or someone else with a knife you were holding? The French term for the self-destructive impulse is "L'Appel Du Vide," or "The Call of the Void." Freud spoke of a "death wish"; modern researchers dubbed it "High Places Phenomenon." I wondered, what if the impulse were directed outward? What if someone had succumbed to the urge—just once? Would they live the rest of their life knowing they couldn't be trusted?

Thus, Sean was born, and with him my desire to do a really tight first-person narrative and give us a glimpse of a life lived just one step closer to the line.

Sean is the ultimate unreliable narrator—his dark past and violent urges make him the perfect suspect in Annabelle's disappearance, yet his clear sense of regret and shame around his previous crimes, and his determination not to cause anyone else harm, are quite convincing reasons to believe he's innocent. Can you talk about what it was like to write such a dynamic, compelling character?

Writing Sean was an exercise in authorial indulgence. I was free from the normal rules of writing protagonists. I didn't need to worry about keeping Sean a "good guy," forcing him to stick to the hero's journey. He is both good and evil, both trustworthy and unreliable. He is a character with whom I had freedom to explore and act in big ways, and writing him was a pleasure and a relief. I miss him all the time.

What is a "good guy," anyway? Is it someone who naturally does no wrong, or is it someone who fights the potential for evil within himself? What should we be judged on, our nature or our efforts? What's a little murder between friends?

What was your greatest challenge writing this novel? Your greatest pleasure?

This book touches some raw nerves, and I've joked that its actual title should be Trigger Warning For Everything. There are so many layers here: sexual assault, racism, violence against women, police brutality...it was all hard to write, and it all touched nerves for various personal reasons, but it felt good to write these things down and let the light hit them. To be honest, when I wrote this book, I did not know it would get published, so I didn't worry about what anybody else would think; I just wrote my guts out, and then later I had to deal with the reality that it would be public. There's a lesson in there about the authenticity of art when you dare to expose your most vulnerable self, strip down to your skin and let your truth show.

My greatest joy in this book was the love story, which was a tribute to "Annabel Lee," the Edgar Allan Poe poem that got me writing these types of stories in the first place. I wanted to write a truly gothic romance. Blood-and-dirt-smeared kissing scenes with corpses nearby? Check. Murder-makeout-murder scenes? Check. Psychotropic roofie sex scene? Check. Look, it's inspired by Poe. It's going to be dark, twisted and maybe just a little bit wrong, but that's what makes it so, so right.

Can you describe the writing process for this novel? How did the story evolve as you worked through it?

I always write a ton of drafts. My agent says that for me, the magic really happens in revisions, and this is very true. Each time I run through the manuscript, I strengthen the characterizations and settings, fine-tune the mystery elements, and all that other good stuff. I think this book went through a grand total of thirteen drafts. As I revised the book, I came to more deeply understand Sean and his mother, who was the most elusive character for me in this piece. I felt this antagonism coming from her, but when I realized there was an ocean of love and fear underneath that mask of control and cunning, I understood her (sometimes self-centered) motivations for keeping a lid on Sean's behavior. Annabelle was clear to me from the start, and I have a whole draft of this story just from her perspective so I could keep the timeline and clues *straight. Maybe someday I'll put it up on my website. If you think Sean's mind is a twisted place, you should check out Annabelle's inner monologue.*

You've set this story in Texas in the 1980s—what made you choose this time and place? Why were these choices so crucial to the narrative?

I lived in San Antonio for four years in my twenties, and I'd been wanting to write about the experience of being a fish-out-of-water Californian living in Texas. For craft reasons, I wanted to structure the story so Sean was racing against the clock, waiting for the detectives to get ahold of his juvenile records from another state, and that would be boring in 2017—it would be a matter of sending a single email. I also wanted this ambiguity of not having cell phones, this hunting around, scrawling phone numbers on scraps of paper, fumbling change out of pockets to shove into pay phones. I also thought the grittiness of the eighties served as a metaphor for the grittiness of the content. In so many ways, the eighties were a perfect fit, and the second I considered setting it in that decade, I knew I had hit on the right idea.

Do you read when you're working on a project? Or does it distract you from your stories?

I'm always working on something, whether it's edits or a draft, so I have to be able to read while I write. That said, I read things that inspire but do not compete with what I'm making. For example, while writing Hunting Annabelle, *I was able to read and be inspired by many domestic thrillers, crime thrillers, sci-fi thrillers, British procedurals and historical mysteries, but I was unable to read American*

Psycho or watch Dexter, *both of which were recommended to me as "must-consume" for the writing of this book but which felt too close to my concept. I did read quite a bit of work from the 1980s for research as well as devour a lot of film, music and TV from that era.*